Best of the 20

Penknife Press Short Story Writing Contest Entries

Best of the 2006 Penknife Press Short Story Writing Contest Entries

Compiled by
L. C. Redmond, Jr.

Penknife Press   Chicago, Illinois

Copyright © 2007 by L. C. Redmond, Jr.
All rights reserved under International and Pan-American Copyright Conventions.
Published in the United States of America by Penknife Press, Ltd., Chicago, Illinois.

ISBN 1-59997-001-5

Manufactured in the United States of America

TABLE OF CONTENTS

Stories are listed in the order they were submitted.

SUMMER OF THE OLD WOMAN

That was the summer I wanted to die. Wanted to, but I didn't have the courage, and it was absurd, there was no reason to. None to live either, is all.

Up here in Vermont you're meant to love summer; it's like a religion -- probably left over from sun-cults in pagan times -- picnics, parades, everybody cooking outdoors. Reminds me of when I was in Sweden: all the benches in public squares face the sun – I wanted shade. Summer's always seemed shapeless and sullen, doesn't have that springy texture the other seasons do.

That summer I was within two years of my mother's age when she died. Gradually, so it took a long time till I noticed, I was overtaken by dullness that later I could call despair. It wasn't painful active grief like when I left Rob. I hadn't broken any pots or wet the brushes with my tongue, which would've told me right away -- I use them to apply cobalt and other metals, nickel, cadmium, lead. But it drifted in and wrapped me quietly, so I wasn't aware for a long time.

There didn't seem to be a reason to do anything.

Nothing to devote myself to. I'd felt like this when the children left, but by that summer they'd been gone a long time, and hateful into the bargain, too busy to phone or visit. Their casual brutality when I needed surgery: I'll do a quarter.

They said Christmas? Home's freezing and raw, there's all that traffic. At the last minute they gathered at Sarah's, down in Maryland and I was alone up here. Lord! I thought, I'm not even dead yet.

A lot of people say they'd never've had children if they'd known, and now I find myself -- not ready to say that, no, but it's clear enough: I must've done it all really badly.

I've given this a lot of thought. Even if you knew what you'd done wrong, you'd make mistakes next time, because of course next time would be different.

I should've been more protected against them, but you don't want to have to defend yourself against your own flesh, and I don't think I'd know how. For years I thought it was my fault, I'd given them too much liberty. In the sharp present of a hurt, I was sure I'd done something to provoke it. Then like lightning -- as if I were awakening from sleep? -- one day I thought, in words, they had a father.

But that summer it wasn't only the children, because they're supposed to leave; they have to. I just wish they had gone about it with a bit more kindness. No; it was the end of important work.

In that sense it was the children.

It was the end of possibility, which is a kind of hope.

Always -- without knowing I believed it – I'd thought there'd be new men, new work, new people who'd fill my life with noise and laughter and their stories, but everything began to empty out, like the sky going white before a storm. Even travel didn't appeal – that was a bit scary.

Maybe this is preparation, so by the time you die you don't leave a lot behind. Makes it easier?

***

I'd started late, what with the children, and when my work flourished in my forties I thought it was the beginning of a long ongoing arc.

It never occurred to me that friends would leave. Of course they weren't leaving me, they were making new lives: they moved to the desert or the west coast or other countries; they left cities to find mountains, or villages to find cities. Maybe when you're past making children you remake your surrounds. One by one my old friends tried out new lives, and I was fixed in place. I couldn't imagine leaving – it would be a hardship. I have my work here. And I haven't anybody to go to. And not enough gumption, it must be said. I say it to myself, because part of the difficulty lies in having no one to tell my heart to.

Everybody says I'm so creative – a word I never use. How could I live without the clay, my walls, floor to ceiling, with jars of glazes -- metals, rare earths and common ones, dolomite and potash and Cornwall stone and feldspar and whiting? My kilns. One's portable, but only as a last resort, which this probably was, if I had recognized it. What happens when a person lives beyond her last resort?

Myra's daughter-in-law's a cocaine addict who regularly endangers the lives of her children and has caused Myra and Sam – and their son -- infinite misery. Myra said once, I wish she'd die. I'm fortunate: I don't have anything like these horrors in my life, which is about as interesting as a duck-pond. An occasional deer might come to drink, but mostly it's decorative, with a few water-lilies, and a breeding ground for mosquitoes.

***

I was slow to realize there'd be no more men. My body was thickening and my skin, like porcelain, people had said all my life, coarsening, and the flesh on the upper part of my arms began to crinkle and I knew -- I'd known since my periods stopped, and people quit noticing me: I was old.

I'd become someone people no longer attended to. And it was getting clear, even to me, that the children wanted me to be quiet, to speak less, to move quietly into the background. Don't call attention to yourself, I thought they were saying. Old people grow silent -- because silence is required?

At first I hated it with raw animal fury, but I suppose you can get

3

used to a lot.

Once in a while it's not true. Occasionally an attractive man watches as I walk by and I can feel his interest like a mild electrical current. But when it was part of my daily life -- this takes my breath -- when it happened all the time I never thought about it.

And if I had, could I have held onto it longer?

Attention from men was part of the world, like wind and rain and sunlight. Then it stopped and I burned with its absence. Loss like sheets of fire streaming over the ware -- you can't see it of course, but you know what goes on in the kiln.

Last week I ran into Nancy and Tom in the village. It's odd to know people that long and have nothing binding you to them. I've known them since they married, forty years ago. They were what Ben, my first husband, called a proper nuisance. They used to drink too much and fall all over each other in public – they lived with a kind of common -- but I'd have to say appealing -- abandon. The day I saw them they had a grandchild by the hand, decorous as can be. You could've watched them for forty years and still you wouldn't know anything meaningful about them.

I wonder if one of the things that separates young people and us, the older ones, is a kind of knowing. We know we will die, and soon, and they don't yet. So they skirt the spaces we occupy, as if we carried a contagion. I've noticed this.

And, truth is, you are what people think you are. I used to be unwilling to acknowledge that, but now I haven't any choice. Barely into my sixties, vibrant but unnecessary, all my best work done, I'm at an age -- a number -- with a bizarre reality that has nothing to do with the way I hear my voice in my head. But there are changes, my legs are thicker now, and sinewy. I used to have great legs.

4

So I've told myself, Look, this is what it is. Don't carry on; it's graceless and accomplishes nothing.

Over the last half dozen years my grief changed. It got, I think, less foregrounded. It began to be like my favorite glaze, a soundless gunmetal color you can miss, but gleams here and there. When light strikes it just right, or when your glance lands on it, a quiet unmistakable surprise.

***

Alia, my last local friend, would say I had a chance recently to change things. She'd met a lovely man, she said. He'd seen my work in her home – she's got a couple of my good pieces on a shelf beside the fireplace – and he wanted to meet me, could he call?

Sure, I said. We talked on the phone and he sounded fine, reserved and thoughtful, even introspective, which was impressive, in a couple of short phone calls. I suggested lunch at Grosso's Orchard, a pretty farmhouse-turned-restaurant on the road north. In nice weather they serve at a scattering of tables set in a grove of trees. I thought it would be lovely to sit under trees in the wind and get to know each other a bit.

It was a nice sunny day, and we did eat outdoors, under giant maples hung with colored cloth like little canopies. The table was set with crisp white linen, French china and heavy silver. There's something very appealing about furniture outdoors --

We were both a bit nervous, I think, but the talk was easy enough, and I caught myself watching his hands – so I knew I was interested; I never notice a man's hands unless. And he held my attention. What he said about politics and the government, and what he said about his own life, showed a kind of self-awareness that's rare in anybody, and especially men my age. So later I realized it was his way of making himself available, of saying, I'm open, maybe even vulnerable. But then he mentioned all his money, houses here and in New York, and in St. Thomas, and the apartment in London. I could feel myself drawing in. On the way home I actually thought, You can't buy me.

So when we said goodbye and he gave me his card and said, Call me, I smiled and thanked him for lunch, and I knew I would not.

***

During that lunch I'd imagined huge waves, the pull of riptides. It was a transitory thing: I told myself there was an undertow. He was dangerous in ways I couldn't know, and forgot it, until I saw a nature show on TV the other night. The program was about seals who'd just delivered their pups -- on a rocky coast in the Outer Hebrides, all crags and wind-driven sea spray. I looked it up: it's very far north, only about five degrees from the Arctic Circle, but the Gulf Stream goes by so temperatures are moderate, the voice-over said. The camera focused on a baby seal alone on a rock, and a bird, a skua or gannet, one of those northern seabirds, came and stood there stabbing and sticking the seal pup with a long curved beak.

The baby seal lifted its head, but it didn't move away.

Didn't know how to?

Wouldn't it try to save itself?

The seal didn't make a sound in all that crashing wind and sea.

Finally the mother came back, heaving and barking and drove the bird off. This continues to fascinate me: how animals care for their young – by instinct, without thinking. Maybe without feeling. The announcer said mothers nurse their newborn pups for three weeks and then abandon them and go to sea. Two weeks after they give birth they're receptive again, the bulls come ashore, and they mate. They don't spend much time on land, the voice said.

Something else I learned from these nature shows really bothers me, and that's how much energy goes into pure survival. These creatures don't choose. Everything's in service to the going on. They reproduce and nurse the young and set them free and reproduce again. Some live to great age in communities, like dolphins and elephants. After they show the young how to swim and hunt, they have no purpose, but they're still around, using up resources. All their energy goes into staying alive and I want to know why.

BROWNIE

Angie was feeling shaky and low—she'd just been dropped by a married man named Dick Spencer, a big-wig lawyer in Fresno—so I went over to cheer the two of us up.

I'd met Angie at the Miracle Spa on Blackstone. She was lots of fun, with a figure as good as mine, short blonde hair, and a real pretty face. She had a heart of gold.

That was her problem. She was from the country. She was too trusting. I could see that, the few times we had double-dated. Spencer didn't deserve her. I knew Spencer. He'd been a friend of Nick's.

Angie was renting a townhouse out beyond Herndon, past St. Agnes Hospital, near the tracts of big houses just south of the Bluffs where I lived then. I had a place right above the San Joaquin River, a three-story brick and timbered stucco, the kind with rounded eaves, like a thatched roof. I had half an acre of lawn.

Nick had bought the house for me when his divorce came through. On one side was a doctor, Jeb Fisher, and on the other a builder, Grant Lord. Spencer lived down the street and sometimes he and Angie had met at my place during lunch. Nick and I were separated now.

Like Angie, I was a bit at loose ends. This was before Grant and I got together and moved to San Francisco, before Angie went back to the dairy in Hanford to live with her parents.

That afternoon Angie was worried about money and I asked her to move in with me. We lived together for six weeks, before she got sick and had to move home and Grant and I finally decided to get married.

Angie always reminded me of myself, when I was younger and just starting out. I guess I felt protective of her. I was ten, maybe 12 years older, but except for the difference in our hair, we might have been twins. Like all my friends, Angie called me Brownie.

I found Angie in her nightgown sitting on the sofa, with a glass, a bottle of white wine, and a Kleenex box. There were crumpled tissues all over the rug. The curtains were drawn and the room was stuffy and dark.

She had on a soap opera, the one that starts with the big egg timer and the guy saying, *"Like sands through the hourglass, so are the days of our lives."* Angie began to sob every time the heroine, something Seaforth something, had a flashback of her husband kissing his first wife. In real life, Seaforth and the guy who played her husband were married.

"Honey," I said. "How about changing the channel?"

I gave her a hug but she cried harder and I got up and sat in the chair next to the coffee table.

She began to surf around the dial, round and round, crying again each time the soap came on.

"No, Angie," I said. "I mean the topic of conversation."

I took the remote and snapped it off.

"Let me tell you a story. I think it'll ring a bell." I lifted an imaginary hammer. "Ding," I said. "Okay?"

Angie looked at me with her swollen eyes.

I smiled at her, reached over and took the wine bottle from the coffee table.

"You want a glass—" She dabbed at her eye.

I raised the bottle to my lips. I took a big swig, then set it down, wiping my mouth with the back of my hand, like a cowboy in a movie.

"'Fasten your seat belt!'" I joked in my Bette Davis voice. "'It's going to be a bumpy night.'"

Angie began to giggle, before she remembered Spencer and broke into fresh tears.

9

"You're not a good audience," I teased. "Can't you read the sign? 'No Weeping Until the Feature Starts.'"

Angie blinked, looking at me.

"How can I get your attention?"

I unbuttoned my blouse and Angie giggled again as I leaned forward in my bra and grabbed the bottle. I took a gulp.

"'What do you say, Pilgrim?'" I did my John Wayne imitation.

"Go on," Angie said. She blew her nose.

I began to tell her about the afternoon that Anders finally proposed, how it came out of the blue, just at the right moment, when everything seemed like it was coming apart.

I told Angie how it was a lesson to never jump to conclusions—bad luck can look like good and vice versa before things play themselves out.

"Who was Anders?" Angie said. She wiped her nose with a fresh tissue.

"My first husband," I said. "It was a Saturday and we were working alone at the office like we often did. Anders was all upset. Let me set the scene--

"'Do you think he knows?' Anders said, he'd said it ten times. I had my file out. I was working at my nails. 'Brownie!'

"'I don't know!' I answered. I made short, quick strokes. In my mind, already I'd left him. I was already in love."

"You were in love with someone else?" Angie's red eyes were open wide. I nodded and went on.

"'I get the feeling he does,' Anders said. 'Don't you?'

"'From what he said yesterday?' I kept working the file. I was just waiting."

Now Angie sat forward on the couch. I was the soap opera that had her attention.

We used to joke a lot at the spa between exercises and then afterward, in the shower. We'd loofah each other's backs as I'd tell her some of the screwy things dates had said and done. Angie had a good sense of humor.

"You're kidding!" she'd say, like a high school girl, then hit me with the sponge.

I went on:

"Anders frowned and ran a hand through his hair. 'That,' Anders said. 'And other things. Something Griffith said.'"

"You were in love with Griffith?" Angie asked. I shook my head.

"'What did Griffith say?' I said. I held out my hand to make sure the nails were even. I thought about the Wednesday before, when I'd met Griffith after work for drinks at the Butcher Shop. He'd asked me if Anders and I were breaking up, insinuated he'd like to go out with me. I told him 'No way,' that anyway Anders and I were just friends."

"But you were sleeping together—" Angie sat on the edge of the couch.

I winked at Angie. "'It's just a feeling,'" Anders went on. "I can't pin it down."

"'I don't think he knows,' I said, I was testing him, touching my nails to my palm. They were smooth and even.

"'Well,' Anders said. He dropped his arm to his side, then patted his leg. 'We better hope he doesn't.'

"'He might use it.'"

"Use what?" Angie said.

"'Broomfield would!' Anders said.

"It could be bad," I agreed, turning the file. "Not good. I felt like rubbing it in. I was sick of Anders. Sexually, he wasn't very exciting."

"Who's Broomfield?" Angie said, but I kept going.

"'Not good?' Anders said suddenly, he was mimicking me. He leaned forward, raising his brows and jutting out his chin. 'Are you kidding?'

"'Terrible, a complete disaster,' I said, I stared back at Anders. 'He could hurt you,' I went on, I looked back at my nails. 'Especially now, with the Board.'

"'You bet he could hurt me,' Anders said. 'Why—' Anders turned. 'Broomfield could ruin me.'"

"Who was Broomfield?" Angie said again, she was confused, but I went right on, to lay out the beginning of the story.

"'He doesn't know,' I broke in. I said it as if Anders were a child who wouldn't stop. I put down the file to look at Anders. 'He couldn't.'

"'How could he?'

"'There's no way.'

"'Unless—'

"'He might suspect . . . .'"

"Suspect what?" Angie said. "Brownie!"

"'He might,' Anders nodded. 'That's the trouble. Everyone's touchy. They don't want it in the company.'

"'I know,' I said."

"Affairs," Angie said. Her face lit up. "That's it, isn't it?"

I nodded to Angie.

"I shook my head so my hair swung back and forth, with the part falling the right way. It was my best feature, people said, dark and shiny. Everybody called me Brownie.

"Like now, I was trim and pretty but it was my hair people noticed. For a second, I saw Anders looking at it under the office lights."

Now I could see it all again, for a second I forgot Angie was there watching me swing my hair, admiring it. But then I was telling the story for Angie, to make her feel better.

"'He does or he doesn't,' Anders said. 'It's as simple as that.'

"'You have to assume he does.'

"'You bet your life,' Anders said. He turned to look out the picture window. Except for his car, and my Honda Accord, and someone's big blue Lincoln, the parking lot was deserted. Yellow leaves were falling along the front walk to the office. It was fall, October.

"'You've been very foolish,' I said. I rubbed it in some more. 'Remember? I told you. That time at the retreat, at the lake—'"

"What happened at the lake?" Angie asked eagerly.

"We made love in the women's bathroom, during a speech."

"You're kidding!" Angie said. She started to giggle.

"'God,' Anders said. He hit the back of his hand against his forehead. 'How'd I get into this?'

"'What about me?' I said. I'd begun to leaf through the rolodex on the desk. 'I can't believe I'm talking like this.'

"'Well, you are.' Anders looked back out the window, at the office across the breezeway. At a window, a man and woman in business suits stood talking. From my desk I couldn't see them clearly. I didn't pay any attention. 'You better believe it.'

"'All right,' I said. I skipped past the punched plastic cards of names and numbers with my fingernail. I pretended to look up Broomfield's number. I already knew it. 'No need to roll around in it.'

"Anders swiveled and took two quick steps toward my desk. He reached across the computer and grabbed me by the shoulders. Real hard.

"'It's your fault,' Anders said, his lips were stretched tight. He shook

13

me once, then again, so my head jerked back. I thought for a second he was going to strike me."

I moved my head back and forth, showing Angie how it was.

"God," Angie said.

"'You started this,' Anders said. 'You. You. I'm the one to lose.' He let me go, then reached toward me, to touch my arm. 'Brownie—'

"I pulled away, lifting my hand to stroke my throat. He could have broken my neck."

"God yes!" Angie said.

"'You're crazy,' I said.

"'Get his number,' Anders growled. 'Get Broomfield on the phone.'"

"Who's Broomfield?" Angie repeated. "I'm getting confused."

"'You do it.' I spoke just above a whisper. I kept my face turned to the side.

"'Look, I'm sorry,' Anders said. He lifted his hands, but I leaned away. 'I don't know what's got into me.'"

"I guess not," Angie said. She shook her head. She had a grim look on her face. "Because he was pissed at Broomfield?"

"He was afraid of Broomfield, of what he might say."

"About you and Anders—"

"That's right. 'I don't know,' I mumbled. I shook my head, looking at the wall. It didn't hurt that much but I acted like it did. In a way I was playing 'possum. It was already over and now it was his fault, not mine. If I wanted, I could sue Anders."

"Sexual harassment," Angie said.

"'Brownie?' Anders said. My hair whirled as I swiveled in the chair, looking up at Anders. I set my jaw.

"'I'm sorry. You know what you mean to me. Why, you're closer to

14

me—'"

"That's what Spencer said," Angie said. "Whatta rat!"

"I lifted a finger, pointing at him. 'Never do that,' I said, my voice was shaking. 'Ever.'

"'I didn't mean—'

"'I'll spill everything myself,' I told him, 'you won't have to worry about him.'"

"Broomfield," said Angie.

"'Sure, sure,' Anders said. He edged back toward the desk. 'Of course.' He reached out to touch my hand but I pulled it away.

"'I'm not myself,' Anders said. He stepped across the carpet, staring toward the window. In the other office the man and woman stood close together, head to head. They were about the same height. The man waved an arm in the air so his white cuff flashed. I couldn't see his face.

"'I haven't been, since this came up. Remember,' Anders said, 'at the start, how everything was?'

"'I don't care,' I said. 'That was uncalled for.' I looked down, plucking at my blouse."

I started to do it, to show Angie, but my blouse was already undone. I went on.

"'I apologize,' Anders said. 'You hear me? Brownie?'

"'I hear you,' I said. 'I wish I didn't. Don't touch me again. I mean it.'

"'I won't.'

"'You better not.'

"'It's just that, you know—'

"'Blame yourself. You're the one who started it all. You're the one who couldn't keep hands off.'"

"That's right," Angie said. She was angry.

"'I won't, I promise to God I won't,' Anders said. 'Trust me.'"

"Just like Spencer," Angie said. "Just like him!"

"I turned back to the rolodex. Everything was working out. 'I've got his number,' I said.

"'Yes, I need to call him, I guess—' Anders moved back toward the window. The man and woman were having what looked like an argument. You could tell, the way they stood. I was glad they were arguing.

"'Here,' I said. 'I've got his home phone.'"

"Whose?" Angie asked. "Broomfield's?"

"Wait a second, honey," I said to Angie. "You'll find out.

"'What's their problem, anyway?' Anders said.

"'I'm going to call,' I said. 'I want this settled. Now.' I said it just like that.

"'Come look,' Anders said. 'Just for a second. It's fascinating.'

"'What is it?' I frowned, then got up and stepped to the window, leaving a space between myself and Anders. He and I were definitely through.

"'See?' Anders said. Now the woman in gray was waving a pointed finger. She looked familiar but I couldn't place her. A redhead. She stepped back, picked something off the desk. She shook it. She opened her mouth in a shout. I could almost hear it.

"'She's going to throw it!' Anders said as her arm came back, something glinted as it flew from her hand. With a reflex, Anders stepped away from the window as the man in the blue suit jerked his head to the side, the thing went past him, a paperweight or something."

I watched Angie's blank attentive face.

"'You see that?' Anders said. 'That was close.'

16

"'God,' I said then. I took a step back. Anders watched the two square off. They stood still, six feet apart.

"'Do you think they're going to kill each other? Maybe we should call the police.'

"'Wait,' I said. I was trying to think.

"'I wonder who cheated on who.' Anders grinned, watching them. 'I feel better. Things are rough all over.'

"I didn't answer. I could hardly breathe.

"'I don't think he'll hurt her.'

"'No,' I said. It was all I could say. I could barely talk. You could have knocked me over with a toothpick. I stood to the side, close by the drapes away from Anders. I couldn't believe it."

"What?" Angie asked.

"'What's wrong?' Anders looked at me by the curtains.

"'It's him,' I said, looking."

"Who?" Angie said.

"'Who! Tell me, Brownie—'

"'Him,' I hissed. I was half afraid they'd hear in the other office.

"Anders squinted, shading his eyes, then moved fast to the other curtain. 'Are you sure?'

"'Of course I'm sure.'

"'This is something.'

"'I can't believe it,' I said.

"'Whose office is that?' Anders said. 'What's he doing there?'

"Anders and I stood on either side of the picture window. Broomfield and the woman stood apart. They were talking now, not shouting."

"Broomfield was having an affair?" Angie frowned.

"'I don't know,' I answered. Like Anders, I peeked around the bunched curtain. 'It's been empty, until a week ago.'

"'A week ago? What firm?'

"I shook my head.

"'I don't know!' I said. 'I think I've seen her at the deli.'

"'I wish I could hear what they're saying,' Anders said.

"'Tell me about it.'

"'I wonder. No,' Anders said, 'I don't think he's talking about me.'

"'Who is she?' I said. 'Who is it?'

"'Never seen her,' Anders said, raising his voice. No one could hear us. 'She's attractive, though.'

"'Her?' I said. She wasn't even pretty.

"'Sort of,' Anders said. 'I can't see her clearly.'

"The two of them gestured, now Broomfield started to swing down his arm, then brought it back and with an open hand smoothed his dark hair.

"'That's not his wife, is it?' Anders said. 'What's her name?'

"'No,' I said. 'I've met her.'

"'When?'

"'At a reception.' The woman turned her head. 'At least they're not friendly,' I said. I was talking out loud, to myself. 'That's a good sign.'"

"You were in love with Broomfield!" Angie said now.

I smiled back at Angie.

"'No,' Anders said. 'Something's wrong.'

"'It is.'

"'But what?' Anders said. 'It could be anything.'

"'It could.'

"'Do you think he knows?' Anders asked again. 'About us?' Anders' nose was pressed to the glass as Broomfield turned and stepped away from the woman. Now Broomfield moved toward the window.

"'Look out,' Anders said pulling back. 'Here he comes!'

"'I don't care if he see us,' I said. I was furious."

"I don' t blame you," Angie said. "What a shit."

"'Get back,' Anders hissed, waving an arm, and we both stood to the sides of the big window, our shoulders to the wall.

"'What's he doing?' Anders said. 'Can you see?'

"'He's taking off his coat.'

"'Oh. What now? Brownie?'

"'He's, he's—' I stared.

"'What?'

"'This is crazy,' I whispered.

"'What?' Now Anders stood in full view of the window.

"'Look at that,' Anders said, with satisfaction. 'There it is.'

"'I can't believe it,' I said. I stood at Anders' shoulder. I nearly fell over.

"'Me either,' Anders said."

"You're kidding," Angie said. "They were doing it? Right in front of you?"

"Broomfield and the woman touched one another. Then they kissed again, holding each other.

"For a second I remembered the feel of Broomfield's face against mine, when we'd stood together in the parking lot of Sundowners' after drinks. I smelled his cologne. I'd told him what a jerk Anders was, how I was having an affair with Anders and it was a big mistake. Broomfield promised that he and I we're going to be together, it would just take a little time. We went to a motel.

"Then the woman's hand pulled the curtain shut."

"That's so sad," Angie said.

"'Well,' Anders said, he was still looking out the window. 'I don't know what to say.'

"'No,' I said. I stared at the pulled curtains. I thought of Broomfield and the red-haired woman with the freckled face, of what they were doing. 'This changes things,' I said. Now everything was different."

"I can imagine," Angie said. "You must have felt sick."

"I felt naked, the way you do now," I told Angie. She looked at me with her big blue eyes, then away, at the wall.

Just then the phone rang. She jerked her head back so our eyes met.

"Answer it," I said. "If you want."

"No," she said, "I don't want to."

There was a beep and Spencer came on, in his understanding, caring-hurt voice he used for special occasions.

"God," Angie said. She made a face and put her legs up on the couch. She wrapped her arms around her knees. She put her head down.

"Pick it up, Angie," I said. "I'll go upstairs."

"You're my friend," Angie said, looking up. "He's not. He's, he's—"

Spencer finished his message and the answering machine tape rewound.

"Well," I said. "Do you want to hear the rest, about Anders?"

"Yes," Angie said. "Tell me."

"I told Anders the scene with Broomfield and the girl had changed things.

"'Changes things?' Anders said, suddenly, so I stepped back. I thought he was going to grab me again. 'That's an understatement.'

"'And lucky.'

"'Lucky?'

"'For you,' I said. I lowered my face, shy, like I was embarrassed.

"'For us,' Anders said.

"'Is it?' I said. I looked up at Anders, waiting.

"'Sure it is,' Anders said, he was beaming. 'In a big way. Broomfield's not Mr. Clean. He's got a few kinks. We should have a drink. We should—'"

"Oh no," Angie said. "Here it comes. Just like Spencer, just like him. That's why I didn't answer the phone."

"I turned my back, glancing toward the bookcase of leather-bound books. I waited.

"'Let's have a drink.'"

"Sure," Angie said "That's how it starts."

"I didn't turn. I felt Anders staring at my back.

"'Brownie?'

"'You grabbed me,' I said. I said it like that, like a little girl. 'You grabbed me and shook me. You hurt me.'

"'I didn't mean to,' Anders said, stepping toward me. 'Why, I've never struck a woman in my life—'"

"What a liar," Angie said. "He's Spencer's twin."

"I moved away but Anders touched my shoulder and I stopped. I let Anders bring me to him.

"'I didn't mean to, Brownie. Brownie Brown,' he teased, he put his cheek against my hair. 'My Brownie.'"

"How sickening," Angie said.

"'Didn't you?' I said. I kept my head turned from Anders.

"'No, I didn't,' Anders said. He gripped my arms, turning me to him. 'I love you. I was just worried,' Anders said. 'About us.'

"'Us?' I said. 'I don't understand.'

"'You know, that Broomfield knew.'

"'Knew?' I said, I stared up at Anders. 'How could he?'"

"But you told Broomfield, about you and Anders—" Angie stared

21

at me.

"After that we went to my apartment. Once I thought of Broomfield and the woman in the other office, how they were doing the same thing and in my mind I switched with the other girl, I was the one with Broomfield.

"Then Anders asked me and without thinking, I guess I was all turned around, I said yes. He drove me straight to Clairissa's and I picked out a big clear diamond with a platinum band. Anders wrote a check for $10,000. That night he moved in and the next Monday he had his lawyer start the divorce.

"It was almost as big as this," I told Angie, holding out my hand. "Ten carats." Angie sat straight on the sofa looking at me. She didn't look at Nick's ring.

"Anders and I were together for two years," I told Angie. "Before he had his second heart attack and I met Nick."

"You were married when you met Nick?"

"I'll always have a soft spot for Anders, though I knew he was too old for me. If I hadn't been with him I would never have met Nick. At the San Joaquin Country Club, Sunday brunch."

"I didn't know that," Angie said. She looked confused and sweet. "I thought Nick—"

"Nick is all right," I said. "In a way. Maybe we'll get back together again. Anyway, last spring I saw Anders, in a restaurant in Cambria. He looked a lot older and sort of bewildered. His hair was white. Martha and he had got back together but she seemed more like a nurse than a wife.

"'Brownie? Is it you?' Anders said.

"I asked about Broomfield, if he were still with the company.

"'Broomfield,' Anders said. 'Broomfield?' His face got red. I thought he was going to have a stroke. Before I left Anders for Nick, I had a fling with Broomfield, Anders knew about it.

"Martha gave me a hard look, then led him away. She pulled his arm when Anders stopped and tried to turn back. I watched them get into a little Toyota, it was parked next to the Infiniti Nick had bought me for Christmas."

"You're making this up," Angie said suddenly. "To make me feel better." She smiled now. She looked relieved. "None of it's true. Admit it. It's straight out of Days of Our Lives."

"It must have been hard on Martha," I said. I didn't smile, I was serious, remembering the scene at the restaurant. "The way things had turned around. But it was a lesson."

"A lesson?" Angie asked.

"To stay on your toes."

It was hot in Angie's apartment, the wine and the talking had dried me out, so I reached back and unhooked my brassiere.

Angie watched me from the coach. She was staring at me.

"Come on," I said, "it's just a story." I swiveled in my chair, so the straps slipped from my shoulders and my breasts swung back and forth. I have pretty breasts. Lots of men and women have told me so. "How 'bout offering me a glass for my wine?"

But Angie didn't get up. With one hand she touched the neck of her nightgown. Her face looked white. Her eyes shone even bluer in her white face.

"It is true," she said. Then, like a kid: "You better hope there's no life after death."

"I'm not stupid," I snapped.

Angie looked shocked. Her eyes got bigger. Then I giggled. "Brownie!"

23

"Come on," I said, "don't you know when I'm kidding?"

"You had me going," Angie said. She shook her head so her short blonde hair touched her cheek, the way it did at the spa when she pedaled the exercise bike. "I feel like a fool."

"Sure," I said. "Come on. Get real."

"But what if there is a hell?" Angie said. She frowned. "Think about it."

I took another drink from the bottle. "Doesn't every boss need a secretary?"

Angie couldn't help laughing at that. I remembered again what a funny girl she was as she jumped up and ran into the kitchen. From the back she looked just like me, same shape, same movement when she ran. I could hear her laughing from the living room. I knew she'd be okay, that my story had done the trick. It was better than sitting in front of the stupid TV.

The phone rang again, again Spencer's gooey voice came on, but Angie didn't pick it up. When she came back I was sitting on the couch.

She started to go to the chair and I said, "Come on, tell me all about it, girl to girl." I touched her wrist. "I don't believe Spencer was that hot."

"You know," said Angie, seriously, standing in front of the sofa, "he really wasn't."

"I'm not surprised," I said. "Did I tell you he came on to me?"

"He did? When?"

"It's a long story," I said.

"I want to hear it," Angie said. She put down the wine glass. "That s.o.b."

"You first," I said. I lowered my eyes. "Let it all hang out."

Angie smirked, then dipped her head and slipped off her nightgown and tossed it in the air so it floated for a second like a scarf. Her face was flushed. I poured more wine.

"Screw Spencer," I said.

"Screw him," she said, clicking my glass. "If you want to."

"Are you kidding?" I said. "I already have."

Angie stared at me for a second and then we both broke up. We couldn't stop laughing. Angie rolled on the floor. She wore only her panties. The phone rang again and we both laughed even harder, making jokes as Spencer left his third long, heartfelt message.

"I wuv you dwearly," Angie said.

"It's been so soft without you," I said, making Angie laugh harder.

Finally, I patted the cushion and Angie sat down to tell me all about it. Pretty soon she began to cry again and I put my arm around her. Our breasts touched.

She was upset over money, rent, never getting married, not having kids, getting old, going out with too many men, too many lawyers. What Spencer had done, dropping her like that. She suspected there was another woman.

"Hush," I said, "hush. It'll all work out. Trust Brownie."

I felt her hair against my cheek. She was like a little girl, like my daughter or younger sister. Like my other self.

I kissed her once, on the forehead, and she snuggled closer. When I asked her she said she wanted to move in with me, she didn't want to be alone anymore. After a while I got her up. I helped her pack a bag. While she was in the bathroom Spencer called again.

I told Spencer to leave Angie alone, that he'd hurt her enough already. I told Spencer if he didn't I'd tell Angie about him and me. I'd tell his wife and she'd take everything. He begged me not to. I told him I'd ruin him if he peeped a word to anyone. He hung up as Angie was coming down the stairs.

"Who was that?"

"Fireman," I said.

"Fireman?" Angie said.

"Sure," I said. "Policemen don't have—"

Angie doubled over. It was good to hear her laughing again. "Brownie," Angie said, wiping her eyes, "you're a devil!"

"Come on," I said. "Let's roll."

"Isn't that a song?"

"'C'mon, Baby, Let the Good Times Roll'?"

"Yeah," Angie said, thinking for a second. "That's it."

I squeezed her arm, then took her bag as she locked up and we went out to Nick's long silver car.

PRIDE AND JOY

Vittorio Stepharelli stood at the window of his apartment and watched his wife, Rose Maria, as she wearily climbed into their '93 Impala to head for her custodian job at a Days Inn in Palmdale. His eyes burned in an effort to hold back tears that had been held in for too many years. He rubbed a calloused hand over his worn cotton shirt, massaging the growing ache in his heart as the rattle-trap car backed out of the driveway and lumbered off down the palm-lined street. He hoped it would get her to the motel without breaking down again.

A hard March rain fell from a tarnished silver sky, promising several more inches by nightfall—more bad news for the unfortunate rich in the canyon, moaning in piteous horror as their three million dollar mansions collapsed under the ruthless crush of dense mud. But Vittorio had no sympathy for them. They were morons to keep rebuilding in such a treacherous place. Instead, he worried about Rose Maria in her cheap K-Mart flats and the half-price raincoat she'd picked up at the Salvation Army the first winter here in America. If the car broke down, and she had to walk any distance, she would be soaked through.

After her taillights disappeared into the gloom, Vittorio shook his head and turned away from the window. It would all work out. God willing. Of course, that's what he'd believed when they'd left their small village in Sicily a decade ago, thinking that California would be the answer to all their problems.

But nothing had changed, even after he and Rose Maria and 18-year-old Chiara had become American citizens. They were barely getting by on his wife's income while Chiara went to public high school

27

and worked an after-school job at McDonalds. Three years ago, Vittorio had been laid off by UPS, and while he drew unemployment pay, Rose Maria had started the job at Day's Inn, leaving him to stay home to take care of Paolo.

Vittorio's gaze fell on the boy, and a familiar sadness settled upon him like the weight of the protective apron the X-ray technician had slipped on him two weeks ago during an exam. Not sadness for himself—but for Paolo.

The boy sat on the threadbare carpet, his dark, curly head bent over a wooden pre-school puzzle. In his slender, artistic hand, Paolo held a wood piece shaped like a star. His lips pursed, he stared down at the puzzle for a long moment and then slowly fitted it into the correct place.

In the past, Vittorio had felt a lifting of his spirit at Paolo's accomplishment--and something akin to hope--despite what all the doctors said. But that hadn't happened for years. Now, when he watched his only son painstakingly put one of those puzzles together, he felt only a sense of loss. And he wondered what might've been.

A sudden stench permeated the room, and with resignation, Vittorio turned to the boy. It was time for his diaper change. He trudged over to Paolo, bent down and slid his hands under the boy's arms.

"Come on, Paolo, let's get you changed, son." Using the strength of his upper body, Vittorio heaved Paolo to his feet, trying not to breathe in the ripe, pungent smell of fresh feces.

Paolo towered over him, four inches taller than Vittorio's 5'9". Liquid brown eyes stared vacantly as Vittorio maneuvered to his son's side, keeping one arm fastened around his shoulders as he guided him toward the bedroom. Paolo moved with slow, plodding steps as if somehow his body had a memory of this ritual. And who knew?

28

Maybe it did.

Inside the bedroom he shared with his older sister, Paolo positioned himself on his back on the narrow twin bed and waited, his eyes fastened in boyish delight on a mobile of Sesame Street characters. Grinning up at them, he clapped his hands in delight.

Vittorio reached for the giant-sized tub of Wet Ones and grabbed an extra-large Depends from the box on the dresser, noting that there were only three left. Should've bought more, he thought. But he dismissed that thought with a shake of the head. It didn't matter.

Working with long-practiced efficiency, Vittorio pulled Paolo's sweatpants down past his knees and removed his diaper. The Depends people tried to make it easy by putting the diaper's fasteners on one side, allowing them to be put on standing up and without removing your clothes. But Paolo had been having it done this way since he was an infant, and change wasn't something he easily accepted.

Vittorio briskly cleaned Paolo up with several moistened wipes and slid a fresh diaper under the teenager's rump. His gaze focused on his son's flaccid, man-sized penis, and that's when the pain knifed through him—pain so intense it momentarily took his breath away.

His boy would never use that healthy-looking cock for anything other than pissing out of. He would never know the intense pleasure of making love to a beautiful woman...of impregnating a wife and feeling his heart swell with pride at the birth of a beautiful daughter or a strong, spirited son to carry on the family name.

Tears blurred Vittorio's vision as he fastened the diaper and tugged Paolo's sweatpants back up around his girlishly slender waist. The youth grinned up at the mobile and began to mutter gibberish—the only sound he ever made—not Italian, not English...but some unknown language that made sense to no one but God.

29

16 years ago in Italy, Vittorio had been the nervous young father of a two-year-old when Rose Maria went into labor with Paolo. The village midwife had arrived and ushered Vittorio out of the bedroom. Angelina, a neighbor from down the road and the local busybody, had seen the midwife rushing by with her medical bag. Within five minutes, she'd appeared at their door to take Chiara home with her until the baby was born. That's how it was in the old country. Neighbors—even busybodies—helped each other out without being asked. It was different here. They'd lived in the same apartment on Clair Del Avenue for ten years and still didn't know their neighbors' names. Of course, it was rare that any of them stayed longer than a few months.

Paolo had been silent when he came into the world on that sunny February afternoon. Vittorio hadn't even known he had a son until the midwife came out of the bedroom with bloody hands and a stone-like expression on her obese face and asked him to sit down.

The baby had been blue upon delivery, she told him, and Vittorio, naïve young man that he'd been, had taken her words literally, wondering how it was possible that an Italian couple could create a baby with blue skin. But the midwife had gone on to explain that Paolo had been born with the umbilical cord twisted around his neck, that he'd been without oxygen for an extended period of time, and though she'd managed to get him to breathe, it was likely there would be brain damage. With those words, life had changed for the whole family.

Vittorio straightened, took Paolo's hands in his and gently pulled him to his feet. "Come, darling boy," he said in Italian. "It is time for 'Barney.' I will get your apple juice."

And then it will be nap time for both of us.

Vittorio could almost believe Paolo understood him. The teenager gave a vacant grin and talked to himself as his father led him back into the living room and sat him down on the floor with his puzzles.

Vittorio turned on the TV and went into the kitchen to pour Paolo's juice. He hoped the government wouldn't cut off Rose Maria's food stamps. He'd done some research and had been reassured they wouldn't. But governments were known to lie, especially this one.

He'd thought America would be different. He'd believed California would be the answer. He'd swallowed it, Homer Simpson-style—the so-called American dream. D'ohhh! But the doctors here had failed them, too. Nothing they could do, they'd said. Paolo would always have the mentality of a toddler.

Vittorio gave Paolo his juice and watched as he greedily drank it down. The boy handed the glass back, his eyes glued to the TV where Barney flounced around, singing one of his dopey songs. Paolo loved it. He grinned at the TV in obvious delight and occasionally clapped his hands.

Vittorio sank onto the old tweed sofa—another relic from The Salvation Army and with trembling fingers, lit a Camel. He took a long draw of it, then released the smoke in a flat, blue trail. His gaze fastened on the TV screen, but he wasn't really seeing it.

The phone call had come a week ago, late afternoon, long after Rose Maria had left for work. Vittorio had made the appointment for the following day. There had been no one to look after Paolo, so he'd taken the boy with him, riding the bus to Lakewood. In his accented English, he'd explained the situation to the pretty lady behind the glass window. She'd glanced into the waiting room where Paolo sat scribbling on a coloring book, and nodded. And while his boy made meaningless marks on a wall-climbing Spiderman, Vittorio listened to an Indian doctor, ten years his junior, tell him he was going to die.

No one is ever prepared for news like that, and that afternoon, he'd been no exception. Lung cancer, the young doctor sadly informed him. Vittorio had searched his mind for the correct English words; even after ten years, he still thought in Italian. "How long?" he finally blurted.

A shrug and a downward cast of the doctor's dark, foreign eyes. "Six to eight months…maybe less."

In a state of shock, Vittorio ushered Paolo out of the waiting room and headed for the bus stop. As they made their way back home, one continuous thought ran through his head.

I cannot do this to Rose Maria. She has been through enough.

What kind of God would burden a beautiful young woman with a mentally disabled child, force her to work her fingers to the bone, cleaning toilets and scrubbing floors to bring home a meager paycheck, and every day, growing older before his eyes? Only 40, she looked 55, her once lustrous black hair streaked with gray, her legs deformed by a railroad map of varicose veins. And now, she'd have to watch her husband die a slow, torturous death from cancer, leaving her with a bright, attractive teenage daughter who dreamed of going to college and a helpless toddler trapped in the body of a teenage boy.

No. It would not do. All his life, Vittorio had lived by God's terms. It was time now to die by his own.

By the time "Barney" was over, Paolo's lids were starting to droop. Vittorio's heart jolted as he realized how late it was. He got to his feet, waited a moment for the dizziness to pass, and then went to his son.

"Come on, my boy. Nap time."

Paolo didn't protest as Vittorio hauled him to his feet. He never did when it came to bedtime. Vittorio wondered if it was because in his dreams, Paolo was a normal boy, playing soccer, kissing girls, doing homework, sneaking smokes and drinking beer. Leading a normal life. Vittorio wanted to believe that.

In the bedroom, he changed Paolo's diaper and covered him with his grandmother's hand-embroidered quilt that had accompanied them from Italy. Through the small window looking out on a wet parking lot, Vittorio watched the rain fall. The numbers on the digital alarm clock on the bedside stand glowed red—3:30. It was so dark in the room that it seemed closer to nightfall. For a moment, Vittorio peered down at his son. His eyes were already closed, his long lashes curling upwards like a girl's. Vittorio felt as if someone had reached a hand inside his chest and manually squeezed his heart, sending a reverberating ache down through the soles of his feet. Turning away, he stiffened, his gaze fastening upon a framed picture on the nightstand. He'd seen it a million times before, of course, but he couldn't stop himself from picking it up.

Paolo, at two years old, stared back at him, his dark hair tousled, brown eyes wide-spaced and luminous. The frame was blue porcelain etched with the words "Pride and Joy." A stranger looking at the photo wouldn't have seen anything unusual about the boy. Only his parents saw the blankness in his eyes, and knew that their "pride and joy" would forever be two years old, even as his body grew.

And yet . . . it was true. Paolo was their pride and joy. He'd been cherished from the very beginning, cherished now. By all of them—Rose Maria, Chiara, and yes, by Vittorio. But he couldn't, he wouldn't leave Rose Maria the burden of caring for him alone. In a year, Chiara would be off to college. She'd already been accepted by Southern Cal on a full scholarship. Her dream was to be a doctor and work in the mental health field. There was only one way now for that dream to come true.

Vittorio would wait until he was sure Paolo was asleep. With a soft sigh, the boy turned toward the wall, clutching a stuffed beagle to his chest. His breathing grew deep and even. Vittorio wanted to believe—he had to believe—that even now, Paolo was lost in a dream where he could do all the things he'd never do in this life-time. And soon…God willing, that dream would be a reality. Together, Vittorio would make the journey with his son, and they would talk to each other as they never had before—man to man. And Paolo would thank him for releasing him; he would understand that it was the only answer—the only way to save Rose Maria and Chiara from a life of drudgery.

Vittorio brushed a lock of black hair away from Paolo's forehead and gazed down at him through blurred eyes. The boy didn't stir.

It was time.

He glanced at the clock. It was just after four. Rose Maria wouldn't get off work until 11:00, and with the rain still coming down as it was predicted to do throughout the night, it would probably take her at least a half-hour to get home. That left seven and a half hours. Plenty of time.

He walked into the kitchen and pulled open the utensil drawer, staring down at its contents. That's when he heard the voice of his conscience. *What if you're wrong? What if, by doing this deed, even if it is to give your beloved wife her freedom, you condemn yourself to eternal hell?*

His Catholic upbringing still held a powerful sway over him. Rarely did they ever miss Sunday Mass. He went to confession on a regular basis, and recited the Stations of the Cross with Rose Maria every Easter. And yet…here he was, getting ready to commit two of the deadliest of sins.

He reached into the utensil tray and took out a paring knife, running his thumb along the blade to make sure it was sharp enough. A thin line of blood welled from the cut. He wiped his thumb on a dishtowel and turned toward the door. He'd read somewhere that bleeding to death was a peaceful way to go—and unlike pills, it would be reliable.

Before his prognosis, it would never have entered his mind to do such a thing. But once he realized he had only months to live, and Rose Maria would be left to carry the burden alone, Vittorio felt as if God had broken a contract with him. All his life, he'd been a good man. He'd worked hard for his family and cared for Paolo with loving hands. Never had he ever been bitter about the trials thrust upon him. He'd taken each one like a man, a strong man who believed that God dealt out hardships to make him a better man. And yet, even now, God was still dealing out the blows.

This time, it was too much. Not for him. He had the easy part. What could be easier than dying? Anyway, he truly believed that death was only a journey into a better place. And despite all the teachings, he just couldn't believe that he would go to Hell for this, for rescuing his family. But even if he did, then it was a price he was willing to pay so that Rose Maria and Chiara—and Paolo—would have better lives.

Clutching the dishtowel in one hand, the knife in the other, he stepped into Paolo's room. The boy still slept, but now, he was on his back, breathing slowly and deeply. It was a sign, Vittorio realized. And just like that, all his doubts disappeared into the ether.

Paolo was giving him permission to do what he had to do. For a moment, Vittorio stared down at his only son, and this time, he allowed the tears to brim over and slide down his cheeks. Finally, he moved, placing the dishtowel beneath Paolo's chin and tucking its ends under his shoulders. It wouldn't do to have Rose Maria be forced to clean up such a mess. He reached out and brushed Paolo's hair back from his forehead.

"L'amo, il ragazzo di darling," he whispered. *I love you, darling boy.*

Flattening his palm on the top of Paolo's head, Vittorio poised the tip of the knife to the left side of his throat, under his ear. Just as he started to thrust the blade into his skin, Paolo's eyes opened. It wasn't an accusing look or one of fear. Just the usual blank stare of an unconscious mind.

Still, Vittorio felt the need to reassure him. "Shhhh," he whispered. "Ritornare dormire, il ragazzo di angelo. Quando lei si sveglia, sarà tutto migliore." *Go back to sleep, angel boy. When you wake, it will be all better.*

His hand slid down from Paolo's face to gently cover his eyes. With his other hand, he thrust the blade into the tender skin of his son's throat.

***

Black spots danced in front of Vittorio's eyes. He had no feeling below the knees; his arms felt like concrete. Yet, he still registered the cold of the porcelain bathtub against his naked skin and the slickness of his blood in which he lay.

It was taking a long time to die. With the same knife he'd used on Paolo, he'd cut deeply into both wrists, allowing the lifeblood to drain from his cancer-ridden body.

He wasn't sure how much time had passed. His thoughts had eddied and flowed, taking him back to his boyhood in Catania, revisiting some of his happiest days. Like the one when he'd first laid eyes on Rose Maria as she stood on an arched stone bridge gazing down at the turtles in the stream. Her black hair had glistened with blue highlights under the summer sun. And when she'd turned and smiled, he'd felt as if he'd been struck by lightning.

And later, their wedding day in the village. Rose Maria's hand had trembled as he'd slipped the plain gold band onto her finger. Other wonderful days and beautiful memories...his hand touching the lovely mound of her belly as their first-born kicked in her womb...the glorious day Chiara burst into the world, full of fire and robust health...the first tender moments cradling his son, knowing he would never be "normal," but finding it nearly impossible to believe that as he looked into the baby's perfect little face.

Lost in the memories, it took a moment before he realized he'd heard a sound that he shouldn't be hearing—a key rattling in the lock, and then the opening of the door. He blinked sleepily and tried to sit up. But his muscles refused to work.

"Vitto? Il mio amore, I'm home," Rose Maria called out. "They sent us home because of flooding on the ground floor."

Alarm flickered deep inside Vittorio, but it seemed as if his brain was the only thing left working in his body. No, he gave a silent shriek. This is not the way it is supposed to happen. I do not want to know. I do not want to hear!

But he could hear clearly. Her footsteps coming down the hallway.

"Why is it so quiet in here? And why are the lights off, Vitto? It is too early for bed."

She would check on Paolo first. She always did. Vittorio squeezed his eyes shut; he wished he had the strength to move his hands so he could cover his ears.

For a moment, there was nothing but silence. And then, Rose Maria began to scream. Vittorio knew it was a sound he would hear throughout eternity.

Chiara Stepharelli methodically tore the acceptance letter from Southern Cal into tiny pieces and watched as they floated down into the wastebasket. Her eyes were dry, her hands steady. All the tears had already been cried. She had no more. She'd finally come to terms with her destiny. After all, some dreams were never meant to be.

She turned to the mirror and swept a hand down her crisp, pink blouse embroidered with "Merry Maids." It was her day to work while Mama stayed home with Paolo. Tomorrow it would be her turn to stay at home. Chiara pulled her long, dark hair back into a ponytail, and left the room.

She stopped at the threshold of Paolo's room—the one she used to share with him before what the police called "the incident." Mama had moved in there, giving Chiara the master bedroom, saying, "A girl your age needs her own room."

Mama had just finished changing Paolo's diaper. She looked up at Chiara, lavender smudges of fatigue under her dark eyes. "You leaving for work now?"

Chiara nodded. "You need me to pick up anything at the store on the way home?"

Her mother shook her graying head without looking up. "We're out of food stamps. We'll have to make do until next month." She pulled up Paolo's sweat pants and gave him a gentle smack on his thigh.

Paolo scrambled up into a sitting position and grinned with delight when he saw his sister. The healed scar along his throat stood out starkly against his pale skin. Chiara stepped into the room and went over to give her brother a hug.

"Will you stop and see Papa after work?" her mother asked.

"Of course," said Chiara. "How was he last night?"

38

Mama shook her head, her dark eyes glimmering with sadness. "Not good. He did not recognize me. The doctor says his time is growing short."

Chiara couldn't look at her mother. Instead, she kept her eyes on Paolo's innocently happy face. "It would've been better if he'd just died that day. How can you do it, Mama?" She finally forced herself to meet her mother's gaze. "Feed him, change his diaper, stay with him until he falls asleep? After what he did to our helpless Paolo? Please tell me...how can you still love Papa?"

Maria Rose didn't speak for a long moment. She simply put her hand on Chiara's shoulder and gazed at her son. "Simply because I do." She paused a moment, then added, "Do not hate him, Chiara. He did what he thought would be best for us. He did it because he loved us."

Chiara digested her mother's words, trying to force back the bile rising in her throat. Finally, when she managed to rein in her emotions, she turned to her mother and said quietly, "And that is what makes it so appalling. He did it out of love."

She turned and walked quickly out of the room. A few minutes later, she waited for the bus that would take her to Merry Maids. It pulled up in front of her, and she boarded, taking a seat in the back. Her eyes fastened on one of the ads on the panel running along the length of the bus. It showed a young man in a graduation gown holding a diploma and wearing a happy grin. In huge block letters, the caption read: "It's All About Education!"

Chiara stared at it a moment, and then pulled an Entertainment Weekly magazine from her bag and began to read about Jessica Simpson's divorce from Nick Lachey.

MOMMA DIDN'T WANT HER GIRLS PLAYING WITH GUNS

I didn't even shoot Cousin Jeremy with a real BB because they were banned in our house because my brother kept shooting things he wasn't supposed to, like me or my other sister who now had a BB permanently sticking in her lip. Of course, Cousin Jeremy wanted revenge against me for shooting him, but he wasn't quick enough, because he ate too much and watched too much tv while sitting in his underwear on the couch all day, every day for the entire summer. Cousin Jeremy was always eating, from the moment he woke up until right before he went to bed. He ate gross stuff too, like spaghetti and cake for breakfast. I wished he would just go back home, but he didn't have a home no more. I'd tell you why but we weren't supposed to talk about how Uncle Larry was no good and drinking all the time and how he didn't even buy a tombstone for Aunt Mary. I was mad because there was this big fat kid on our couch twenty-four hours a day, and we couldn't even say why. We were just supposed to say he was visiting. We couldn't even say why Mom had to take the cushions off the couch and dry them in the sun every day because Cousin Jeremy peed on them every night. He wasn't allowed to drink any liquids after eight at night, but when that didn't work, Mom banned him from drinking after seven, then six, then five, and when that didn't work, Mom tried waking him up during the night to pee, but when didn't work neither, we got the neighbor lady who cleaned up shit in that old folks home to bring us these big plastic sheets that zipped up around the sofa cushions, which was stupid anyway because the cushions already stank like pee. I didn't even like to sit on that couch no more. The plastic sheet crinkled when you sat down, and it sounded gross. One time, I had a bowl of ice cream, and I sat down and that sound just turned my stomach so much that I had to give mine to Cousin Jeremy, who then had two bowls, which he ate before anyone was even done with their one bowl. One time, Mom told me to wake up Cousin Jeremy and make him go pee early in the morning as I was going out to get in some good fishing before it got too hot, and when he got up, there was a puddle of pee in the dent his fat ass made in the couch. It was gross. Mom wouldn't even let us swim in the public pool in town, because she said everyone peed in it, which didn't make sense because we weren't supposed to swim in the lake right outside our front door because everyone's septic tanks leaked into the water so much that the water gave us gross ear and eye infections when we swam in it or even floated on inner tubes. We went swimming anyway when Mom was at work, but if we got caught, we got punished. Mom called us disgusting for wanting to swim in shit, but then Mom let that fat ass Cousin Jeremy pee all over our couch. I just couldn't understand it. She even made our dog Puddles sleep in the shed, because he peed in our house once when he was a puppy on the first day we got him, and that was how he got his name, because he made a little pee puddle on our kitchen floor, and then he got named Puddles and was forever banished all at the same moment. And it wasn't even a lot of pee, just a little puppy puddle no bigger than a wad of spit. I just couldn't understand why my Mom let Cousin Jeremy piss all over every goddamn thing. I used to like to watch tv before his fat ass showed up.

The day I shot him, Cousin Jeremy came out on the back porch to get my brother's action figures to keep him company on the couch while he watched tv and ate all our food all goddamn day. The sight of his dirty, pee-stained yellow, what used to be white, underwear made me angry for some reason, so I shot him. I was out there pumping up

41

the BB gun six or seven times and dry firing little puffs of air at the back ends of ants and sending them flying. It was really hard to pump the BB gun because I was still pretty little for my age. The first two or three times, I could get the pumper down, but then after that, I'd have to put the stock on the ground and the barrel in the air and then kind of lean down to get the pumper down. I liked that gun being all pumped up with air and ready to explode. It just felt good in my hands. So anyway, Jeremy came outside and was leaning his belly over the toy box. This wasn't a fancy toy box at all, but rather just some plywood nailed together to make a big crate outside our backdoor. The sides were pretty big and he had to lean way over. And the sight of his big flabby ass made me angry for some reason, so I picked up a little stone and put it in the barrel and shot him right in the asshole. I didn't mean to shoot him at all, because I couldn't imagine that the pebble would fit in the barrel for one thing, and for another, BB guns weren't supposed to shoot rocks. But it did. It really did. At first when Cousin Jeremy was jumping around, I kind of laughed, because I didn't expect the gun to shoot at all. I didn't get scared when he was dancing around and yelling, because my brothers shot me up with that very same BB gun a lot of times. I never got shot in the bare flesh, because they knew better than that after Mike got shot in the lip and all, but it sure did hurt when you got shot through your clothes. It stung a lot and left a red welt, but that was it. I thought shooting Cousin Jeremy was kind of funny to be perfectly honest. I was also very proud of myself for being ingenious enough to put a little rock in the BB gun too. Then I saw the big red spot of blood blooming through his underpants as if a big dark red rose suddenly got painted there. Then I took off running and hid the BB gun in the coal shed and got my fishing pole and just went away for the afternoon. When Mom came home from work at three, I could

42

hear her and my brothers and sisters yelling for me. Then I saw my brothers coming down to the lily pads where I liked to fish for bass, but by that time, I was down where the lake fills up from the creek, which was where I liked to fish for sucker fish. I knew I had to go home sometime, but I put it off as long as I could, till the fancy people walked their dogs around the lake in the evening on the fancy path they collected money from the other summer people to build. When it got really dark and the bears came to root through garbage cans at the volunteer fire house, I knew I had to go home and get what was coming to me, which I knew would be bad, because Mom hated it when I fished, and she never ever wanted me to shoot guns neither.

In the fall, when I begged to go along hunting with Dad and my brothers, she always told me no, even if they said yes. I couldn't hunt no way, because everyone knew it was the law that you couldn't hunt until you were twelve. When I asked to go along hunting, Mom would call me a lezzy, which really hurt my feelings, and then I'd stay in my room all day or walk through the woods to grandma and grandpa's house and eat their stale-ass cookies they always had in that pumpkin-shaped jar on their table. Their cookies went stale by getting soggy not by getting hard, which was how cookies got stale in our house. But I'd eat a few of them and look at all the taxidermied bass on the walls of their house inside, then I'd go outside and look at all the deer horns nailed up out there. About three years ago, grandma had a picture of herself in the paper standing beside the deer she killed, which was hanging upside down in their yard. Grandma was on the front page wearing her red and black checkered coat and her red hat and the deer's eyes were red too. All the neighbors cut Grandma's picture out of the paper and hung it on their fridges, because people from around here rarely made the paper except for high school football scores and shit like that. Everybody cut it out except Mom, who said it was embarrassing and just plain gross for a woman to hunt or fish, which hurt my feelings, because I really liked fishing, and I always thought I'd like hunting too.

I never went over to grandma and grandpa's house to visit them or even look at all the taxidermied fish, I went to steal corncob pipes which grandpa made to sell at the flea market every Sunday for one dollar each. I'd go say hi to him whittling in the yard. He hardly ever talked, and when he did, he called me Mountain Man, which was what he called all his grandkids. Sometimes he called me Mitch, which was my oldest brother who was in the army and hadn't been home in a year. I liked when he called me Mountain Man, and I didn't even mind when he called me Mitch. I liked it because if I ever got caught stealing a corncob pipe when he went to the outhouse to piss out the warm Old Milwaukee beer he drank all the time, he'd blame Mitch, and then everyone would think he was crazy, because Mitch was overseas somewhere. I'd steal a pipe and then run into the woods and smoke dried leaves until Dad and my brothers came back home with all their kills. I liked petting all the pretty dead pheasants and the furry cold stiff squirrels. When Mitch was home I'd get to pet dead grouse and quail, because he was the only one who could hit them. Or he was the only one who'd go into the brush to find them, I guess. My other brothers mainly liked to shoot rabbits and deer in the cornfields around our house. Shit, you could throw rocks at bunnies and kill them, they're so easy to sneak up on. And deer just walk right up to you pretty much. Mitch hated the way my two other brothers hunted, which was to wait until sundown or maybe a cold rainy afternoon, and then just walk over to the field across the road and shoot a deer. Mitch always climbed a tree a mile into the woods and then he shot them with arrows. Mitch thought it was a pretty shitty thing to shoot a deer in the cornfield across the street. I liked the way all my brothers hunted because I liked deer meat. I liked deer meat and eggs the best. I even liked deer chili and deer spaghetti sauce. Everybody else liked deer baloney but I didn't because it got slimy real fast. We all teased Mitch and called him the Noble Hunter and Mountain Man. But it was true that no one else in the family could even get close to wild turkeys except for Mitch. My other brothers took their dead deers to Adam's Meat Market where you got a free beer and a cheeseburger for bringing in a deer. If you gave the butcher a lot of the meat, he'd cut up the deer and make sausage and baloney for cheap. Mitch butchered his deer himself in the yard with a hacksaw and his razor sharp buck knife. At first it was kind of gross to see him saw off a deer's head, but then I got used to it, and then I got to hold the horns while he sawed. The worst part was when the deer head was hanging by one strand of stringy something or another. Mitch wouldn't eat anything from Adam's Meat Market because he said Adam mixed a little deer meat with a lot of pork fat, which was true, because all that deer sausage was greasy as hell, then Adam would steal most of the deer meat for his own use to sell at the fancy farmers' markets he drove to in the city every week.

So I went home as late as I could after I shot Cousin Jeremy. Mom forbidded me to touch guns or fishing rods ever again, and then she called me a lezzy, which made me cry. She said I liked to kiss girls, which was a total lie, because I thought most girls were very stupid, if you asked me. Mom said no one invited me to slumber parties because I was a gross girl who fished and shot guns and stank bad because I always wore the same red sweat pants everyday. Then she asked me if I wanted to grow up to be a homicidal killer. When I said, no, she called me sick. That's what she said -- "You're sick!" Mom got so mad that she hit me a few times and grabbed my hair and beat me against the door frame until she started crying. Sometimes Mom made Dad beat me, but since he started driving truck he was never home no more, which was fine by me. Mom said I'd get punished good when he got back, which would be in like a month or something, so I didn't care too much about that. He'd just take the BB gun away from me the way he took it away from each of my brothers when they shot something they weren't supposed to, like me or other kids or momma birds that had babies up in the trees.

I cried a lot and screamed that I hated her or Cousin Jeremy or everyone. I don't remembered what I yell when I get mad like that. Then my older sisters played hospital like we did when they were little like me, and they bandaged me up by tying rags around my head to hold the ice on, and they tied popsicle sticks to all my fingers like splints and wrapped toilet paper around my legs. They put tin foil around my teeth. I guess they thought they might as well fix my buckteeth while they were at it. I slept like that, perfectly still, because my jaw throbbed from being beat and the back of my head was completely numb from being beat against the wall. I stayed in bed while Mom yelled at Cousin Jeremy for peeing on the couch again. I stayed in bed until Mom went to work. I stayed in bed while my sisters got on their bikes to ride down to the horse farm to flirt with the boys there. Sometimes, they hitched a ride to the Indian Gap Army Base down the road to flirt with the soldiers there, but if they got caught Mom beat them and called them whores, because Mom's sister got pregnant by an Army man, which was how Cousin G.I. Joe got to be around. I stayed in bed while my other brothers fired up the car to go do who knew what. I stayed in bed until there was nobody home but fat ass Cousin Jeremy. Then I went and got my Dad's .22 rifle behind his bedroom door. I pulled the bolt back like I had a bullet in it and pointed it right at fat ass Cousin Jeremy on the couch until he screamed, then I left the house without saying one goddamn word. Because of gun safety, Dad kept his ammo locked up all the time, but in the green truck there was a box of .22s under the seat everyone forgot about. I filled both pockets of my red sweat pants with bullets and just started walking around the lake. I heard some people laughing at me because my head was all wrapped up in toilet paper and there was tin foil on my teeth. I kept the bandages on because my face was all swolled up and green with bruises. I walked to where the stream flows out of the lake. We were not supposed to go there because copperhead snakes hung out all over there. I got through the snakey part alright, only seeing a few hanging in the tree branches and a few more on the rocks. I didn't mind the snakes by the stream too much, but I hated seeing snakes in the lake when you were swimming and they'd swim fast at you like some slimy alien. I walked right along that stream and into the thick brush where you weren't supposed to go, because it was Boy Scout Land, and they prosecuted any of the locals from going into their woods and their lake area their ... their ... their ... their there. I hated them, because they had this nice lake in there that no one ever fished and the bass in there were really big. I hated them because they had all these retarded city boys come and stay in fancy cabins and run around our woods in their queer ass uniforms. I sneaked up on them a few times before that and watched them canoe and play their gay games and shit.

I can't really put what happened all together, but it was kind of like shooting Cousin Jeremy in the asshole. I mean, I know I loaded up the clip and put in it in the gun. I know I pulled back the bolt and loaded a bullet into the chamber. I know I aimed across the lake and right into

47

that crowd of faggoty ass boy scouts marching around like sissy-ass faggots. I know I shot, pulled back the bolt, loaded another bullet, and shot again. Then I followed the stream back out. When I got to the road by our lake, I started limping for some unknown reason. I imagined myself to be like one of those Revolutionary War soldiers. I don't know why I imagined that, because a couple times a year crazy people came out here to do Civil War re-enactments. But I thought of myself having that banged up guy beside me playing a drum and another banged up guy on the other side of me tooting on that flute or whatever. I whistled and limped home.

I put the gun back and was sitting in the front yard by the plastic pee sheet drying in the sun when the cop car came up. The police were stopping folks and asking them stuff, but they didn't ask me nothing. I had my head all bandaged up with toilet paper and my teeth in all wrapped up in tin foil, and I was smoking my corn cob pipe full of dried leaves, and they didn't ask me shit. But I guess the neighbors down the road said they saw me with a rifle that afternoon. So when the cops came to talk to me, I said that I was just getting Dad's rifle back from Cousin Jeremy who had stold it and went into the woods. I said that I didn't shoot guns at all or even know how to, because I was a little girl, and I guess they believed me. The cops yanked Cousin Jeremy right off that couch and hauled him away in his pee-stained underwear. Mom said he was sick and that he got put into foster care. I didn't feel too bad about none of that stuff, because I just nicked one of those faggot ass boy scouts and didn't kill no one.

Scarf pushed like a black helmet almost to her eyebrows, the wide sleeves of her black manteau hiding her freckled wrists, Mollie hesitated in the arrival lounge, trying to decide which of the dark-haired, dark-eyed men was Hassan Nouri. Still unused to wearing hajib, she checked her reflection in the glass partition, making sure no hair had slipped from under the scarf. Then she realized that a lean man in a gray suit and blue shirt with no tie was studying her -- one of the few clean-shaven Iranian men she'd seen.

"Mr. Nouri?"

"Mrs. MacDonald?" When she nodded, he asked, "Where is your husband?"

"He had a heart attack - last week, in California. He was mowing the lawn. Died before he got to the hospital -- the paramedics couldn't save him." She resisted the impulse to slide the scarf away from her face so she could see his reaction more clearly and knew enough not to try to shake his hand. "They did the best they could. I came anyway."

"Alone?"

His spare features showed disapproval.

"I want to see Iran." She risked a small smile, then realized it was a mistake.

"But . . . alone."

"Stephen already made arrangements for the trip - and I brought the cash to pay for it."

She knew there were no banking links between the United States and Iran.

"It's not the money," said Mr. Nouri. His voice had a gravelly edge. "But a woman traveling alone...."

"I won't be alone. You'll be my guide."

"We can't stand here talking. Let me take your luggage, then we can discuss this...situation." He spoke perfect English, with an accent that reminded her of somebody, an actor, probably. Then, as if remembering proper etiquette, he added: "I am sorry about your husband. It was very sudden?"

"Thank you. Completely unexpected. But he did smoke." Again, Nouri's expression suggested that she'd said something he thought was odd. "Bad for the heart," she explained. "Causes cancer, too."

"Ah yes, so it is believed."

He frowned and she realized that he was shocked because she didn't seem to be mourning. Should she be at home beating her head with her fists? Well, she thought, the scarf and manteau were black, weren't they? Her feelings toward her husband were none of his business.

Suitcases at their feet, they perched at an airport café table with small glasses of amber tea. She was able, now, to study him more closely as he stirred two sugar cubes into his tea. Not a bad looking man, older than she'd thought, with a strong nose, graying hair, dark circles under his eyes - maybe forty-five, she decided, a man who worried a lot. Stephen never worried about anything; he always knew he was right. However, she was sorry Mr. Nouri disapproved of her.

"Since you are here, I will find a woman guide for you."

She peered over her tea at his black-speckled chin. "Why?"

"It is more proper." His tone allowed for no argument, but she argued.

"I want you to be my guide." She set the glass into its tiny saucer. She tried to find a reason he'd understand. "It's important to me to do this trip as I would've done it with my husband."

"I don't understand."

50

Hypocrisy didn't come easily to Mollie, but she made the effort.

"He wanted us to see your country. He can't be here, but if I do what he planned, as he planned it, it's almost as if he's still alive."

Had she gone too far?

"I see." Mr. Nouri looked thoughtful.

"My husband hired you because you're the best. He'd want me to have the assurance of your experience and...expertise. We can keep to the same schedule. The only difference is that Stephen isn't here. If anybody asks, tell the truth. He died suddenly. What's wrong with that? Won't your wife understand?"

"My wife is dead, also."

"I'm sorry. But, you see, we have that in common. You must understand my feelings. I need to do this. Everything will be okay if we stick to our plans."

"How American you are: so sure that 'everything will be okay.'"

"But I am American."

"That is why - one reason - everything may not be 'okay.'" He observed her for a while, until she began to wonder if he was trying to unnerve her, then said: "Perhaps we can do this. Not many tourists are coming to Iran just now. But we will have to be very...circumspect. We must be careful that we don't do anything that appears improper. It is unusual for a male guide to take a single woman around Iran. A few years ago, it would have been impossible. We must never touch. You must always ride in the back of the car. We must be formal with each other."

"Of course. I will forget that I am an American."

"I never will. But I am glad you understand the situation. Now, I will take you to your hotel."

He picked up her two suitcases and led her out of the café. Slinging her handbag over her shoulder, she followed, not speaking again until they were in his car, a Mercedes, clean and shiny, although several years old.

She wanted to discover the boundaries of his reserve.

"Why," she asked the back of his head, even though she knew the answer, "must we be so circumspect, so afraid?"

His reply surprised her: "Do you want the official answer or....?"

"Never the official answer, Mr. Nouri. Always the other one, whatever it is."

"We are an ancient tribal culture. In the tribes, women were property that could be stolen and therefore needed to be protected." She saw him look at her in the rearview mirror. "In some places, it is still that way."

The way he lifted his eyebrow told her a great deal about him, or so she suspected. Then she wondered: did he know she was watching his reflection in the rearview mirror?

"I've never been a man's property, not even my father's. I'd never want to be."

"You are from the West, but here we must respect tradition."

"Why?" she asked with false innocence.

He looked at her as if to say, how can you ask that question, then replied, "Because we have no choice." He added: "It is more complicated than that, of course. Fear, power, respect, religion - many factors are involved. That doesn't mean that women cannot be doctors or lawyers, have careers. Half of our university graduates are women."

"But they must obey their husbands and fathers."

"Naturally. That gives them safety and security."

They drove through the night without speaking. Tehran was larger and the traffic heavier than she'd expected, with, she noted, a ferociously masculine approach to driving. Even the women drove that way, but at least they were allowed to drive, unlike the women of Saudia Arabia. She was glad she wasn't behind the wheel. Clouds of pollution hovered above the traffic.

"Since we are being frank, Mrs. MacDonald," he said, finally, "why are you here? Really?"

So, he didn't believe the trip was to honor her husband and his wishes. Good for him.

"I don't know. Maybe I want to see for myself."

"See what?"

"How it is."

"And are you?"

"I'm starting to."

She pretended not to notice the looks she got when he checked her into the high rise hotel - once part of an international chain headquartered in Dallas. He told her what to do about dinner and breakfast and that he'd meet her in the lobby at nine o'clock the next morning. With a partial bow, he left her alone, room key in her hand. When she reached her room, her suitcases were already there.

Stripping off everything but her underwear, she pranced around the bed and chairs, reveling in the freedom. With the door locked, she could be liberated from the scarf and the ankle-length coat known as the manteau, but even to open the door for a bellboy or maid she'd have to put them on again. She'd even had to wear them on the Iran Air plane from Heathrow. She had no idea how the flight attendants managed so well in their long coats and scarves. She'd also been fascinated by the Iranian movie shown during the flight, a love story during which the young couple didn't touch once. While putting away her clothes, she found a Koran, a prayer rug, and a small prayer stone in a drawer. An arrow on the ceiling pointed to Mecca.

Exhausted, Mollie fell asleep almost at once, but in the morning hunger drove her to cover herself and search downstairs for breakfast. Passing a couple of souvenir and carpet shops, she encountered a crowd of men on their way into the dining room. She was surprised by how intimidated she felt, as she watched them move ahead of her. Then she realized that, covered as she was, she was invisible to them.

A few of the men were armored in western business suits, but the group included Africans in white robes and colored turbans, Arabs in tan or white galabiyyas and various headgear, and brown-skinned men in loose shirts and baggy trousers. It seemed that a conference of the Oil Producing Islamic Countries was in progress. In the lobby, miniature flags of the two-dozen participating nations marched across a snowy tablecloth.

Angry at her unusual shyness, she made herself maneuver through the men to the breakfast buffet, then felt guilty when several men stepped aside for her.

After breakfast, Mollie ventured out for an exploratory stroll. The sidewalk and street were jammed with commuters. Drivers ignored traffic signs and lights, weaving in and out of lanes, speeding up, slowing down, darting here and there with crazed energy, and pedestrians were nearly as erratic as they wove among the moving vehicles. Most of the women wore either black manteaus with trousers underneath and scarves over their heads or the standard black chador. A few women stood out in shades of gray and green - rebels, apparently. On the buses, the women sat and stood at the rear, with the men in front, regardless of where the empty seats happened to be. She returned to the hotel just in time to make a quick trip to her room to wash off the grime from the air before meeting Hassan Nouri in the lobby.

She saw him standing by the plate glass window, taller than she'd remembered, with straight posture, before he noticed her. Would he recognize her in her scarf and manteau? It was hard to show individuality in this costume - but, of course, that was part of its purpose.

He looked across the lobby in her direction, but seemed reluctant to acknowledge her or move toward her. Finally, with no change of expression, he walked over.

"Good morning, Mrs. MacDonald."

"Since we're going to be together for three weeks, can't we use first names?"

"Not in public."

"Fair enough. But please, let's relax when we're on our own or I'll go nuts."

He didn't respond to that, just pushed open the door and followed her out to the street.

Once they were in the Mercedes, she safely in the rear seat, she asked him: "Aren't you even curious about what I look like?"

"I know what you look like. You are a slim, attractive woman of about thirty-five, with blue eyes."

"Blue-green, actually. But what color is my hair?"

"Reddish, I think - you let a lock slip out from under the scarf."

"Strawberry blonde, actually. That's what we call this shade in America."

She saw him smile for the second time. "Strawberry blonde," he repeated. "Okay. Now, we go to see the State Jewels, so you can learn about the corruption of the Pahlavi family."

"I can hardly wait."

The jewel collection of the late Shah and his family filled many rooms in a bank basement. It was so huge and excessive that soon her eyes began to glaze over.

"Yes, yes," she begged, "I agree, the Shah was terrible, paying for all this with the blood and tears of his people -- can we go somewhere else?"

Without further comment, Hassan took her to the National Archaeology Museum, interesting enough Mollie supposed but not what she had in mind. However, she was the object of stares and giggles from a group of secondary school girls in black trousers, long black coats, and scarves. They resembled a group of novice nuns, she thought, although a couple of them wore blue jeans under their coats.

"Where are you from?" asked one bold girl in passable English. When Mollie said America, the girl hurried over to pass on the information to her companions, who peered at Mollie from under their scarves.

Mollie started to walk over to them, but Hassan spoke sharply: "If we're finished here, we can go to the Islamic Arts Museum. The calligraphy exhibit is world famous."

However, Mollie rebelled. "No calligraphy," she said. "I'm starving. How about lunch while we talk about what we do next?"

Yielding to her plea, Hassan took her to a restaurant downtown. The walls were decorated with large photographs of Persepolis: stark beige columns assaulted a blue sky and stone emissaries from foreign lands knelt before the Persian monarch, tributes in their arms, fear and respect on their stylized faces. She longed for wine to go with the kabobs and rice, but had to settle for scarcely tolerable nonalcoholic beer. She was the only woman in the restaurant.

"Museums are fine," she said, "but I want to meet people, learn about Iran today."

Again, Hassan studied her across the table. She'd never thought of herself as complicated, but he seemed to be having difficulty understanding her intentions.

"Are you interested in carpets?" he asked.

"No," she said. "I'm interested in human beings."

"What about your husband?"

That was the last response she expected from him.

"Stephen was not interested in human beings. We met at law school - two lawyers, but very different. I work with non-profits. He preferred corporate clients. I suppose I should've stayed home and mourned when he dropped dead, but I felt...restless. So I came here. Are you shocked?"

"It's not my place to be shocked."

"He wanted to come to Iran because he visited here when he was a boy - his grandfather worked for Standard Oil. That was in the days of the Shah."

"Yes."

"I do a lot of pro bono work - for organizations that help the unemployed. In the United States, we have many people who can't find work."

"I have heard that."

"I've also helped women sue companies for discrimination. Stephen hated me working for free. He despised my lack of ambition." She looked up at Hassan's bony face. "What I'm trying to say is that I care about people more than things. The statues and jewels are beautiful, but dead. At least, to me. It's probably my own deficiency. I'd rather meet people. I don't want to cause trouble, but there must be some way I can talk to ordinary citizens. Like those girls in the museum - they were so sweet."

"Please be patient. This situation requires patience from both of us."

She wanted to squeeze his hand, reassure him that she understood, but all she could do was sit there with a blank expression.

Mollie wasn't a vain woman and rather enjoyed not having to worry about what she'd wear each day, but she was discovering that it was hard to express herself when her body was covered and she couldn't even touch another human being. It was okay for her to touch another woman, but she didn't know any women in Iran. She'd seen girls and women holding hands as they walked, even men holding hands, but the one person she knew in this country was off limits.

"I was a lawyer," said Hassan. "I, too, represented people who were in trouble, who suffered because of injustice, but I quit legal practice. As time went on, I found it...difficult. And I make more money as a guide - or did, until recently. We still get tourists from Europe and South America. Even Asia. But not from North America."

"I think we have a great deal in common, Hassan." She corrected herself: "Mister Nouri."

"Come, let us go to the Bazaar. You will see people there."

He led the way out of the restaurant. Suddenly, she felt happy and reckless, but Hassan looked irritated and tired, she thought, when they started zig-zagging through the covered Bazaar. She enjoyed dodging donkeys and carts and clusters of shoppers and was fascinated by the crowds, by the gaudy and banal merchandise in the shops, by the vendors calling to her and offering tea, and by the women struggling with children, shopping bags, and chadors. Several women, she saw, held their chadors closed with their teeth in order to free a hand to cope with their kids. Ordinarily, she would've been annoyed, even outraged, but now it seemed charming and colorful.

She found herself babbling, making silly remarks about the shops and shopkeepers, the crowds, even the spicy smells assaulting her nostrils. The more she talked, the faster Hassan walked, as if trying to escape her mindless comments. This, too, seemed humorous to her.

I guess I'm ordinary, she thought. And Hassan, he's ordinary, too. We're both so ordinary, even though we're here, in this exotic place.

Impulsively, she accepted a shopkeeper's invitation to drink tea. A plump, chain-smoking man in a hideous purple shirt, he spoke enough English to make rudimentary conversation while Hassan lurked nearby. He had five children, he boasted, and seven grandchildren, and he was sorry she didn't have kids of her own. However, he said, she should not give up: a woman is happiest when she has children. She bought two scarves from him.

"Thank you," she told Hassan, as they dodged a handcart loaded with huge rolls of fabric on their way out of the Bazaar. "I enjoyed this."

"Time to go back to your hotel," he said. "We have an early plane tomorrow."

"I don't understand," she replied.

As Hassan regarded her, the shadow of a man riding a donkey crossed his face - his elegant face, she found herself thinking. The face of a poet, of a philosopher. Oh, hell, just a face.

"It's in the program," he said, with a tone of either irritation or resignation. "You must have a copy of it. I sent it to your husband. No matter," he added. "I will give you another copy tomorrow morning."

He said nothing more during the drive across the city and she felt rather chastened and afraid to risk more words. When he left her in the lobby, he told her to have her suitcase outside her door at seven-thirty the next morning and to have breakfasted and be ready to leave by eight-thirty.

"I am responsible for everything else, but you are responsible for that."

He turned away, so she saw only the side of his face as he talked to the desk clerk. She wondered how many times a day he shaved that aggressive beard.

The next morning, she stared at the back of his neck and asked, as he maneuvered the Mercedes through morning traffic, "What was she like - your wife?"

"I can't talk, now. I have to watch the street or we'll miss the plane."

"Yes, of course." With difficulty, she stopped herself from apologizing.

On the small plane to Mashad, a former Aeroflot jet, he sat several rows away from her. She spent much of the flight comparing the old Cyrillic notices with newer information in Farsi. Although she couldn't read either language, she found the exercise calming.

"If you want to understand the Iranian people," Hassan told her, as he arranged their luggage in the trunk of the rental car in Mashad, "this is the place to make a start. One of the holiest shrines in all the country is here. Twenty million people make pilgrimages every year."

He seemed to be challenging her to discover a rapport, a sympathy, for his people. Later that day, they drove to the enormous holy complex, golden domes and minarets glittering above every other building in town. When they parked, he gave her a chador to drape over her scarf and manteau.

"Like this," he said, showing her how to hold the black cloth over her head and under the chin, while keeping it closed across the front of her body.

"Now I understand why those women use their teeth," she said.

No matter how she tried, she couldn't move as easily as the black-draped women who glided like shadows among the wide courtyards and tile-sheathed buildings. You must learn as a child, she thought, to move with modesty and grace. I learned to be a tomboy and a rebel, and that's how I move.

Hassan seemed to want her to experience something here, so she did her best not to disappoint him. She watched the other people, the men and women separate, studied the way they knelt and bent over in prayer, and listened to the emotion in their voices, the intensity of their devotions. Some people, she was sure, were weeping.

I wish, she thought, I felt anything as fervently as they seem to feel whatever it is they feel, but she wasn't a religious person. She also wished that Hassan didn't watch her so closely. Perhaps it was part of his job, but the way he followed her with his eyes couldn't all be professional. At least, she reminded herself, she didn't have to worry about an uneven hem or a panty line showing.

The next morning, when Mollie saw Hassan across the hotel lobby, she felt a spark of pleasure followed by intense embarrassment. Turning away, she found herself staring at a photograph of the lobby before a recent renovation. It showed a large "Down with America" poster in both Farsi and English above the old front entrance. An American flag rained black bombs over the glass doors. How odd, she thought, that they took down the sign but kept this record of it. A country of schizophrenic gestures - or people.

Hassan walked up behind her. "Please don't judge my country by the extremists. Contrary to what you may have heard, we do not all think alike."

"Neither do we." She turned to look at his dark, shadowed eyes. "Despite what you may have heard."

He turned away, with an almost angry movement of his body. "Let's go," he said.

"Oh, yes - we must stick to the program."

He started to reach for her scarf, then stopped.

"Fix your scarf," he told her. "I can see your hair - your strawberry-blonde hair."

With both hands, she reached up and tugged her new navy blue scarf forward, smoothing her hair beneath it, then tightening the knot.

"Sometimes, I don't mind wearing hajib. It saves time. But I'd like to have a choice."

"Eshrat - my wife - felt the same way."

"Your wife. You must miss her." Then she quickly added: "Freedom is having choices, isn't it? That's why money is important - it gives people freedom to make their own choices. Sometimes, anyway."

He nodded. "I think you are a good person, working to help the poor in your country."

"I don't do enough."

"One never does enough." He looked at his watch. "You will find today's program interesting."

I should feel overwhelmed with responsibility, she thought, but I only feel happy.

They drove south, to the white marble tomb of the great Persian poet Ferdowsi. On the way, Hassan surprised her by singing some of Ferdowsi's verses. He sang in a stylized, high-pitched manner that made Mollie tremble. Staring at the sun-blanched road, he filled the car with music, history, and emotion.

"That was beautiful," she said, when he stopped. "And strange. I wish I could understand the words."

"Ferdowsi is a hero to our people. You will see - even today's

62

students love him. They may be drawn to western ways, but they still kneel before Ferdowsi."

The monument was crowded with adolescent students, the girls in the familiar black coats and scarves, paying respects to the great poet and reading aloud the verses carved into the marble walls. Mollie watched them, touched by their reverence toward the founder of the modern Persian language, by their respect for the past. Thoughtlessly, she put her foot onto the lowest white marble step leading to Ferdowsi's tomb. A young man gently gestured for her to remove it. Embarrassed, she moved away. Then a girl approached her.

"You are from where?" asked the girl.

"San Francisco," said Mollie. "America."

"Welcome," the girl said. Then she signaled for a friend to come over and whispered something in Farsi. The friend pulled a small camera out from under her black coat. "Please," said the first girl, standing next to Mollie. "Okay?"

Before Mollie could react, the friend took their photograph together.

"Thank you," said the girl. "Have good visit in our country."

Mollie wondered what the snapshot would look like: a pair of faces peering from two dark caves. Would her expression give her away, make her look bold and American beside the delicate, darker features of the teenager, or would the garb turn them both into anonymous shadows?

It always seemed to be the girls who were brave enough to speak. Perhaps there's an underlying defiance, here, Mollie thought.

Not letting the student and her friend get away, Mollie grasped their hands, asking them about their school, their families, their ambitions. Hesitantly at first, then with laughter and enthusiasm, they answered her questions and, in turn, wanted to know about America. They talked for several minutes, limited by the students' English, but with energy, until the girls' teacher led them away to join the rest of their class. However, even he smiled at Mollie, as he herded the students toward the exit.

All this time, Hassan had been standing back, watching; then, as he walked with Mollie to their car, he whispered: "You see? They don't think you are a devil."

"I don't understand that way of thinking - how can someone be a devil just because he believes differently than you?"

"It is not only beliefs, Mrs. MacDonald. It is also actions - history is made of actions, and we live with the consequences."

"But look at Salman Rushdie - condemned to death because he dared to disagree."

"It was more complicated than that."

"I'll bet most people in this country were on his side."

"My brother-in-law believes that Salman Rushdie deserved to die."

"Because he wrote that book?"

"Yes. Rushdie claims he is no longer a Moslem so he should be able to write whatever he pleases, but my brother-in-law says once you are a Moslem you are one for life and must obey the rules or pay the penalty. Many people agree with my brother-in-law. Perhaps the British used Rushdie for their own purposes, but he should have known fatwa was inevitable. I don't agree with my brother-in-law, but I understand his reasoning."

The rest of the morning, they drove through small dusty towns populated, it seemed, only with men. The rare woman Mollie saw on the streets was always swathed in a black chador. She was more likely to see clusters of young men shuffling among the flat-roofed mud brick buildings, aged vehicles, and tired-looking animals. Hassan had told her that the average age in the country was only fifteen. Occasionally, when she caught people staring at her, she wondered what gave her away as a foreigner, under her dark coat and scarf. Maybe it was the fact that she dared look them in the eye.

After a couple of days exploring the eastern regions near Mashad, they flew again on a small Iran Air plane south to Kerman. This time, Hassan sat across from Mollie. They exchanged only a few words, leaning slightly across the narrow aisle, but looked at each other often - raising their eyes from open, unread magazines on their laps.

Another rental car, another hotel, another attempt to grasp the deeply held convictions of the people of this ancient, yet new country. A blue-tile-covered twelfth century shrine loomed magnificently, its arched gateway, dome, and minaret dominating the historic desert town. Barefoot, Mollie followed Hassan into a cool, shadowed courtyard, but before they reached the mosque, a boy about ten years old trotted up, opening a paper-bound book. It was his English class workbook, she realized, as he turned the smudged pages, showing her where he'd filled in the blanks of various lessons. Then he gave her his pencil and pointed to an empty page.

"Please," he said. "Name here."

Feeling like a fraud, Mollie autographed his workbook.

When Mollie and Hassan came out of the mosque later, the boy ran over to her again. "Goodbye," he said. "Friend."

Mollie found that she had no voice to respond, so she waved to the boy, then blew him a kiss. (After, she hoped that the Morality Police wouldn't arrest her for that - he was an Iranian male, after all.)

For lunch, they stopped at a café on the main street of a nearby town. A simple store-front place of plastic-topped tables on an aged tile floor, its only customers were local men. With their sun-darkened skin, black hair, heavy moustaches, stubbled chins, and clouds of cigarette smoke, they suggested to Mollie a gang of villains from old thrillers. Some of them wore beards and turbans, patches of sweat stained their shirts, and their hands were toughened from physical labor. She and Hassan sat near the back of the café, where they could see the stoves and copper kettles in the kitchen. While they ate salad and yoghurt and lamb and rice, more men crowded into the café, some of them glowering at her, others staring through the smoke, as if they couldn't figure out why a woman was eating in their café.

"Don't be afraid," Hassan told her.

"I'm not afraid," she replied.

One of the older men came over to Hassan and asked where his female companion was from. Was she a Moslem? When Hassan said that no, she was not a Moslem, the man asked why then she was covered up. "To show respect," Hassan replied.

"Ah," said the man. "Good." He smiled at Mollie and rejoined his companions in their tobacco smoke haze.

Following the ancient caravan route of the Silk Road, Hassan and Mollie continued westward. When they stopped for a break within the golden ruins of a twelfth century stone caravansary, he poured tea from a thermos, then produced a small drum and accompanied himself as he sang another traditional song.

"I used to play and sing a lot," he told her, "but for fifteen years it was forbidden."

"What do you mean? Forbidden?"

"The revolution - the Islamic revolution. The mullahs were afraid of music, that it would corrupt people, lead them from the spiritual life. But now it is allowed again."

The goat-hide instrument, he explained, was a daf. The rhythms he produced on it seemed both complicated and austere. Looking past the broken wall as he played and sang, she saw a herd of black goats crossing the dusty road. Far beyond, on a barren hill, she glimpsed a small mud-brick house. She could imagine a camel caravan plodding across the naked landscape, stopping within these thick walls for the night, then continuing on its journey the next morning. Little had changed in all these centuries. And why should it?

When he stopped playing, Mollie turned to him: "Tell me about your wife, your marriage."

"Eshrat was killed by a missile during the war with Iraq, a missile given to Saddam Hassein by the United States. We never had children. We were afraid to until there was peace again. Now, I wish we hadn't waited."

"I don't know what to say."

"You don't need to say anything. None of it is your fault."

A few feathery, wind-blown clouds drifted above low dry mountains that hunkered in the distance against a huge blue sky. No advertisements lined this highway. In the car, the road stretching in front of them like a pale brown ribbon, they told each other stories.

"Eshrat's mother tried to arrange a marriage for her. She refused that man. Her father was a lawyer and supported her ambitions. Because of him, we were able to marry. He died not long after she was killed."

Mollie was curious about large billboards on the outskirts of the towns and cities on which were painted idealized faces of young bearded men.

"They died during the war with Iraq," Hassan explained. "Martyrs." He shook his head: "Today's young people don't remember. Many of them were not born. They need to be reminded of the sacrifices made then. Life is more than satellite dishes and mobile phones."

He asked her about her past life. She tried to explain it to him, but it seemed trivial to her, now.

"I'm from Montana - that's in the northwest of the United States. My father owns a Wild West History Museum in Butte. When I went to the University of Montana, male students playing at being cowboys used to come into the dorms and lasso girls. They thought it was funny. Their idea of a serious book was Zane Grey. You've probably never heard of Zane Gray. I escaped to California and met my husband at Hastings Law School. He seemed suave and sophisticated after the Montana lads. His fingernails were clean and he liked sushi."

Hassan stopped the car at the side of the road, resting his forehead against the steering wheel for several moments. Then he sat straight, staring ahead.

"I am going to get another guide to finish the trip. This isn't working. I know a good guide, a woman - you will like her. She can show you Persepolis, Esfahan."

"You must be very afraid of me."

"Afraid? Of you? Yes, I am."

"I'm not a bit scared of you - I trust you with my life."

"Maybe that's why I'm afraid - one of the reasons."

She was beginning to believe she could read Hassan's emotions from the back of his neck. The emotions that she didn't understand were her own. Gloom one minute, hope the next, then remorse, followed by intense happiness. She had never been this happy, she felt, or so miserable. Confusion, she decided, must be the human condition. Or else, since being in Iran, she'd been infected with the national schizophrenia.

He looked at her over the back of the car seat and a feeling of danger slapped her in the face almost as if he'd struck her with his hand. Then he turned and started up the car. The engine sounded to her ears like a machine grinding human hopes and desires to dust. For a long time, they drove silently.

When people stared at her as they passed through the little towns, she wondered how much they saw in the mask of her face surrounded by the dark blue scarf. Did they, could they, perceive her guilt - their shared guilt, the guilt of desire, if not of action, the sin of selfish willfulness in the face of moral inflexibility?

Maybe he was right, maybe it was best to end this game, but no female guide for her. She would cut short her trip, flee to San Francisco, pretend that she was mourning Stephen. She already had mastered the art of hypocrisy. Maybe it was even her fault - Stephen's death - because she hadn't loved him. That was nonsense, of course, but so was every thought that passed through her head.

As they passed through yet another windy oasis town, she saw a man bent over sweeping trash in the gutter using a handmade broom of twigs. Why didn't he have a better broom? Was it a matter of cost or did he prefer that awkward, antiquated one?

She realized that he was studying her reflection in the rear view mirror.

"You should be watching the street," she told him.

"I am - enough. You looked like a school girl then." He glanced away, adding: "The sun is bringing out the freckles on your nose."

Just then, peering through the dusty window, she saw that they were passing a statue of a young soldier striding forward with an anti-tank missile launcher on his shoulder.

"What is that?"

"A monument to the sons of this town who died in the war with Iraq. You wonder why so many billboards and monuments? That war lasted eight years. We fought alone, the world against us, Saddam Hussein using weapons provided by the West. More than eight hundred thousand people in this country were killed - sixty-five percent of them civilians. My brother-in-law was an air controller, then. He and my sister lived on the fourth floor of a building in central Tehran. Sometimes, there would be two or three bombings during a night. They had to run down four floors to the basement, no elevator, with their children - one barely four, the other only two years old. One evening, when he was downstairs with my sister, the bombing began. When he ran up to get the children, he discovered that my four year-old nephew had dressed his little sister and, sobbing the whole time, was trying to get her downstairs to the shelter."

Mollie wasn't a sentimental person, yet this man had touched her and there was no place to escape, unless she flung herself into the stony desert.

"Most families lost somebody, sometimes as many as four or five in a family. My brother-in-law finally quit his job because he couldn't bear to be away from his family night after night."

Mollie clutched the back seat of the car.

"I don't know what to do," she said. "There is so much injustice - everywhere."

"You do your best. So do I. We've been soldiers, you and I - our own kind of soldiers. We've changed lives, done good. Remember that."

"Yes."

Their gazes met, then separated as if their eyes had been burned.

Mollie pushed tears from her eyes. Then she began to laugh. When

70

she saw Hassan's alarmed expression in the mirror, she laughed harder. He shook his head and she realized how much she'd frightened him.

Mollie didn't understand what had happened - they knew each other so little. Yet she believed she could say anything to him and knew he could say anything to her. But one thing neither of them had to say. Scarcely more than a week had passed, their worlds were totally different, and they had never even held hands, yet they knew and understood each other intimately.

She wasn't surprised when he didn't arrange for another guide to take his place. Now, they were alone crossing the great Dasht-e Kavir Desert, not a sand desert such as the Sahara, but more like Nevada: dry, dusty, studded with sharp rocks, with low hills and tough plants that had adapted to the harsh environment. From time to time, they passed mud brick caravansary ruins. Sometimes, they spoke to each other of their lives or of the country through which they were passing, but often they were silent.

Mollie found that she'd become obsessed with small aspects of Hassan's appearance, since she'd never see him naked. His long earlobes, the way the hair grew over the back of his neck, his thick eyebrows when he turned to look at her, the way his Adam's apple moved, his bony hands gripping the steering wheel, and his eyes - those dark, dark eyes.

"They say we train and finance terrorists," Hassan said, staring at the bug-splattered windshield. "Lies. We give money and food and medicine to Palestinian organizations - humanitarian aid. But not for killing. And what is terrorism? Isn't it terrorism to blockade a country so the people can't get food and medicine? Isn't it terrorism to deny a country access to financial markets and business so it can sustain its economy? Isn't it terrorism to sell your enemy weapons and then prevent anybody from selling you weapons to defend yourself?"

Mollie watched the back of his neck and his hunched shoulders and, when he turned slightly, saw his jaw clenched with anger and pain. In her mind, she touched his face, telling him that she understood.

After a long day, as the sun was pulling its orange rays behind the rough gray hillocks, they reached the ancient oasis city of Yazd. The hotel there turned out to be a cluster of bungalows among trees and gardens, a relief after the harsh sun scorching the brown desert. Parting in the courtyard, they went to their individual bungalows. She didn't see him when she went to the hotel restaurant for dinner. Feeling unsettled and exhausted from the drive, she crawled into bed but couldn't sleep.

I can never understand this country, these people , she told herself. I can never get close to them. To him. I'll always be a stranger. I have no choice but to remain a stranger.

The next day at breakfast, Hassan seemed the same, telling her about plans for the day. And the week. After Yazd, they would drive south to Shiraz and Persepolis. She would find Persepolis impressive, he promised her. Everyone did.

Shut up, she thought, just shut up. Stop telling me history, stop describing places, stop holding yourself away from me.

"Yes," she said. "It sounds interesting."

Walking through the narrow, twisting streets of Yazd, between the leaning mud-brick walls, she felt sure that the people who lived here three thousand years ago would've recognized the place - except for the electric wires and television antennas swaying above the flat mud roofs. She followed Hassan, staying close to the walls to avoid the sun, resting frequently under arches that threw down blocks of shade like spilt India ink. How did women live like this, covered in black? Why didn't they die from heat prostration?

Tall, angular wind towers, their slits catching breezes and sweeping them down into the houses, cut into the brutal sky. Occasionally, she was brought back to the present as she leaped out of the path of a motorbike speeding down the narrow, crooked streets.

"See these doors," said Hassan. "From a thousand years ago. Two differently shaped knockers, one for men and one for women. The metal hitting the wood made different sounds to warn the people inside whether a man or woman was visiting."

"So?"

"If it was a man, the women in the house hid in back rooms."

"The tribal culture, again."

"If you like."

"I don't like."

"So be it."

In the afternoon, they drove to Yazd's Zoroastrian Fire temple. Although this building was only a hundred years old, Hassan explained, the flame had been nurtured and transported from temple to temple for more than two thousand years. The winged figure gazing down on them, he said, was Ahura-Mazda, ancient god of the Zoroastrians, who created the heavens and earth. The god of wisdom, Hassan said, and the god of order.

"We need him, now," Mollie replied.

"Maybe he is still here," he countered, "if we could see him."

From the temple, they continued to the ancient, rocky Towers of Silence, where until recently the Zoroastrians performed their "sky burials."

"Zoroastrians believe the earth is holy," Hassan told Mollie, "and should not be corrupted by decomposing bodies, so they put their dead on those towers for the vultures."

"I can understand that," said Mollie.

"You're not disgusted?"

"Why should I be? If you think about it, it's much cleaner, that way."

"You're the first westerner I know to feel that way."

"Don't you understand by now I'm not your ordinary westerner?"

"Yes," he smiled. "I do understand that."

At first, against the late afternoon sky, the two Towers of Silence could've been weathered buttes in the American west. But, as Hassan took Mollie closer, she saw that the round, flat-topped stone structures at the crests of the two steep hills were man-made. Several much smaller mud brick buildings clustered at their bases. Here the bodies once were prepared for sky burial atop the towers. Mollie followed Hassan up a rough and broken path to the top of one of the towers.

"Why aren't they used any more?" she called to him.

"The city grew too close to the towers. When the vultures flew over neighborhoods after their feasts, they dropped bits of human flesh. People didn't like that."

"Narrow-minded of them."

"Now, the bodies are put in mausoleums to decompose without touching the earth. There aren't many Zoroastrians left, anyway."

Climbing through a large hole broken in the curved stone wall, Hassan and Mollie stepped onto the wide stone floor where for centuries bodies had been left for vultures. It felt peaceful there, she thought, surrounded by the tall, circular wall, the empty sky overhead. In the center of the rough floor, she found a pit into which cleaned bones had been dumped year after year, century after century. She gazed into the blackness, then faced Hassan. For the first time on the trip, they were alone, in a place where no one could see or chance upon them. They stood without moving, staring at each other, the late afternoon sun stretching their shadows across the stone floor and onto the rough surrounding wall. The shadows could reach toward each other and touch, why not they?

Mollie knew without asking that she couldn't stay in Iran and he couldn't leave. She looked up at the blue sky, as if she expected a cluster of crook-necked vultures to be circling above them.

"My life," she said, "has been a closed door waiting to open." She laughed: "Maybe you saw that in me: the door that looked as if it wanted to open."

Silently, he stepped up to her and embraced her. She put her head on his shoulder and they held each other, as an evening breeze descended around them. When they finally drew apart, their hands clasped, she turned her face away, suddenly shy.

"You really don't know what I look like. You've only seen my face, nothing else."

"A beautiful face - and I see everything in it. And your eyes. And don't forget your hands." He lifted her freckled hand to his lips, pressed it against his cheek. Then he drew back abruptly. "Men and women are not allowed to touch in public, not even husband and wife."

"But this isn't in public."

"Technically, it is. And adultery is punishable by death in this country."

"I read about that - but only if you're a woman." She shrugged: "I'm not afraid. Everyone has been kind to me."

"We have too much pride to be rude. And too much sense. No one here has anything against you personally, but that doesn't make them your friends. Not now or ever. Besides, tourists bring money. We want your dollars, but not your way of life."

"But what about us? You and me?"

"You are unfair to me, Mollie." He didn't even notice that this was the first time he'd used her given name. "You give me hope for happiness that can never happen. Love is only an emotion. It has little to do with reality."

She broke away and moved toward the pit in the center of the Tower of Silence, staring into the blackness. "I wonder how many bones are down there," she said. "How many skeletons that were picked clean by the vultures?"

"Be quiet, Mollie."

He took her hand and led her back through the hole in the wall and down the slippery broken rock path to the rental car. Only when they stood beside the sedan did he remember to release her fingers.

"They are watching us," he told her, as they drove back to the hotel. "We do nothing they don't know about. The Morality Police are everywhere. We can never be too careful. The time has come, I think, to end all this."

"That's such a funny idea," she said. "Police to monitor morality."

"Believe me, there is nothing funny about it."

"In my country, people try to enforce their own kind of morality. It doesn't work."

She should've been afraid, but wasn't. She knew that he felt as she did, even if nothing could come of it, even if the mullahs and Morality Police fed them to the vultures.

The next day, they flew back to Tehran, a week early. She would miss Persepolis and Shiraz. She would leave Iran without seeing the great square in Esfahan.

"I don't want you to lose money on account of me," she told him. "I'll pay for the hotels and tickets - everything, just as if I'd stayed for the entire three weeks."

"Don't be stupid. Of course, you won't."

He arranged for a taxi to take her to the Tehran airport for her plane to London. He thought it would be easier for both of them. But when the time came, he was at the hotel. He put her in the cab, closed the door. They looked at each other through the taxi window as the car separated from the curb and penetrated the furious river of traffic.

Staring through the speckled glass, as the cab shifted lanes, she looked up and saw, on the end of a flat-roofed high rise building, the last of the giant anti-United States signs: an American flag, many stories tall, the stars white skulls, the red stripes transformed into streamers of blood dripping black bombs.

NO EXIT STRATEGY

I had started thinking perpendicularly. I was so absorbed by and obsessed with my routine. Maintaining routine meant continuously pruning alternatives. What would happen if I did something I would never think of doing? Every intersection and offramp I passed on my way to and from the lab where I worked, for example, was a perpendicularity to explore. The streets that looked the most interesting were the most plausible, but what about the streets I didn't notice? And so my mental exercise while driving, or engaged in some routine and tedious dissection, became to try to identify precisely the last thing I would think of doing. Which didn't turn out to be the worst thing I could do. For example, while performing an autopsy, puncturing my rubber glove with a syringe of infected monkey blood was the worst thing I could do, but by no means the furthest from my mind. Survival in the lab meant constantly identifying and scrupulously avoiding the worst thing you could do, a simple accident that could kill you. When you break a test tube, you have to find all the pieces, because if you stepped on a piece of glass it could cut through the booty straight to the food, exposing your bloodstream to whatever had been in the tube, whatever was in the air, on the floor. When a simple accident could kill you, you learned to forsee incidents, to remember the futures to avoid. So, spending fifty hours a week in the lab or more, my life penciled itself in somewhere between the worst thing I could do, and the things I always do. And the last thing I would do, I finally discovered, was to quit my job. But the last thing I would think of doing, was quitting science. To abandon my research into the mystery of life in favor of life.

When I discovered this about myself, I was squinting through the visor of my spacesuit through the electron microscope into a tangle of imperceptibly minute, inconceivably destructive viruses. I still didn't know whether a virus was creature or machine. At that moment I saw a flash of movement, but it wasn't the slide, but a reflection in my helmetglass. I looked up, and blinked to bring the room back into focus. I saw nothing moving except Jacob in his suit, oxygen hose trailing from above, maneuvering carefully toward the door to the autopsy room. I wondered whether I had imagined the movement, and, since I was not imaginative, wondered whether it would be more disconcerting if I had or hadn't. It was then that I heard my breathing lurch as my eyes fell upon an open cage door.

The lab was a level four biocontainment core in which we tested deadly diseases on monkeys. There were no doors or windows. The room was depressurized so that, if there was a broken seal, air would enter and not exit. To leave, you had to pass through a sterile airlock and bleach shower into a grey area, dropping your clothes into a laundry chute leading to the incinerator. The lab had two rows of cages on opposite walls of the small sealed space. In one row were monkeys infected with our latest variant, in the cages opposite were uninfected monkeys. We hoped to see whether the agent was airborne. A plexiglass partition eliminated the possibility that the disease could be transmitted through flung excrement. The open cage door was on the infected side. Somehow, an infected monkey, one we had given the name William Patrick, had escaped.

I shouted to Jacob and that noise startled William Patrick such that he leapt on top of the electron microscope and bared his fangs at me, emitting a fierce guttural trill I had never heard before. Before I could stumble back he was two more places, then began jumping up and on the row of infected cages instigating a monkey riot. Even the monkeys in the final stages of death gurgled their support, twitching their dissolving musculature. Their shrieks drowned out whatever Jacob and I tried to say to each other. He was proposing we evacuate, instead I reached for the net, hoping to protect the experiments in progress. It was the wrong decision. You have never seen a more talented monkey. As I approached William Patrick with the net, cooing sweet lies, he clambered headfirst down the side of the cages and darted between my legs. Jacob had the tranquilizer pistol and barked at me to stay back, leveling it at the desk where William Patrick now poised as if studying my papers. But the first dart bounced off the wall. William Patrick retrieved it, and threw it directly at me, it bounced off my faceplate and my net swept air. The next moment, William Patrick had wrapped his tail around Jacob's neck, yanked his air hose out, and knocked him to the floor along with a tray of pox-smeared microscope slides. With his strength, claws, and teeth, William Patrick could have done much worse damage to Jacob, but hopped off, chattering. He wasn't trying to injure us, just let us know how it was in the jungle. Even in the throes of his shrieking tantrum, his eyes, already pink from the onset of the virus, showed only disappointment. To show his powers, William Patrick, as I swung the net down, leapt over my head and sailed across the entire room so quickly I could not tell whether he found handholds on the ceiling or simply flew. The other monkeys bounced, turned in circles, and covered their eyes.

When it was all over, William Patrick sedated and back in the cage where he would die, our biocontainment suits were covered with rips and infected or uninfected human or monkey blood. The damage to the lab was impossible to survey. The monkeys would be destroyed, along with all the remaining samples in the lab, which would have to be sterilized top to bottom before testing in there could resume. Jacob and

I were both sterilized, quarantined, and debriefed through glass. Then I saw nobody for two weeks except the nurse, lying in isolation, deriving new ways to outlast the clock as I waited to see whether death would punch me out. I was bored enough to think about my ex-husband, how space travel must feel like solitary on death row, waiting to see if the odds will commute your sentence. Although no human had ever contracted this disease—it was in fact brand new, our team had engineered it—I had some idea of what it would do to me. If I became infected, I would have wanted euthanasia to spare myself the agony of the symptoms, but that would have been a betrayal of the project. Instead it would be my duty as a scientist to allow the disease to take its course so it could be studied in a human. But more than that, I thought that if I decided for euthanasia the others would believe it was because I was a woman. I'm glad I never had to make that decision.

So instead of thinking about dying, I thought about other jobs I could have. They brought me my journals, and others I requested. I had heard of a team that was investigating the neurologic basis of memory, hoping to isolate neural inhibitors preventing prememory. Their theory was that it made no sense, with regard to what was known about the physics of time, that our minds would allow us memory of the past but not the future, and that this inability to remember the future was an evolutionary adaptation, because organisms with no memory of their own deaths would be more motivated to survive. I had read an intriguing article about mice who knowingly avoided the place where they would be killed. The government had shown no interest in sponsoring this research, though it had provided at least one test subject who "reproducibly made improbably perspicacious estimations of her immediate future." My quarantine room had windows of wire-reinforced glass and in the grid of wire I mapped a timeline, the

81

steps I would need to take to remove myself from Project Pandora, without endangering the project. Finally I had to chart two futures, because my leaving the project was contingent on Jacob's being able to continue, as he held most of the knowledge I did.

But our fifth day in the "slammer" it was reported to me that Jacob showed traces of the agent in his blood, but that I had escaped infection.

A strange feeling I could not name changed the focus of things. It had the flavor of relief but was not exactly. I had never felt anything like it: I wanted to quit my job. The thought was dangerously addictive. I worked twice as hard to find a solution to the puzzle we had been assigned, lost sleep. And so it was that I found myself making wrong turns. The quarantine wing where I visited Jacob as he died in isolation was enough off my normal route through the gigantic complex that I found myself wandering tiny catwalks and cement labyrinths under the city. The game was to walk until faced with a forking path, then to choose a direction without thinking. Not thinking was a state I was able to achieve only fleetingly.

The center was huge and my clearance allowed me access to almost everywhere. It was built in concentric rings to contain the level 4 core, where I worked. I was familiar with most of the building except the area directly beneath where I worked, the bottom of the core, which was off limits to everybody. It was all like a city, a city without space, and somewhere outside its cool silence was the noisy gridlocked glare of California. Corridors unfolded into cantinas, a lounge (with smoking), and cold locked doorways bearing red biohazard flowers. A post office, apartments, a library. And a veritable zoo of laboratory animals: mice, guinea pigs, ferrets, rabbits, birds, and of course apes. Most of the animals seemed happy. Some seemed asleep or dead, and a few were clearly in the throes of diseases they had contracted naturally while waiting to be infected with an experimental disease. The building had everything I could think of except windows or plants.

The core, sealed in brick, used to be the entire building. Then the old building was refitted and became the level 4 core, and around that brick building another building was erected, with dizzying Star Trek-esque catwalks and exposed cable and ductwork running along beneath them. In the grey tiled corridor whose vertical space extends up the outside of the old building, its windows now sealed, are glass cases depicting various projects ostensibly sponsored here: agribusiness miracles, new cures for deadly diseases (partly true), and the like, most of it perhaps factual if misleading. Broad steps led up through vertigo-inspiring emptiness to the upper catwalk where suicide could be considered. Colored banners bearing the SP logo hung two stories down to the tiles traversed by only the handful of us who had security clearance. Complex arrays of arched beams held in place a metal roof. Walking the catwalk I looked across the void into 3rd floor laboratory windows. The clash between the old brick building and the new metal building was unsettling and seemed to reveal to me how in secretive government bureaucracies things are layered on top of things in an organic accumulation of scientific advances and foreign policy imperatives nobody could have exactly predicted, but tearing down and rebuilding was blocked by those whose power might be overturned, ensconced, afraid of the velocity of advancement. Pandora virus wasn't a curiosity to show school children, some rare specimen of parrot or tropical fish. Neither was it mustard gas, to be sprayed on a Cold War battlefield. It was a monster. It made nuclear bombs look like shiny pistols. It was a tiny keyhole through which, if one squinted through an electron microscope, one could glimpse a future without people. It was perhaps wrong to be bringing it out of theory and into the world at all, even if our primary purpose in engineering samples was to find a vaccine. Two bland combed-over white technocratic misfits walked past, beslacked, beclipboarded, windbreakers whispering. I ignored them, feigning absorption in a colorful computer graphic-laden wall display promoting incomprehensible research involving mousepox. A photo of a smiling child attested to the wholesomeness of these advances. Behind it, a locked closet's sign read DATA. I turned my attention to a few abstract paintings hung in unseen corners like a half-hearted afterthought, then went to see Jacob.

Jacob was somewhat chipper until his mind started to go from the hemorrhaging. He tried to cheer me up, strangely, claiming that I needed to observe him because when would we get another human subject. He described his suffering with an attempt at clinical precision but enough subjectivity that it was clear it was a ploy for company, tight and desperate, which I responded to, though I found it almost impossible to take notes on the progress of the disease. My enthusiasm faltered. His family had been told that he had already died, and had been given an urn they were told was filled with his ashes. Though Jacob and I weren't exactly friends, and I would rather not have known what our virus would do to a human subject, I had to sit across the glass from him, listening to him rasp through the speaker. I was the only one who could offer company. I had security clearance, and had seen enough monkeys crash and bleed out that I was still able to look him in the eyes even after they were becoming swollen and pulpy with the onset of symptoms it would have been impolite of him to discuss with anyone but me. "We built it," he said, "and now I'm trying it out. And I have to say that we did a fine job, because this sucks. Write down that it turned out to be slightly more devastating in a human than a monkey because the psychological effects, as parts of the brain shorted out one by one, were more pronounced." He seemed surly and delusional. He showed symptoms of classic senility. He would go away into his memory and come back, and passed through different times in his life, mistaking me for various people at one point. "I have mnemonia," he moaned, "My dreams are a mirror of the future because I can't tell," he started to cough, "when I am. Or whether I'm awake. Because if I had different futures, I must have different presents."

We never figured out how the monkey escaped. The locks on the monkey cages were electronic. Did the monkey resolder something, Jacob joked, choking on his own detaching throat, as he in vain replayed the events leading to his death. Could an electrical failure have unlatched the door? A surge, spike, or momentary outage? And what would such a malfunction mean in the case of a sustained blackout? Jacob had been my favorite coworker because of his open contempt for our employers, the military, and "Mr. White Man" as he often referred to Adam White, our boss. "You just know those fuckers would go to all the trouble of building a state-of-the-art level 4 biocontainment zone, and fuck up on monkey cages. Those cages are every bit as important as the airlock. Did they pick those computerized locks to impress the generals with the blinking lights? A padlock doesn't malfunction."

"William Patrick could have opened any lock," I joked, and some of Jacob's mouth tried to smile. "We should have named him Harry Houdini."

I had made visiting Jacob a regular morning and afternoon ritual, really the first breaks I had allowed myself since beginning work there, and I continued to take the breaks long after Jacob had dissolved, leaving only a deadly, hot, contagious stain in a mattress destined for testing and incineration. In the back of my mind I was trying to complete a proof and I was unable to concentrate as well as I had been. I developed a mild narcolepsy, and would prop myself on hallway benches for brief dreams in which I looked for exits.

And so I came awake discovering I had wandered perpendicular into the security hub and struck up a conversation with a large and amiable guard named Mac, who addressed me as "Ma'am." A reassuringly solid African American, Mac would have made a good bartender or priest. He personally apologized for the escape of the monkey and wanted to know how security could respond to future monkey escapes. I searched his eyes for irony and found none. Studying his nametag more closely I saw that he was security director, not a guard. And he obviously knew who I was.

"Funny you should ask, Mac, because I had a lot of time in quarantine to write up my recommendations. I'll print out a copy for you, I'm disappointed you never received one. But please, don't call me 'ma'am,' it sounds so formal. Just call me Doctor. Doctor Adorno."

"Okay Doctor, I look forward to reading that. There's usually lots of time to read," he smiled, at this and I decided to visit him again. What could be more perpendicular than to try to befriend someone not a scientist? Someone whose world was visible to the naked eye, the world I never saw.

I considered social intercourse a generally trivial level of the natural order, though I had to admit its trivialities were endlessly vexing. Mac had charisma. Charisma was social, but was clearly an adaptation that would lead to proliferation of its gene, if it were genetic. But being stimulating, likable, genuine, persuasive, was a good idea, and a good idea could perpetuate itself through generations, or even emerge simultaneously in disconnected social clusters, without any Lamarckian genetic encoding. But bad ideas also had a staying power. Why didn't bad ideas die out? To be fair, many bad ideas had, like smallpox, been contained and eliminated forever from the language. But what about, say, war, that uniquely human social cancer. The word thrived. Why hadn't war died out like slavery? That that bad idea was bad was well documented. In few cases was war fought and won for survival, so how could it perpetuate itself? Rethinking this, if ideas were species, they were certainly parasites, as they were dependent on human minds for survival. It is not always the most beneficial parasites with the holding power. So perhaps war was somehow beneficial for the survival of the human species, or perhaps again predatory parasites had an edge over beneficial ones. Suicide, for example, was an idea that could not effectively perpetuate itself, it seemed. But then an idea like that wouldn't be concerned with survival.

Security had been concerned that the young man with the jeans and white V-neck Tshirt with gold crucifix was a bomber of some kind. I watched Mac's men interrogate the young priest over his monitor. Mac had called me over to see whether I recognized the man, and because, respectfully, he sought my opinion. Security had picked him up spraypainting our building. LIVES EVIL, he had begun. That anybody would notice our building had never to our knowledge happened: streets around the complex were reportedly filled with plainclothes security posing as city workers of various sorts, and of course the building had no address or entrance save the underground parking tunnel that one entered through a guardpost half a mile away. Not even those of us who worked in the building would recognize it from outside. They told us it was in a dangerous neighborhood. And of course it had no markings or features of any kind. Its outer layer was weathered brick, to fit the neighborhood, and to disguise the bombproof concrete shell. All this security for a laboratory facility, we had been told, was to foil animal rights extremists. It was surrounded by a razorwire crowned chainlink fence which the interlocutor had clipped with wirecutters and stepped through.

He said he was a priest, that his name was Joe, and claimed there was evil in the building. The interrogators could get nothing more out of him, though the priest story wasn't believable. When the interrogator asked him whether there was a church who would vouch for his identity, he claimed to be an unaffiliated, freelance priest.

What put the interrogators on shaky ground, to my mind, was that this youth with the neatly trimmed beard was crazy and correct: there was evil in the building. How could one plausibly deny it? First of all, for security reasons none of us really knew everything in the building. The things I knew were pretty frightening. If there existed a Satan, some of our virus samples would belong in the same category. How else would you categorize a fragment of protein smaller than a nucleus, too simple to be considered life much less conscious, that could possess a person and reduce them to jelly, in the process feeding off their flesh, reproducing itself, and spreading its violence to everyone who tried to help its victim, until there was nobody left to touch. Viruses were not malevolent, they were mechanical—as unconcerned as a rock—but were as close to evil as I would want to get. I was fascinated by the man in the room. How vexing this social intercourse, fathomless, and yet somehow funny. This guy just had no access to appropriate behavior, oblivious to intimidation.

They left him alone, with a pack of cigarettes on the table he didn't touch, and I studied him through the screen as they returned to the office, conferring quietly. This lone zealot had somehow defeated the most elaborately contrived security system in southern California simply by calling its bluff. By dragging him into the debriefing room they had essentially confirmed his suspicion that something was going on, whether he was delusional, a lone man bent on seeking out and eradicating bad things, a spy for China, or, as he claimed, God. I was intrigued. He stared through the wall in the general direction of the core. If he was a spy, I was the one he wanted: I may not have known the most terrible secrets, but, what secrets I knew, I was the only one with the technical knowledge to understand. If he could see evil, as he reasoned, then I wondered how he would react to me.

I asked Mac to let me talk to him. Mac was reluctant and picked up the phone to contact Adam White to request permission, but did not restrain me as I walked down the corridor the guards had entered from, found the room, let myself in, and sat down across from the priest. A guard entered behind me and positioned himself in a corner. Sharp blue eyes looked into my eyes. His gaze was direct as only the gaze of an animal, child, or psychopathic can be. Like staring into the sun, one could not look at it.

"Mr. Priest, I was wondering if you could answer a few questions."

"And your name is?"

"Doctor. Mr. Priest, I am concerned that you think there is evil here. If this turns out to be true then we will certainly have to take whatever steps are necessary to clean it up. I'm sure there are theological waste disposal teams who specialize in that sort of thing. But, if your story is true then why aren't there other men of the cloth surrounding the complex?"

"Most priests," he said, leaning forward, "don't see evil. They set their sights high, heavenward, hyperopic. To be God's agent, you have to take your eyes off Him."

"What do you mean by evil?" I asked.

"Rational murder. I see shimmering rifts, borders between futures. One of these futures has people, the other is the end. These rifts intersect here. Soon it will be too late to choose."

Behind me I could hear the security man clear his throat to deflate the creepy silence, because I had felt a click. Something I wanted to talk about, or was this his charisma? I longed for privacy in which to talk to this man. Security would never allow it.

That night I left through the tunnel and the sunset did indeed look like a shimmering rift where two futures met. Those making the decisions in the research program ought to have perfect foresight or common sense but there was no evidence of either. I, on the other hand, an isolated workaholic who devoted more thought to smaller topics than all but a handful of schizophrenics and molecular physicists, agreed with a lunatic re "evil."

And, Priest or no Priest, this is what it boiled down to, exiting the expressway beneath the sky of colliding futures, and being waved through my subdivision gates by a new guard I did not recognize: my life was my results, and my home was an avalanche of data, to be spread out over any domicile I might rent or be assigned. At night I would arrange their piles, by day my kitten Ebola Reston would rearrange them.

Was this his charisma I felt? Evil in dialectical struggle with good? or mutual loneliness? How would I find this young man? Well, if there was evil in me, I supposed he would find me.

And what about quitting? It occurred to me that I had no exit strategy. One did not simply retire from well-paying, high-level top secret military research. If I quit, it could kill the project. Whoever's project this was wouldn't like that. This is something I should have brought up during the hiring process.

Somewhere underneath a gigantic windowless casino, in front of rows of tiny monitors, I conduct an orchestra of surveillance cameras. On an empty staircase used mostly for access to conduits, I see a monkey. But when I zoom in I am startled to see it is a dead woman descending the stairs. Either that or she survived our experiments.

I close my eyes and when I open them his penis has a symmetry seen only in textbooks and is pleasingly oversized with a pronounced head such that it is easy to see the spread of arteries, especially when so engorged. Kneeling in the antiseptic shower, as I lift it to scrub it I inspect it for blemishes, but find none. As I stand up it feels hot on my breast. But when I push my wet hair from my eyes it is not Joe Priest but Lenin. I see I am not in a proper lab: through gaps in its planks I see desert.

I woke up scared. Something about working in that place, perhaps. There was much kept inside. And I didn't much like living and sleeping alone, not like this, not when I also worked alone and ate alone. During the few months of marriage when my husband and I lived together, I enjoyed sleeping with him more than I would admit, bodies locked, fused in a heat so primal as to seem solar. But I was never into having a long-distance relationship with anybody--not a writer, not my husband, and especially not the longest-distance relationship in history--so when he left Earth and broke that warmth that infused the marriage certificate with life, it died like a winter leaf. Ebola Reston could be depended upon to sleep with me inasmuch as a kitten could be considered dependable, but it was the crazy hour when the hallucinations must be routed from every room.

I was not at liberty to discuss my work with anybody, in fact, and so I talked about it with my cat, which was still probably illegal. I was probably the leading virologist in the world but perfectly isolated from the larger genetics community. In fact I had signed forms promising never to publish. In my sealed employment contract, I was technically an immunologist, identifying vaccines for potential viruses, focusing on those that were most lethal. But I didn't really know. I was alone in the lab these days, but I didn't know what happened to my research after I handed it off to Adam White. It was not clear who we were working for. Though my paychecks came through Monsanto, we entertained occasional visitors from the federal government. And my boss was always flying to the University of Washington.

Beginning with smallpox, Marburg, and Ebola, we developed permutations of their genetics, and tested the new variants on monkeys. Then the parameters of the disease (such as how many particles of virus were necessary for infection, how quickly and by which means the disease was communicated, and how quickly the infected people would die) were fed into a computer, which would randomly generate factors such as weather, wind drift, and human movements, to simulate how any given virus might spread through a human population. The computer would take the parameters of disease. When the simulation consistently reported global catastrophe, comprehensive depopulation, it was a cause for celebration.

And so I found Mr. Priest's talk of evil somewhat refreshing. I did not believe in evil, per se, but it was somewhat satisfying that someone had noticed and taken an interest in the unmarked building, because what went on there was truly of interest.

I was invited to an elite club by my boss Adam White. I assumed it was for a professional meeting, though I did not know how I would respond if it was meant to be a dinner date. A valet leaned down to my descending driver's side window, and I half-expected him to tell me that my brown Oldsmobile could not be allowed in the lot due to the exclusive establishment's dress and vehicle code, but instead I was looking into the eyes of Joe Priest, wearing a vest and nametag that read Joe Flist. His eyes met mine though they showed no signs of recognition. Flustered, I got out and handed him the keys to my car. As he drove off, too late I remembered my briefcase in the trunk. I tried to think what papers were in it and considered retrieving it. Just then Adam pulled up in an obnoxious red Porsche. He unfolded himself from it, popped the trunk, tossed a tennis racket in, and handed off his keys without looking at the valet, coming to shake my hand with both of his, beaming.

Adam White: amateur pilot, tyrosemiophile, vecturist, labeorphile, cigrinophile, iconophile, record collector, entrepreneur, epidemiologist. I wanted to ask him to take the sunglasses off his head while we ate. They seemed affected, a token to prove he was always a man of leisure, accessories at the ready. But I knew full well that leisure was out of the question for the man who daily mediated between scientists and unknown underwriters, and who was probably entrusted with more secrets than I could understand. But he seemed the perfect bachelor with his red car, white hair, business casual, and, I wondered, glancing around, bodyguards. While he regarded his immediate surroundings with childish excitement, as though he might at any point jump up to go hang gliding or scuba diving, I was sure his skis and crampons were getting no more action than a regular dusting by a hired housekeeper in a home he seldom saw.

A waiter hovered and I asked for any red wine. The waiter nodded, and did not try to overwhelm me with a luxury of alternatives. Adam White ordered an appetizer and water for himself.

As if sensing my thoughts, Adam admitted: "I have a lot of interests but I regret I'm not a colorful conversationalist. My dad had dozens of stories. He worked for Pinkertons. He killed a bear with a pistol. But I didn't inherit his gift for hyperbole. I'm afraid I brought you here to talk about work."

After the waiter reappeared with wine and water, took our dinner orders, and disappeared, Adam White cut to the chase. I felt briefly foolish for suspecting this man of wanting to date me, and felt begrudging respect.

"I have an offer to make you. We are looking for scientists involved in the project—especially women—to promote to the next level. The next level of, of course, salary, as well as security clearance. You are one of our best candidates and I wanted to take this opportunity to interact with you socially and get a sense of your ambitions."

I squirmed at his use of the word socially, but any suggestion that the two of us might enjoy one another's company was over quickly enough. My ambitions? This was the time to discuss quitting then.

He seized and began buttering a piece of bread, continuing.

"What it boils down to is that in the event of an outbreak, immunizations will be in short supply. There will have to be ring containment, of course, through quarantine, but should that fail, the question of who gets vaccinated will be... nontrivial. Are you following me?"

"An outbreak of what?"

"Pandora, for example."

"Are you telling me that you anticipate an outbreak of a virus that we synthesized this year, in total secrecy?"

"The point of our work is to be prepared for a worst-case scenario."

"How could there be an outbreak unless we sponsored it?"

"It's unlikely, very unlikely, which is all the more reason for secrecy. And for keeping you on the team."

"Those agents are serious. You know that. We've seen Ebola eat equatorial villages, but what we're working on is worse. I don't even feel comfortable talking about an outbreak. That would be a crisis of unprecedented proportions, unimaginable."

"Unimaginable," he smiled, "but calculable."

My attempt to introduce my discontent was stumbling. "If something went wrong in the world, like an epidemic of a deadly genetically-engineered virus, I suppose I'd be one of the last to hear about it. To be more isolated than I am in the lab, you'd have to work in that reactor on the moon."

"Yes, but, on the positive side, in order to be safer from an outbreak than you are in the facility, you would indeed have to be on the moon."

The shrimp scampi appetizer arrived. Pink chromosomes swam in oily yellow cytoplasm. The promotions were happening to me quickly enough to inspire a certain cynicism. I realized that, if I was to negotiate a new contract, I might also reopen the issue of my retirement.

"So to return to my proposal, in such a worst case scenario, inoculations will have to be rationed and distributed rationally to preserve the infrastructure of government and commerce." Two shrimp on my plate seemed engaged in meiosis as I stared down at them. Infrastructure? "We won't be inoculating, for example, murderers on death row." He smiled at this seemingly rehearsed reasoning.

"Not at first," I offered.

He paused, his nostrils testing the odor of my comment.

"But of course," I continued, "preserving all human life will be a priority for us all. In this worst case scenario."

"Of course. A priority. But strictly infeasible. But by agreeing to be part of this team, you will of course ensure that you are among those to be inoculated." He chuckled and looked off, into his memory, peeling a shrimp. "Believe me, some of the men, military men, involved in planning worst case scenarios were not interested in choosing women based on their talents as scientists."

I stared at him.

"Oh, you know how some men are," he smiled. "But in any event Doctor, there is human survival to consider. You are young and your medical records indicate perfect reproductive health. This is something we are looking at with the men too. Jacob, incidentally, would have been wrong for this next phase of things."

I wonder if my mouth hung open as I stared. Professional mind meanwhile wondered how to broach the subject of retirement in the light of this more urgent matter of the invasion of my privacy, and all the implications of what he was telling me, all with regard to a project that was framed as, essentially, being one of those whose lives were spared. Infrastructure. In a worst-case scenario, retirement means death. Another question regarding professional poise had begun to gnaw at me: When is it appropriate to throw burgundy in your boss's face? When is it imperative? Would I be immediately taken down by Secret Service? And: how perpendicular is that?

"The Olds. You don't need to get it for me, I can drive."

Joe handed me my keys and walked with me to my car. I watched him out of the corner of my eye. He caught my eye and unexpectedly smiled. They're all crazy, really. Would he attack me? Did he recognize me?

"Is this your day job? Or is there evil here?" I ask.

"Your building. I can see it from here."

I looked off into the lattice of cloud beyond. Serrations of mountains stamped the indigo sky. We were thirty miles from the complex.

"I see a shining plume," he said, "of glowing smoke. It's bright enough to read by. But I suppose you don't see it."

Was it possible he could see the smoke from the bioincinerator, where used monkeys were destroyed? Were there people who could see infra-red? But even so, there must be hotter smokestacks than ours in the city's industrial sprawl. I looked at him. He was looking at me. He had striking blue eyes. A recessive gene. Is a genetic code, I thought, a destiny? Truly the way things will go, things that matter, life?

I did not remember a lover so affectionate. Obviously a spy, professionally trained. Did he get up while I was asleep to photograph my scribbled genetics with a camera concealed in his eyelid? Did brave, lazy Ebola Reston defeat him by knocking the papers behind the desk earlier while rolling on his back during a catnap, dreaming that an outbreak of Australian mousepox had left the apartment scattered with tasty morsels? Were foreign spymasters listening to my snores, needles scrawling my beta waves onto printouts? When would he kill me? Would he do so respectfully, mercifully, quickly? And would he kill me to obtain military secrets or to destroy them? In order to build a bomb or to defuse one? Certainly a submicroscopic speck capable of replicating itself in a human host at dizzying exponential speed and radiating through the entire species was a credible deterrent. Because if you're willing to destroy yourself to defend yourself then one ought to take you seriously--right?--this shows that you are a serious person. Or was he a spy for God, copying our DNA? This is why I needed to publish, because God subscribed to the Journal of Genetic Research and Virology Annual. God probably stole the whole idea from us. Maybe Joe could get me a better job in God's lab, splicing genes to make more intoxicating hyacinths, cuter kittens, phosphorescent fish. And what would I tell Adam White? Because he knows he does better research than God. And where could I get a job when my only reference was classified? It would appear as though I had simply not been working for five years. It was perfect, because God is omniscient and wouldn't ask for a reference. Wasn't having sex complicated enough without worrying about your lover being a spy? And would it worry me more if he was working for the Chinese or if he was actually working for God? From whom was I keeping the most secrets? The Chinese would reward me for my knowledge. God on the other hand could only be displeased at my hackery. And it feels bad when God hates you. How could I explain to God that my employer had forbidden me from signing a petition against a nuclear reactor on the moon? Was it too late for me to learn nuclear physics and to transfer to the moon? And would God be jealous that I was hooking up with one of her staff? Or were priests allowed to fool around with atheists now? Was sex as a sin contingent on the denomination? And, wait, what if a worst case scenario came about? What would happen? Or: how could it have happened? Or: who could have prevented it? Adam would have me believe that preventing it was my job. I should have asked him what his best case scenario is. It was childish, the way Joe clung to me all night, turning when I turned, childish and nice.

I want to leave the complex but they took my car away from the parking lot and cut the lights. I am walking out through the echoing underground tunnel following a faltering flashlight beam when I hear a car approaching from behind, its headlights flooding the tunnel, showing its endlessness. There is no place to hide or run so I stand and wait for it. Adam White leans across the front seat and opens the passenger door for me. We drive on as though we have someplace to go together. He seems pleased and won't stop talking about the project, trying to tune in something on his car radio. In the desert where the wind rattles a windsock on a lone hanger beside a biplane tethered to the ground, he pees with practiced ease beside the car. I start the engine and put it into gear. He doesn't even shout as his delighted face, red from the taillights, is engulfed by the blackness behind me. He looks like a struck match and is gone. I turn perpendicular to the way we were going, and exit. Then the only thing to see is the highway's stripe and the flare of odd fierce meteors.

When, in the morning, Joe was gone, I had to search the house. A reflexive flash of rage gave way to relief, since, all things considered, I preferred having him gone. The note said "Love life and the moon, love Joe." How he could have made it out of my neighborhood was another question, but I wasn't about to ask the neighborhood guard if the priest I fucked had left before dawn.

The new genetic codes were called, collectively, Pandora. Since watching Jacob dissolve, more than once I believed I had been exposed, and felt that peculiar weightless nausea of possibly having fallen off the edge of a very tall building. But mostly I repressed such thoughts and focused on the numbers. We had identified the viruses with global depopulation potential and were now testing possible vaccines. Most of these vaccines proved to be themselves lethal, and the rest were ineffectual, with one exception, but I felt closer to finishing the project and being in a better position to broach the subject of my retirement with Adam White, in a stolidly professional manner, without the rage that had overcome me during our dinner meeting.

This new agent took a short time to incubate, but when the monkeys started to crash, the entire room went down in two days—according to my experiments a near perfect fatality rate. Their last day alive the monkeys, though they were falling apart from the hemorrhaging and liquefaction of the tissue, showed signs of aggression. They made horrible gurglings and flung their own infected tissue around the room. Something about the way this bug ate through their brains made them violent. From the looks of it, we had created something scary. But we had no way of knowing whether humans were similarly susceptible, which was fine with me.

My eyes strained as I peered through my helmet glass and focused the electron microscope on the viral tangle that had torn apart the monkey cell, I couldn't tell the shapes on the slide from the afterimages that swam through my tired eyes. I made a mental note to switch from two caffeine pills to three. There was no way to drink coffee in a space suit.

A red light came on. That meant there was a security problem. I shut down the microscope and went through the sealed door into the shower room and let the spray wash over the suit.

The red light comes on. Then all the lights go out and the emergency light's on only halfway. There is a klaxon firing short bursts. A fire broke out of the incinerator. The ventilator system now labors to remove smoke from the building at the risk of also releasing pathogens. I am in intermittent blackness, surrounded by glass and scalpels and monkey corpses and deadly viruses, my pressurized space suit going limp as the pumps have quit. I shout through my helmet to security hoping that one of the microphones works. I prepare to exit through the safe zone and airlock. The bleach showers no longer work, I cannot disinfect properly. Luckily the airlock doors can be pulled open. It is difficult feeling my way out with the gloves.

I came awake and did not know how long I had been slumped against the shower wall. The seven-minute shower had ended. The security alert, another doctor claimed, had probably been a drill. That was not my first narcoleptic seizure in the lab, but the first time I had fainted into a nightmare. Obviously I couldn't tolerate that. I went home to try to sleep.

I have a satchel with the vaccine. I try to get out of the complex. The monkeys have escaped from their cages. Vicious, agile, infectious, they crawl through the ceiling panels and lurk, teeth bared in viscous faces. Thick strands of hairy bloody fluid drool through those grates, the gelatinous, infectious residue of the new dead.

I tried to wake up fully but lay there flattened by dread, my mind unable to release its hold on this problem: what is the difference between holding the virus in your mind and being infected by it. I had had a bad dream and had to reassure myself that the representation in my mind of the virus's structure was not real. But that wasn't true. DNA was real. DNA was in every cell responsible for every simultaneous thought. If the thoughts were made of DNA, then why wasn't the DNA in my thoughts the DNA the thoughts were made out of? Did this mean my mind was infected? Could the virus be transmitted by thought? If the molecules comprised in the virus could be communicated by language then why couldn't the virus? And if I am dreaming, this dream could be my body's way of telling me something about it that not even a doctor could, at this stage, yet detect.

I pushed purring Ebola Reston from my pillow, rubbing cat hair from my mouth. It wasn't even midnight. I threw on a sweatshirt and jeans and drove out the gate and to the Club, needing to talk to someone. I might admonish him for leaving before dawn, if I couldn't think of anything else to say. I thought he would be happy to see me. It was a different valet who stood at the post though.

"We're closed."

"Is Joe working tonight?"

"Joe doesn't work here anymore."

"Why?"

"Missed two shifts. This is supposed to be my night off. They called me in to cover for him."

"That awful little candy red car, that belongs to Mr. White, right?"

"Yes."

"I'd like to go in and talk to Mr. White."

"You'll have to park your own car I'm afraid. I'm going home."

"Are you sure? Because I'd really like to put a dent in that toy."

"That's fine with me, as long as you wait ten minutes for me to punch out."

I found Adam White in the bar. While in the corner gentlemen of means chatted softly, rolling cigars in their jowls, Adam, sitting alone with a chocolate martini, was examining a row of bowling trophies in a glass case. He wore a yellow sports walkman with his designer sports coat and tie, and was bobbing to some beat. His eyes widened at my entrance as through I were a tennis ball unexpectedly served and he moved to intercept me, leaving his headphones on.

"Doctor, what a surprise. I didn't know you were a member here."

"I'm not."

"I'm sorry if I offended you the other day. Have you come here to accept my proposal?"

"I have a couple of concerns. The first is my salary, including full retirement benefits. The second is the problem of completing our research without human testing."

"So I take it you're interested in joining the inner team? Salary won't be an issue I assure you."

One of the men in the corner, I noted, was Mac, who raised his snifter to me in recognition, not quite smiling.

"Because," Adam smiled, "your knowledge is indispensable. As are you, doctor." He gestured to the corner and I followed him over to the men who sat around a table covered by a large unrolled blueprint of a building in the shape of a pyramid. "Our new office," Adam beamed. His watch sparkled as he pointed to a corner of the schematic. "You and I will live here."

I wondered what he meant by "and," and "live." Was this a new laboratory where we would all get new offices? I looked at Mac, who did not meet my gaze, looked down at a pager, unclipped his phone and called in. He frowned, and Adam frowned, watching him. Finally Mac closed his phone. "How are the two women?" Adam asked. Mac shook his head. I don't know, but we have some fires to put out. I'll leave you to your celebration."

In Seattle, Mac had learned, at the university facility where Bertha was kept, a network administrator reported a grievous security violation, in which one of their own employees had set up what was being described as a website for terrorists. This had been brought to the administrator's attention by Federal government officials. Although no top secret data was kept on those machines, this bizarre incident risked undermining government confidence in their whole enterprise. Adam would have to fly back to Seattle the next day to meet with the Feds and smooth feathers.

But the real problem was that someone had sneaked into the California facility.

While Mac presented me with my new keycard and the combinations to the core subbasement doors, Adam beamed like a prom queen. He looked like a catalog page with pink sports shirt tucked into white shorts, socks and sneakers, almost jogging in place with enthusiasm.

"Doctor I am very excited to now be able to share with you this other part of our research. In cooperation with the federal penitentiary system we're offering prisoners a chance at a commuted sentence in exchange for their cooperation doing human testing of the potential vaccine you've identified."

Mac abruptly turned away and sneezed. Adam and I looked at him in alarm as he unfolded his handkerchief sheepishly to remove a spot of blood from his moustache.

"Are you all right Mac? If you feel sick you should go down to the medical wing and have yourself looked at."

"I'm fine, Mr. White, just a little head cold."

He punched some numbers on the wall and the door slid back. Directly ahead was the grey area, where protective suits were worn before going into the core. He led me on a corridor around the outside of the core.

"I think you'll agree that these experiments are most useful, without verification with human subjects, the viral synthesis is just finger exercises. Here's the good news: we have two lucky women, prisoners, who may be our first survivors."

"If that's true then my work here is done."

"Oh the work goes on, Doctor. But you've seen what these agents can do to monkeys. So prepare yourself. Remind yourself that these subjects are rapists and child-killers being spared life imprisonment or execution in order to make a contribution to science."

We passed some wire-reinforced glass. In a blood-soaked bed I saw a wet and shriveled pupa that was once a human. Adam tapped the glass. "This agent continues to amplify even after biological functions have ceased. This person is long dead and still smoking like crazy. I've not seen anything quite like it. As a weapon it is something new:

destroys people and removes their corpses, leaving only bone and connective tissue to clean up. One of your lucky breaks, doctor. We hadn't set out to find a corpseless plague, it just landed in our lap."

We moved to the next window. "This one's still very fresh."

Joe's head rolled back and I saw his eyes were pink and soft. "He went blind early, it seems," said Adam. He had made a bloody mess of his holding tank. It appeared that he had been throwing himself against the walls, which bore his red imprints. His crucifix glinted from the ooze of his collapsing chest cavity. Joe had wanted to let the blind see.

"Doctor White, I know this man. Mac? This man is no murderer or child-rapist. He's a priest."

"Stupidity doesn't become you, Dora. This priest sneaked into the facility hiding in your trunk. He is a friend of yours I understand? We can only assume he was working for the Chinese and hope that he was not able to get any information out of the complex. We have no reason to believe you intentionally compromised our security but we cannot exclude that possibility. If you weren't necessary, it wouldn't be an issue. So, if you have any misgivings about your new assignment, or SP, you should know that it's too late for that. Just decide which side of the glass you want to be on."

Only one half of his mouth continued to smile. He pulled a tennis ball from his shorts pocket and bounced it on the sterile white tiles while awaiting the aroma of my response.

My reflection was superimposed on top of Joe. He twitched. His lesions hovered, burning, on my cheeks.

Into the mirror.

HEAVEN SCENT

As he sat behind the wheel of the Heaven Scent van idling at a stoplight, Rick saw a skinny boy crossing the street, a red backpack slung over one shoulder, and instantly he saw his kid brother Danny, his colorful X-Men backpack shining in the sun as he waited for the school bus. Then he imagined Danny on that last day, weighted down beneath his pack in the cruel sun somewhere south of Fallujah, the grenade cradled in his hands, and Danny lifting up his hands as if he were taking Communion.

There had been a closed casket service at the non-sectarian Willow Grove Cemetery; a Catholic burial service denied Danny, the suicide.

Danny boy, what have you done? Rick thought. Where have you gone?

The light was green.

The driver behind him leaned on his horn and Danny's ghost disappeared, but Rick knew he would be back.

He drove slowly down the street, watching the signs pass by, looking for 107 McKinley Place. The niece had said she would meet him there. Two blocks later, Rick turned right onto McKinley, a shady street lined with small—a real estate agent would say cozy—houses of 1920's vintage. Number 107 was a stucco and wood Tudor with a tall, narrow gable above the front door. A silver Lexus was parked in the driveway.

A man and a woman got out of the car as Rick pulled the van to the curb. He parked the van, grabbed a red plastic toolbox from the back, and walked up the drive. Rick was wearing the Heaven Scent Cleaners uniform, a dark blue jumpsuit with the company logo, a thin gold band encircling the words Heaven Scent, embroidered over the left breast.

106

He carried a clipboard in his free hand. Rick set the toolbox on the ground and introduced himself to the couple, Tony and Carmela Sorrentino.

"I'm sorry for your loss," he said. It sounded mechanical, he had said it so many times before, but truly he was sorry for them. He knew what they felt.

"Thank you," Carmela said. "Your office said to give you the key."

"Yes."

She dug it out of her red leather purse and handed it to him. "How long will this take, Mister Warren?"

"I'm not sure yet, " Rick said. "I'll check the premises today and see what needs to be done. Then I'll bring a crew in. Usually, we can take care of everything in a few days."

Carmela nodded. "That would be fine," she said.

"Right," Tony said. "We'd like to get the house listed as soon as possible."

Rick noted the urgency in his voice and knew his crew would have to get the job done on time. There had been too many screw-ups since Danny had died. Rick knew they were his own fault, but what could he do? His world had blown apart with Danny's.

"Poor Uncle Mario," Carmela said. She looked up at the gable rising over the front door. "This house was everything to him. He built it himself, you know," she said, turning back to Rick.

"Are you sure you want to sell it?" Rick asked, sorry as soon as he spoke the words. It was none of his business after all.

"Absolutely," Tony said. "We have no choice, now that the old—Uncle Mario—has died in it. We could never live here, no one in the family could. We have to sell it."

Carmela didn't say anything.

Rick didn't question the couple's superstition. After twelve years in the business, nothing surprised him anymore. There were countless ways in which a person might handle the death of a loved one. Who was he to say that any one way was more valid than another? He couldn't find a way for himself, how could he find one for them?

"Would you like to come inside with me?" He didn't think they would, no one ever did, but he thought he should ask anyway.

Carmela shook her head. Tony said, "No."

"All right. I'll call you when we've finished," Rick said.

He waited until the Lexus had backed down the driveway and pulled out into the street before picking up the toolbox and stepping onto the front porch. He opened the box, removed a pair of rubber gloves and a facemask with respirator and put them on. Years ago, such precautions would have been unnecessary, but the threat of hepatitis and AIDS from contaminated blood necessitated the gloves. The respirator was for the smell. Rick removed a camera from the box and slid it into a pocket of his jumpsuit. He tucked the clipboard under his arm and fitted the key to the door. He pushed it open and stepped into a small foyer. It was hot and stuffy inside the house, the windows all closed, the air conditioning turned off. He walked into the parlor.

The uncle had been a suicide as well. Rick had a copy of the police report on his clipboard and he looked up at the ceiling, at the hole there above the Barca-Lounger, where the first bullet had lodged. The man's hand shook so much as he squeezed off the first round that, incredibly, he missed his head, sending the bullet into the plaster ceiling overhead. Cracks radiated out from the hole like spider legs. Somehow, after that failed attempt, the uncle steeled himself and pressed the barrel of the .38 against his chest. He didn't miss that time, but he didn't die right away. He managed to get up and stagger a few feet across the floor where he collapsed before the fireplace, beneath the inscription on the mantel that read: Mine, always mine.

How had he been able to do it? Rick wondered. Why hadn't the reverberation of the pistol echoing through the little room, or the ringing in his ears, or the acrid smell of the powder burning his nostrils, or even the bits and pieces of plaster raining down upon his head, why hadn't any of that jolted him from his death wish? How was it that after that startling first miss, he was still able to collect himself and say yes, I really did mean to die, let's try it again, shall we?

And how is it that Danny, a good Catholic, could have stood there in the sun, the live grenade in his hands, as his fellow Marines dove for cover. Could he really have smiled, as it was reported he did, before blowing himself to atoms?

Rick shook his head and blinked back the tears; there were things that surpassed all understanding.

In addition to the police report, Rick also had a Heaven Scent Cleaners worksheet attached to the clipboard, which he now consulted. He took a pencil out of his pocket and drew the floor plan of the rooms on the form. He walked around the rooms, making notes as he went and taking pictures of the damage for any insurance claim the survivors might want to file. As he went through each room, he removed the personal photos hanging on the walls and stacked them neatly in a closet so that his crew wouldn't be reminded of the person who had left the grisly remains behind.

He snapped a photo of the burgundy colored Barca-Lounger. The fatal bullet had lodged in the man's chest, so there were no bullet holes in the chair, but there was a partial bloody handprint on one of the arms of the chair where the uncle had pushed himself up. Rick bent down to examine the chair and determined that it was covered in vinyl, a material that could easily be cleaned, depending, of course, on whether or not the Sorrentinos even wanted to bother with it. Most of the time, the survivors threw out such damaged pieces.

Rick noted on his form the drops of blood—protein was the term he instructed his technicians to use---that spattered the oak floor between the chair and the brick hearth before the fireplace. A second handprint stained the brick.

There was a large spot of blood, maybe two feet in diameter, on the floor in front of the hearth, where the man collapsed and died. He squatted near the stain, studying it. Six quarts of blood pump through the human body and Rick thought the man had left much of that blood on the floor. The thick stain was almost black in color, except near the center where there was a small mass of reddish tissue that had oozed from the man's chest. Rick noticed that the floors were in need of resurfacing, which meant that the blood would have soaked deeply into the dry wood.

He stood and scanned the room. Rick was accustomed to the incongruity of blood and bone, bits of flesh and tissue, in a domestic setting such as this—last week's newspaper turned to the sports page; a cheap reproduction of Da Vinci's Last Supper hanging on the wall, a dry palm frond stuck behind the frame; a pair of eyeglasses lying open on the table beside the chair. Rick knew that if he went into the kitchen he would find family photos, kids mostly, held in place by little plastic fruit magnets on the refrigerator; a medicine organizer with various colored pills and capsules stored in plastic cubicles, each marked with a different day of the week; a favorite coffee mug, perhaps depicting a beach scene with blue sailboats on the horizon, resting on the counter by the sink. Rick thought that maybe even more than the gore of a messy or violent death, it was these little tokens of a life no longer lived that made it difficult for family members to come back to the house to do what must be done. Still, they could not be expected to enter a place that resembled an abbatoir and that's where Heaven Scent Cleaners came in.

It was a profession that few people knew anything about and, even if they did, few would want the job. Yet, it was a valuable service that Heaven Scent provided. Rick knew that most people understood little about death. They didn't realize that death was messy. The bowels give way, the bladder lets go, there may be vomit, and in the case of violent death, blood, body fluids and fecal matter, bone fragments and hair, tissue, splattered everywhere.

Who would clean up such a mess? The bereaved? Not likely.

It would be me, Rick thought.

As proud as he was of the work he did, reclaiming some dignity for the dead and helping the survivors work their way through grief, it was a job that wreaked havoc on his social life. Dating him was as bad as dating a mortician. He recalled a recent date with a woman named Helen that had not gone well.

"The bones are the last to go, of course," he had said, mistakenly thinking the process of putrefaction fascinated her. He twirled up a forkful of spaghetti.

Helen paused, her fork arrested halfway between her plate and her trembling lips and Rick knew that once again, he had gone too far, too fast. Yes, there it was, the color draining from her face as if she was about to toss what little she had eaten of her eighteen-dollar veal marsala.

Rick knew from experience that once this first date was over he would never see her again. Over her dead body she would say, and he almost laughed out loud at the thought. But there wasn't really anything to laugh about, not when you were a thirty-five year old bachelor with no prospects.

"Don't let it bother you," Danny had once said, in a rare role reversal between them, Danny giving advice to Rick. "You're a great guy, some woman will find that out. It will happen."

That was easy for Danny to say, Rick thought. Danny with his string of girlfriends. And now his widow.

His thoughts of Danny flowed into the gloom of the cloistered little house, weighing upon him. It seemed as though a dense and suffocating fog had suddenly filled the room. He couldn't stay in the house any longer.

Later that night, as he lay on the couch in his apartment, watching the latest news from Baghdad on the television, Danny was with him once again. It had been one of those days and Rick knew he had brought it on himself. In the year since Danny had died Rick had tried to avoid the news as much as he could, but the televised sights and sounds provided some unexplainable psychic link to his little brother, almost as though Rick could bring Danny back from the dead, suit him up in his dust colored uniform again, and maybe this time, someone would rescue him from his demons before it was too late.

Danny's demons came to life for Rick in the last letter his brother wrote him. The letter arrived two weeks after Danny's death. Written in an unfamiliar scrawl, it was an emotional, barely coherent letter, in which Danny rambled on about a nighttime firefight in a small village, bulldozing a wall, finding the bodies of an old man and several children beneath the rubble in the morning. Such a tortured letter from Danny, who had coached basketball at St. Rita's School, who had wanted children of his own someday. How had things gone so horribly wrong?

And now the Church declared that he would spend eternity in hell as a suicide. Rick could not accept that. His brother was a good man, used unwittingly by bad men for bad purposes, yes, but a good man at heart. Rick could not believe that Danny's soul would be damned simply because he had, in one utterly desperate and faithless moment, sought his own justice. No merciful god would allow such a thing, would he?

Rick was back at the house on McKinley Place early the next morning with a crew of four Tyvek-suited, facemasked and gloved technicians. He called Carmela Sorrentino from the house on his cell phone and asked her about the chair, being careful to tell her the lounger was soiled, rather than bloody, and did she want to keep it? As he expected, she answered in the negative. Rick had two technicians clean it anyway and load it into the van. It would later be donated to the local Goodwill store. The bloody rags used to clean it would be bagged and sent to a medical waste disposal center to be sterilized and then incinerated.

The other two technicians were on hands and knees, working rags and cleaning solution over the bloodstains on the floor. Although naturally right-handed, they scrubbed the floor with their left hands, a company policy Rick had established to remind them all that there was nothing normal about finding a dead body in a home, nothing normal in what they were doing and that they should never consider such death to be normal. The smaller stains, the trail of spots from the lounger to the hearth, came up easily. The handprint on the brick took a little more work, but it too was finally eradicated. It was the large blot before the hearth that caused them trouble. They worked on it for hours, but as hard as they scrubbed, they could not remove it entirely. It was no longer as viscous as before and the dark color had faded a purplish-gray, but it was still there.

113

Rick was worried. This was an experienced crew. Maybe if they let the stain dry out thoroughly, they could attack it again the following day. Rick told the technicians to pack up.

The next morning Rick went to the house alone, thinking he could probably take care of the remaining stain himself. After the previous day's cleaning there was little risk of being exposed to contaminated blood, but Rick donned his protective gear anyway. Better safe, he thought.

Inside, he opened the curtains and let the sunlight flood into the little parlor. He knelt on the hardwood floor beside the stain. He ran a gloved hand over it but felt nothing but wood, all traces of pathology—as he called the physical remains—removed. Using the strongest cleaner he had available, Rick carefully and diligently scrubbed the stain, working the cleaner into the wood inch by inch. It took him three hours to work over the entire stain and when he was finished it looked perhaps a shade lighter, perhaps not.

"Damn!" he said, sitting back on the floor.

Again, he let the solution dry overnight and returned the following day. Again, he was thwarted in his attempts to remove the stain. He had no choice but to call the Sorrentinos and tell them what was happening. In Rick's opinion, they would have to replace the floorboards before selling the house.

"What are you talking?" Tony Sorrentino said, over the phone. "That would cost us a bundle."

"The insurance would probably cover it," Rick offered, aware of the irritation in Tony's voice.

"Yeah, maybe. I want to see it first. Can I?"

"Sure, it's your house," Rick said.

Later that day, Rick met the Sorrentinos at the house. He stood on the covered porch, sheltered from a heavy rain that had begun earlier that morning and showed no signs of stopping anytime soon. He watched the Lexus pull into the driveway. Tony and Carmela made a dash for the porch, she holding her purse over her head.

Although wearing his blue jumpsuit, Rick did not bother with any of the protective equipment as he unlocked the door, the threat of disease having long since been eliminated.

Tony and Carmela entered timidly, their first visit to the dead man's house since he had shot himself.

"Oh, Jesus," Carmela said, when she saw the stain. She covered her mouth with her hand and stared. Rick wondered if she was going to be sick.

"Oh, Jesus is right," Tony said, circling the stain, eyeing it, as though looking for a way in. "You guys couldn't get this out?" he said, looking up at Rick.

"We tried everything."

"Jesus," Tony said.

"It's Uncle Mario," Carmela said. She had drawn closer to the mark on the floor, yet her voice sounded far away.

"What?" her husband said.

"He's still here, he's still in this house."

"Come on, Carmela. What are you talking about? You're giving me the willies, here," Tony said.

"Don't you see, Tony? It's a sign. Uncle Mario's spirit is still in this house." Rick saw Tony's eyes dart quickly around the room as if looking for the dead man. "We can't sell the house," she said.

Tony stopped pacing. "Tell me you're joking."

"He's not at peace, Tony, and until he is, we can't sell the house."

"We can just tear up the damned floorboards like Rick said. Put down a new floor."

She shook her head. "That won't make a difference, his spirit will still be here."

Rick stood watching them, listening to their conversation. It was comical at first, but there was something in Carmela's stubborn insistence that her dead uncle was still among them in spirit that tugged at Rick. He was suddenly uneasy in the house, an emotion he had never felt before in all the many houses of death he had entered over the years. Despite the cold rain falling outside, he felt a trickle of sweat run down his back. An image of Danny in uniform flashed before his eyes, startling him.

Tony was pleading with his wife, whining to her about repairing the floor and selling the house immediately, but she was having none of it. This was a woman used to getting her own way, Rick thought, and she did. She politely thanked Rick for the work Heaven Scent Cleaners had done and told him she would mail him a check in the morning. To her husband's inquiries about what they would do with the house, she simply said she had an idea.

Never in the twelve years since Rick founded Heaven Scent Cleaners had he failed as he did at 107 McKinley Place. It mystified him completely. Blood, that's all it was, why couldn't he get it out? He was thinking this all the next day as he shuffled through reports and bills at the office, and he was still thinking about it when he stopped in at Fiona's Café for dinner. On the way back to his apartment he found himself driving down McKinley, as if the house itself had called him back for yet another try. Ridiculous, of course, he didn't even have the key anymore. Still, he slowed as he drew near the house.

There was a car in the driveway and it wasn't the Sorrentino's silver Lexus. He pulled over to the curb and looked toward the house. It was dark, but as Rick watched, a faint light seemed to wash up behind the parlor window. The light grew stronger until a distinct yellow gleam shone forth.

What the hell was that? Rick wondered. Had someone broken into the house? He got out of the van and quietly shut the door. Cautiously, he made his way up the steps to the porch. There was no sound coming from the house, but now he could clearly see the yellow light spilling from the window. From the porch he could peer into the parlor window, the curtains still open just as they had been when he last visited the house.

The yellow glow emanated from a spot before the hearth where a ring of candles surrounded the indelible stain. Rick saw a dark figure sitting on the floor silhouetted by the candles' glow. The figure's back was turned to the window. The rest of the house remained in darkness. This was no burglary, Rick thought, but what the hell was going on?

Almost without his volition, Rick stepped to the door and carefully tried the doorknob. The door slowly opened. He could feel his heart racing. He stepped inside, gently closing the door behind him. The figure across the room never moved. He crept a little closer.

"Please be quiet," a woman's voice said, softly.

Rick froze, startled by her voice. She hadn't turned to look at him.

He slowly walked toward the figure until he was standing alongside her. In the candlelight Rick saw that the woman was probably in her early thirties. She sat calmly, her legs folded beneath her. Her long black hair was fashioned into a braid that hung down her back. It lay like a glistening black snake against her white dress. Her eyes were closed.

"Who are . . .?" Rick said.

She opened her eyes—Rick noticed they were blue—and placed one finger across her lips for a moment. "Sit, please," she said. "I'm almost finished."

Rick lowered himself to the floor and sat beside her, watching. She had closed her eyes again and he wondered how she could be so calm, so trusting in the presence of a stranger in a dark and empty house. The woman was silent and still. He studied her face, inscrutable as a mask. He noticed how the candlelight played upon her hoop earrings. After a few minutes, she slowly opened her eyes, as if only then coming fully awake. She turned to look at him.

"My name is Gwen," she said.

"What are you doing here?"

She got up, walked to the wall switch and turned on the lights. Then she came back to the ring of candles, leaned over and began blowing them out. A smoky scent wafted through the room.

Rick watched in silence. He thought he should be angry with this strange woman, fooling around with what he considered was still his responsibility, the bloodstain on the floor, but he found that he was not angry. He was, in fact, curious.

When she had blown out the last candle Gwen said, " Carmela Sorrentino hired me. She wants this house cleansed."

"That's already been done," Rick said, rising to his feet. "By me."

"No, not cleaned. Cleansed." She collected the candles in a canvas tote bag Rick had not noticed before. "There's a difference," she said. "You remove the physical presence of the dead, I remove their spirits."

"You're a witch," Rick said, thinking that was not exactly the right word, but not knowing what else to call her.

Gwen laughed. "No, not a witch. A psychic."

"You see dead people?"

"Not in the Hollywood way that you're thinking about, but I can communicate with the spirits of the dead, yes. I can help them move on to where they belong."

"And Carmela hired you to help her dead uncle?"

Gwen nodded.

Rick stood there for a moment, thinking. He looked at her. In the bright light he could see that she was pretty in an ethereal sort of way. She was thin and delicate looking, her face pale, but looking into her blue eyes Rick could see reflected there an inner strength that momentarily flustered him. "So, how's it going?" he asked.

"I certainly feel the presence of Carmela's uncle in the house," Gwen said, "but I sense something else as well. I don't know what it is yet. In any case, I'm finished here for tonight. I'm tired."

Gwen picked up her tote bag and started for the door. Rick followed.

"Tonight? Do you mean you're coming back again?"

She opened the door and stepped out onto the porch. "Tomorrow night," she said.

Rick closed the door behind them and walked down the steps with her. "Listen, Gwen, would it be all right if I joined you tomorrow?"

"Why?"

He really didn't know. Was it merely professional interest in an unorthodox stain removal method? Something else? "Just curious, I guess. Is that alright?"

"I suppose so. I'll be here by eight."

They were standing by her car.

"Thanks. By the way," he said, extending a hand, "my name is Rick Warren."

She shook hands with him. "I know."

"That's right, you're psychic."

"No. Carmela told me."

Rick was at the house the next night before Gwen. He waited in the van until her car turned into the driveway, then got out and walked with her to the house. Inside, Gwen again placed the candles in a ring around the bloodstain and lit them. Rick turned off the lights and sat on the floor beside her.

"What now?" he whispered.

"We wait," she said. "In silence."

They sat there for a long time, Rick shifting his weight every now and then on the uncomfortable hardwood floor. He looked at Gwen who, as she had done the night before, sat serenely, her eyes closed. Rick watched the candles flickering in the darkness, watched their shadows dancing, and felt as though they were drawing him in, as though he were shrinking down into the glowing circle of light. He thought dimly of time passing, but didn't know how long he had been sitting there, or even—a very odd sensation—whether he was actually sitting there or not. He felt disconnected, adrift and he thought of Danny, also adrift, wandering, and the hot tears were in his eyes, and then he saw one of the candles move, he was certain of it. "They're here," he heard Gwen whisper.

Rick felt the air suddenly grow cold. A shiver ran down his spine. His eyes were open, but there was nothing to see other than the candles and Gwen. Her eyes were now opened also and she seemed alert, listening, her head cocked slightly to one side.

"Who is it?" Rick asked, softly.

"Mario," she said. "He's confused."

Rick was aware of a strange feeling in the house, a thickening of the air if that were possible, and a light tingling sensation, like a buildup of static electricity. He felt the hairs on his arms rise up. He did his best to ignore these feelings and focused on Gwen. A faint smile crossed her lips and she nodded her head as though agreeing with someone in a conversation. She raised her right hand from her lap and extended it, palm up, to the circle of candles. Rick watched her eyes track something unseen from the dark corner of the room to the halo of light.

"Yes," she said, to the air. Then, after a few moments, she said quietly to Rick, "Mario's gone. Now there's only the other."

"The other?" Rick asked. He had no sooner spoken those words, then his mind was filled with images of Danny. They came in a swirl, a mental blizzard that threatened to overwhelm his senses. Danny on his bicycle. Danny in his baseball uniform. Danny trying to play Rick's guitar. Danny sitting on the porch swing with his first girlfriend, Rachel. Danny in his Marines dress blues. Danny in a dusty tent writing his last letter home. Danny holding the grenade. Rick felt as though his heart would explode. He was no longer sitting up but was slumped over, his head nearly touching the floor, as Danny, Danny, Danny, raced through every nerve, every bone, and every vessel within him. He was filled with Danny. He was Danny.

He felt the pain of the last year, the paralyzing depression, unwinding inside him, uncoiling and streaming through him like psychic surgery. Rick sobbed. He felt a hand touch his back and he knew it was not Gwen. At once, a great calm descended upon him. The images of his brother disappeared and there was now only a light like the candlelight filling him. He slowly rose up and looked at Gwen.

She smiled at him and he noticed the tears in her eyes.

"I don't have to worry about him anymore, do I?" Rick said.

"No," she said. "He's at peace."

Rick sighed. Gwen reached over and took his hand. "And so are you."

FAMILY BUSINESS

It's pretty hard for me to avoid that intersection, since it's where the highway comes into town. Most of the time I try not to think about it. But once in a while I stand at the side of the road and watch the cars and trucks zipping past, and wonder exactly what happened, especially on sunny, frosty mornings like that one was. There wasn't much traffic, they said. Maybe Mom was half-asleep and didn't see the truck coming, maybe the sun was in her eyes. Was something distracting her, they asked us, did she have something on her mind? I couldn't say. At least there were witnesses, I remember thinking. At least somebody saw, and tried to help, did what they could right away. I'm not really sure why that should make me feel better, but it does.

***

My friend Karen and I went into town to go shopping one day. You'd think someone her age would know how to buy a bikini, but she had no idea how much work it was. She thought we'd just be going to, like, one store and picking one. No way, I said, this is going to take some work. So she had this one all picked out after trying on maybe two, and I couldn't believe it. It was so wrong, and she just didn't clue in. I guess it would have taken some imagination to see what a good suit could have looked like on her, because she'd let her thighs get all hairy and wasn't tanned. Still, I could see this one wasn't it.

"What's wrong with it?" she asked.

"Too old lady. Doesn't show enough skin."

"Maybe I don't want to show too much."

"After you get a tan going, you'll look great. Don't worry."

"I don't want one, Sadie. What about skin cancer?"

"As if. You're talking about stuff that happens to old people."

I convinced her to try on a few more suits, ones I'd picked out. She'd picked black and dark blue ones, said they were slimming colours. I guess, if you want to look like a vampire. The ones I picked were definitely better. Yeah, she'd have to get a bikini wax, but that's no big. One really looked good, almost like mine, but in a bigger size of course. It was the same fabric, a blue tropical print with orange flowers, which plays up my tan really well and brings out my highlights. And she had cleavage in front, behind and on the side. What could be better?

"Now that's a bikini with power," I told her.

She still picked the dorky blue one she liked in the first place. I don't know about that girl.

***

If you ask me, there's nothing creepier than empty campgrounds. They remind me of graveyards. They're so quiet, with utility poles sticking up all over like headstones among the black skeletons of trees. And in the fall and winter, with no one around for miles, they're downright depressing. My dad, on the other hand, really gets off on them. To him, they're vast, open stretches of opportunity, every campground's a new beginning for him. To me, they're just more of the same crap.

My dad makes his living buying rundown campgrounds and fixing them up. Then he resells them and buys more. He's been doing it for years, and it never ends, he's like an addict. At first, he still worked at the Ford dealership in Red Deer. He bought the first campground from a friend, and worked nights and weekends for months fixing it up. He fixed up the showers and the outhouses, upgraded the wiring to the sites, repainted and carpeted the office. He regravelled the roads, repaired and painted the picnic tables and then he sold it. Then he turned around and bought another one, same thing. After a while, he quit his job, and now he does the campgrounds full-time. Sometimes he has two or three on the go at once. I mean, who knew there were that many rundown campgrounds around? Who even knew there were that many campgrounds, period?

I hated it, myself. We were always moving from some little town to another, living right on the campground, usually. It was different when Mom was still around. She always insisted we rent a house in town, which you can usually get for shit in these little places. But after she died, Dad said he didn't see the point of renting a place in town when he'd be spending his time at the campgrounds anyway. It's a family business, he said, and we'll both be out there working, so we might as well stay there, too. So he'd drive me in to the local high school in the morning and pretty much the rest of the time, I was at the campground with him.

Family business. Yeah, Mom was out working at a campground the morning she was killed. Dad and I were at another one. It was a cold, bright, slippery Saturday morning and she was trying to turn left onto the main highway when she was broadsided by a tanker truck and hit a power pole. They said she maybe didn't even see it coming, with the glare off the ice and the sun at the angle it was. They said it was a lucky thing the tanker didn't blow up. Right. I mean, how lucky can you get?

Dad carried right on after she died with his big ideas about the business, how I'd be the accounting person after I finished high school, and take care of the books and all that. I never argued with him. I knew there was no point. But I also knew that I'd leave the minute I could.

***

One thing I've learned is that you've got to go with your strengths, go with your power. It's no good trying to be something you're not. Dad's a salesman, for instance, and even though he thinks it's his carpentry skills and stuff that move the campgrounds for him, it's actually just his car salesman personality that does it. And Karen. She's a nice girl and all, but she could never do what I do. Partly, it's because she isn't that attractive, although I keep telling her how much potential she's got. And I really think she does; if she'd lose some weight and get a tan, she'd really be off to a good start. But she doesn't pay attention to the little details like I do, and that's why she'll always be stuck in some joe job like the one she's got now, at the Saan store in Brooks. I mean, you wouldn't want to buy the clothes there, even with the employee discount.

But me, I'm a detail person. I spend time finding out exactly what my clients want, and it pays off for me big time. You wouldn't see me slaving my ass off in some department store for minimum wage. I only work a few hours a day, and I make great money. And when I save up enough, I'm moving to a bigger city, Calgary or maybe Vancouver. More money, more clients in a bigger place. More power. Though you'd be surprised how much business I get in Brooks.

I guess men are the same all over.

***

Like I was saying, Dad used to get me to help him with the campgrounds, especially after Mom died. I didn't mind at first, didn't mind painting, learning how to use power tools, cutting grass, helping him haul lumber around, that kind of thing. I refused to learn how to drive, though. I just can't do that, and I got mad when he kept saying I should learn. But I did everything else. I figured he needed someone to help him after she was gone.

One cold day in the fall, a Sunday afternoon, I was in the office of the latest campground, painting the new shelving Dad had installed behind the desk. It was dark green paint, I remember, and I was

125

thinking how dusty the shelves would always look. Not the colour I would have picked. I heard him come in and stand behind me and I knew he was watching me, probably watching my painting -- he always said I was in too much of a hurry. He didn't say anything and I was just about to ask him if everything was all right when I felt his hands on my waist. I turned around and he looked different than I'd ever seen him before, like someone I didn't know. For the first time, I was afraid of him. I started to scream, and he put his hand over my mouth. Not that anybody would have heard me out there, anyway.

***

After that day we didn't mention it again, couldn't possibly mention it. I wanted to forget it, pretend it had been a dream, or something I'd imagined. And then it happened again, and again. After that, I left as soon as I could.

I guess I could be angry at him. I was at first, but I'm not anymore. For one thing, anger is negative, just drains away your energy, and I'm a positive person. Still, I struggled to understand for a long time why my own father would do this to me. And then it dawned on me: he really couldn't help himself. He's said that, and I believe him, that he couldn't help himself. I have this power, I know, and it has an effect on people. I guess it's just the raw vital life force within me, and people respond to it. Why should he be any different? It's actually amazing he resisted as long as he did. But he couldn't help it. Men are drawn to me, I see it all the time. Women, too; I see them looking, I see the jealousy in their eyes, and the desire. It's just simple magnetism. And only a few of us have that gift.

***

Karen and I went out for drinks one day after she was done with her shift at the store.

"I haven't seen you around all week. Where've you been?" she asked.

"In Calgary. I had an abortion."

"What?"

"Yeah. I was nine weeks pregnant – ugh."

"Well. Geez, you should have told me."

"I didn't want to upset you. Anyway, it was no big deal, just took a few minutes. I asked them afterward if I could see it. They showed it to me in a little pan. It looked like a big clot of blood, or a piece of liver or something."

She didn't say anything for a minute, then she asked me what Mike thought of it. Mike's one of my clients, and Karen thinks he's my boyfriend. It's just simpler that way, to let her think what she wants instead of getting bogged down in the details. You know, she's a small-town girl. It wasn't that I was trying to hide anything from her, or like I was ashamed of what I do or anything. But someone as provincial as she is wouldn't understand, so I figured there wasn't any point in going too far into it. I just told her I had an Internet business, which is partly true. I do have a website.

"Oh, Mike was fine with it. You know, he's not ready for that whole thing. And I don't know if I ever will be. He drove me down and everything, he was really good about it."

"Well, that's good, anyway."

***

Dad was actually the one who drove me to Calgary. I made up some story about a job interview there and he told me to take the bus, he was busy working. Then he asked why I didn't get a ride with one of my boyfriends. Finally, I had to tell him why I needed to go there.

He hardly said a word at first as we drove west to Calgary, just lit

127

cigarette after cigarette. I watched the bright yellow fields of canola roll by, listened to the old Ford F-150 rattle every time we went over a bump. It made me think of him fuming once because he heard a cop make a remark about FORD standing for Found On Road Dead.

Finally, he spoke. "So whose is it?"

I didn't answer.

"Do you have any idea?"

"What kind of question is that?"

"I know what you do. Don't think I don't. Everybody in the whole damn town knows about you."

"That's a lie."

"I heard about you from some of your johns."

"They're not johns, they're clients."

"Don't get smart with me."

"If you don't like the way I live, just remember how I got started."

That shut him up. He didn't say a word all the rest of the way to Calgary, not when we were at the clinic, not all the way home. He let me out outside my apartment building and didn't answer when I said goodbye, didn't even look back.

I guess I told him.

***

I knew Karen about a year before I finally told her about my business. I just hated to reveal myself too much to someone I didn't know that well. She didn't freak out, I have to give her that. But I don't think she really understood, either. What people like her and my Dad don't get is, my clients want a relationship. It's not just about sex. If they just wanted that, they'd find a girl like Karen and be done with it. The reason they come to me, and the reason I can charge top dollar, is that they come to me for so much more. Companionship, advice.

128

Guidance. Compared to a shrink, I'm cheap. And let's not forget beauty. Beauty's kind of the ultimate power, something that sets the beautiful apart. People are glad to pay to bask in that, you know? And it would be small of me, greedy, to limit myself to one man. Is it my fault I'm worth every cent they pay me?

***

I don't hang out with Karen much anymore. After I told her about the business, she really seemed to change. Not at first; at first she was trying to be cool, like it didn't bother her. But then I could tell her small-town judgmental attitude was taking over. Like she started to point out jobs she heard of that were open. Right, like I'm going to take some stupid retail job. But I thought maybe she was just trying to be nice. After a while, though, it started to annoy me.

Then one night we were at a bar having a few drinks and she got on my back about getting some help. She said she knew a really good counselor I could talk to.

"Where do you get off calling me crazy?"

"I never said you were crazy. I said you might need some help. Everybody needs a little help sometimes."

"Let me tell you something. I am the one helping people. These men, if they didn't have me to talk to, they'd be crazy. I help them with all kinds of problems. You have no idea what I do. I know one thing, I don't go around making judgments on other people, I don't go around telling people what's wrong with them."

I walked out of that bar right then, big, wet snowflakes melting in my eyes, and I didn't look back once. Things like that prove I have to get out of here, go to a big city, where people are sophisticated. In a small place, people are afraid of me, they're afraid of my power. I'm sure Karen's afraid, and that's why she hasn't called since that night, two months ago, now. I haven't called her, either. I don't need that kind of shit. She's probably just jealous of my success. People are always jealous when you succeed. She can't stand to think of herself stuck in this little town, stuck in this life, the way I'm so not.

I mean, some people just don't get it.

ORDERING PIZZA FROM A MURDERER

I.

I'm remembering funny things now. Things that are obsolete. No longer useful. That's what I'm remembering.

I bought a gun. I put it in the cupboard on a blue plastic plate with a green bowl turned upside down on top of it.

I called Chris. He answered like this: Talk to me. Is he trying to make me throw up?

I told him to come pick up his son.

He called me irresponsible and then a bitch and a bad mother. Some people lack creativity.

I reminded him that his sperm being half of the boy means he has to pick him up at three.

The court order he said means I have to pick him up on Friday not Tuesday, Carol.

I'm remembering the nausea. I'm remembering vomiting 15 times that week. When I thought about a Stranger's penis inside of my mother, chunks came up like clock work.

I got my kid into the car by giving him a potato with toothpick arms and legs. He goes to montessori school so this type of thing works.

Chris' girlfriend answered the door. I don't know words small enough for her to understand. Find Chris, OK Dorothy? I said.

My kid shows her the potato which he has named Rusty.

Don't do that, I said.

I'm remembering nightmares. Black nights with black fog and black men attacking me on black streets raping me with long black poles or black muzzles of black guns.

When Dorothy left to find Chris, I whispered to the boy that if he doesn't hide Rusty, Dorothy will eat him in a stew.

I'm remembering hiding in a filing closet at the courthouse. I saw him coming. He was fifteen feet away. I freaked out.

When your father gets here, I said to my kid. He had the potato in a flower pot. Are you listening, Conor?

Chris came to the door in a bathrobe. This was to piss me off.

What a pleasant surprise, Conor, he said looking at me with a frown.

I'm not remembering how my mother talked or what expressions she used or the way she told jokes or got angry or laughed or ordered coffee. I can think about it analytically, but I can't hear it the way it was.

Stop being such a damn bitch all the time, he was saying. I don't remember what I was saying.

Nobody was walking up or down the hill. I always looked at the people around me now that the Murderer was out.

II.

Now that the Murderer was out, I thought every black man I saw was him. I was worse than the cops. In college, I protested the Rodney King incident.

He was a young black kid, maybe twenty. He would be a middle-aged black man now, maybe forty.

My kid's montessori school was teaching him to use different color crayons to draw people. I didn't let him talk to black men.

His teacher called me in to talk about this.

We sat down on a mat on the floor. The teacher was a large woman but she sat indian-style. I didn't know how to put my legs: under me or straight out in front. I settled with them to the side and then kept switching.

She offered me oranges. We talked about things, like their plans to

132

make dream catchers, but I sensed she was going somewhere else. Finally, it came.

Conor called a little girl in the class a . . . criminal, she said in a lowered voice.

I peeled the inside of the orange slice away from the skin with my teeth. He's got a good vocabulary if that's what you're saying, I said.

I think he said it because she's -- the teacher looked at me with her lips pushed out like she might give me a stern kiss -- African-American.

I lied and told her about his father, the terrible, terrible racist. The boy has been over there for the past two days.

III.

For the past two days, the Murderer had been out.

I was trying to find parking in the projects. It was the only place near the movie theater that had parking. The rain coming down hard on the windshield made it hard to see.

The boy was running a quarter back and forth over the dashboard.

When you scratch the dashboard, how many allowances will you have to save to buy me a new car? I asked.

The school was encouraging question asking to teach conversation skills.

Daddy gave me ten dollars, Conor said.

Do you have any concept of how much a car costs? I question-asked, backing into a parking spot.

I got out of the car. I struggled to get Conor out of his car seat. The rain was soaking through my blouse.

Conor and I took shelter under an awning while we waited for the street light to change.

There was a man standing next to us. I looked at him. He was sheltering his head with a newspaper. He was black, about fifty years old. This is him, I thought.

The man looked at me staring at him.

Do you recognize me? I asked.

The man looked away like he didn't know I was talking to him.

Do you recognize me I said, I said.

The man shook his head.

You're not going to look at me? I asked.

The man looked at me.

Conor put his arms around my leg. I pushed him behind me.

Aren't you embarrassed to look at me? I asked.

I'm remembering the Murderer's thin hips when I almost ran into him at the courthouse. I'm remembering how in the filing closet I kept thinking about those thin hips, his little naked butt, thrusting on top of my mother. Her face is a grey circle in this daydream.

The man started to walk away. The street light was green now.

I ran out into the rain and pushed him. The man grabbed my hand.

Hey, hey, the man said.

I put my knee into his stomach, hard. He grunted. I thought I might do it again.

His coat fell open. He had been holding it closed, but now, as he started to back away, it opened.

He had on a bus driver uniform underneath.

I covered my mouth.

I'm . . . I'm . . . Oh, I said. I ran back to pick up Conor who was crying.

We got back in the car. As I drove away, I saw the man was still standing there.

Conor, can you stop crying? Can you stop crying, please.

The man picked up his newspaper, but it was too wet to put back over his head. I can't imagine what he was thinking.

IV.

What he was thinking when he broke into my mother's home was important to me.

At the library, I read about murder. And in the newspaper. I watched documentaries.

The Murderer broke into my mother's home in Pacific Heights, San Francisco. It was 10 P.M. She usually watched television from 9 P.M. to 10 P.M., so she had probably just turned off the television and gotten into bed.

He entered through a downstairs window which they broke and then unlocked.

My mother probably heard him. Maybe she thought it was the dog. Or maybe the dog was sleeping at her feet.

He didn't go into the dining room and take the silver. We have a Picasso in the living room, but he left it. He went straight to her room. He raped her. While he took a shower in her bathroom, she choked on her vomit. This was because he had duct-taped her mouth shut. Her hands were duct-taped to the bed frame. He used our own tape.

In court, the Defense Attorney - an ugly, vapid man who had little fingers and probably never satisfied his wife - put the Murderer on the stand. I guess the whole event was a gang-related thing. A right of passage to get these little letters tattooed on the back of your neck.

My mother only had one breast. I wondered if he noticed. Would he know what the explanation was?

V.

The explanation was, according to the books I read, that young people murder for perfectly justifiable reasons that are results of greater societal problems. These problems include, but are not limited to:

Violence in the media,

The absence of a moral compass,

Women joining the workforce,

Healthy teen rebellion gone bad,

The natural tendency for teens to form cliques or,

. . . The breakdown of the nuclear family.

This is how I explained to myself what happened.

VI.

What happened is this:

I waited a year, long enough to get pissed off that every thing was so difficult with the Murderer out.

I looked him up in the white pages.

He was unlisted.

I waited another month.

I called the parole board.

They said to me, No way. No how. Not a chance.

Three months passed.

I met an off-duty police officer at a bar. There was a tan line on his finger where the ring usually was.

He bought me a shot. I bought him four.

The sex was uninspiring.

I waited a week before stopping by his office.

He was nervous, sweating through his shirt, until I told him how easy the deal was.

That Saturday he stopped by the house with the Murderer's address and place of employment. The Murderer delivered pizzas.

I dropped Conor off at his dad's.

I sat by the phone, looking at it.

I picked up the phone and rested it between my shoulder and ear. The dial tone made my heart feel like someone was squeezing it.

I'm remembering this song my mother used to sing to me when no one else was around. It was a theme song from a television show. It went: Kookie, Kookie, lend me your comb... She would shake her shoulders in a sort of dance and run her fingers through her hair like a beauty queen. This is the only thing about her I am truly remembering.

The phone was ringing.

Victor's Pizza? someone said.

I'm remembering how my mother and I had a house-boating trip in Lake Shasta planned for the week after the Murder. I had just started dating Chris. We flew back from Vassar together for the funeral.

She already paid for it, Chris said to me the day of the wake. We were in the basement, by the snack machines.

You think it'd be right? I asked him.

The money is already gone, he said. He was smoothing out a dollar bill along the side of the machine.

I took Chris on the houseboat in place of my mother.

VII.

In place of my mother's picture, I put a picture of someone from a magazine.

I turned on the television.

I washed dishes.

I switched channels.

I looked at myself in the mirror.

I changed my clothes. I put on a turtle neck and khakis. I took that off. I put on a dress. I found a suit in the back of my closet. I changed into that.

I wondered if the Murderer would be suspicious when they told him that I requested him.

Suspicious of what?

I put on my highest heels. I was very tall in them.

I switched channels again.

I checked on the gun.

I called Conor at Chris'. Dorothy picked up.

Conor told me he put Rusty in the garden so that Dorothy would not eat him.

I almost felt bad for being such a bitch.

Almost.

I had second thoughts.

I made plans:

I would...

Not let him in.

Ask him in

Shoot him

Punch him

Stab him

Get an explanation

Get an apology for ruining *everything*

Forgive him

VIII.

Forgive him, I said to the girl. He's rude.

She was a short brunette. She came up to our, Chris and my, table

138

at The Stinking Rose, an Italian restaurant in North Beach. She saw Chris through the window. He was her professor at S.F. State. She looked a little drunk. I could see her friends through the window, out on the street, waiting.

She seemed relieved when I spoke. She gave me a smile.

Just thought I should say hi, she said. It's so nice to meet Professor Stringer's wife.

In the flesh, I said.

She laughed.

I kicked Chris under the table.

He took a sip of his water.

I'll see you in class, Dorothy, he said finally.

She left. I watched her join her friends outside.

Would it kill you to be polite? She's your student, not an alien, I said.

He cracked a leg of the crab. He said, She was drunk.

IX.

He was drunk.

I heard him break the window. I put on a bathrobe. I took a bat with me.

Downstairs, I caught Chris climbing through the window.

Jesus fucking Christ, where are your keys? I said. You think that is funny?

He started to laugh like maybe he thought it was.

I'll hit you with this bat if that's what I have to do, I said.

Chris was now sitting on the floor.

Carol, Carol, he said. He patted the floor next to him.

I sat down where he was patting.

His arms were around me and he was hugging me very tight. He smelled like whiskey. He was hugging me so tightly that it hurt a little.

I didn't understand.

He was rocking me, back and forth, like a child. He was crying. Why was he acting like I was the one crying?

Oh, Carol, Carol, Carol, he said.

What? I said.

Carol, oh, Carol, Carol, he said.

I didn't know whether to push him off of me or close my eyes and maybe feel a little safe for a moment.

I let my eyes close.

Oh, Carol, Carol, he was still saying.

I liked the feeling of the rocking.

Carol, Carol, how hard it must be to be so angry all the time, he cooed to me.

He cradled my head, running his fingers through my hair.

I feel bad for you all the time, I feel bad for you all the time, he said.

These were things he had never said to me.

I kissed his neck. I tasted sweat. I smelled something sweet.

. . . If only you weren't such a damn bitch, he said. He was shaking now.

It smelled sweet like orchids, or perfume.

I would have helped you through any of this if you didn't have to be so mean to me all the time, he was saying now. He unwrapped me from his arms and held me at arms length by the shoulders. His eyes were red.

I didn't say anything because all words had just evaporated in my throat.

It. Is. Not. My. Fault, he said carefully. It is not my fault, he said, shaking me a little.

It was like when you get off of a boat after being on it for awhile; the feeling of water rolling underneath you doesn't go away so quick. Long after he left with his suitcase, I still felt him shaking me most of the night.

X.

Most of the night has come and gone, it seems, before the buzzer sounds. What an ugly noise. I will replace it with chimes later.

I am sitting on the couch.

There is a twenty dollar bill on the table to pay with.

The buzzer sounds again.

When did the air get so thick?

I want to stand up. It's hard to steady my legs.

I went to the trial to watch the way the Murderer acted. He was very still during the whole trial. I watched his testimony on a T.V. from another room.

The buzzer sounds again, this time for as long as five seconds.

I am walking to the door I realize. I have the gun in one hand and the green bowl in the other.

I put my eye to the peep hole.

There is a black man, maybe 40 years old, in jeans and a yellow t-shirt standing on my porch.

Maybe I will feel something, like an electric shock. I don't feel anything.

I don't recognize him. I don't even know if this is the man.

I run the plastic bowl around my fingers. I think about my kid eating Kix out of this bowl. I am glad I am not in jail because then he would not get good kid-tested plasticware. He'd eat out of porcelain bowls at Chris'. That kind of responsibility isn't good for a little kid, I'm

141

thinking.

The man stands there for a minute in the hot sun.

Then, putting the pizza under his arm, he turns around and walks down the pathway.

This is when I see it.

The green plastic bowl hits the floor.

There are three little initials on the back of his neck: L.E.M.

Lillian Eleanor Monroe.

My mother's initials.

My stomach caves in on itself in one giant contraction.

I have to switch to the window to get a good view.

I watch him unlock a blue bicycle. He balances the pizza on the handlebars.

I'm raising the gun. I'm pointing it at his neck, kind of. My hands are shaking so badly that at one moment I am pointing at his neck, then I am pointing at his feet, then I am pointing at the pizza.

The man rides the bicycle like that, carefully, with the pizza balanced, until he is out of my sight.

I slide down to the floor, sitting right on top of the green plastic bowl.

Well, it survived the fall and all one-hundred and fifty pounds of me fine.

I turn it upright in my palm.

And that's what there is to it.

BURNING NIGHT

Supper was sauerkraut with hot blood sausage, and I hated both. I squeezed the black clotty insides of the sausage into the green shreds. Mixing them together was fun, but it didn't make them taste any better.

I gazed at the calendar on the kitchen wall, to the left of the crucifix and slightly lower. The glossy colour photo for November showed a happy uniformed marching band with a banner and shiny brass instruments. Mum had promised I could have it for my collection, but only if I ate up every meal for thirty days. It was only the ninth. I coveted the picture and forced a forkful of the bitter-sour mash into my mouth, half listening to my parents who talked about the need for a new church building and other grown-up matters.

Pa's knife sliced a sausage; fat spurted. His handsome pale face shone with enjoyment. My brother Erwin stuffed his mouth with sauerkraut and smiled as if he liked the taste, which I knew he didn't. Maybe he was after the calendar picture, though it wasn't his turn this month.

Mum patted her freshly permed hair. "It's almost night," she said, and stood up to pull the kitchen curtains against the approaching darkness, the way she always did during supper. This time she paused.

"There's a lot of smoke. It looks like something's burning down by the crossing. It glows. Holy Mother of Jesus, something's burning proper. I hope it's not Menger's shop."

I went to the window to see what she was looking at.

My breath fogged the cold glass. I wiped it with the sleeve of my jumper and saw dark smoke spiralling toward the empty sky. A light glowed a half-mile from our house, like an orange-coloured glimpse of hell.

Pa put his fork down. "I'll go down the road and watch."

"Is it wise to get involved with this?" Mum asked, her voice uncertain.

"I'm not involved." He stood up and took his grey hat and winter coat from the clothes hook on the door.

"Can I come?" Erwin asked, his mouth full of blackened sauerkraut. "I've finished my supper."

Pa was already tying a grey shawl around his neck.

"Yes, you can come, son." He paused, pointing his chin at me. "I'll take the girl, too."

"I don't want to go," I protested, frightened by what I'd seen out of the window. "Please…"

An angry glance from Pa shut me up. His hard hand pulled me away from the table. "You'll come."

Within moments, Mum had bundled me into my anorak, a thick knitted shawl and a woollen hat. "Better do as Pa says," she whispered. "Stay with Pa, don't catch a cold, and don't talk to anyone."

Erwin grabbed his jacket and cap and ran down the wooden stairs, and I followed.

Pa forced me into the black metal seat on the bar of his bicycle, so that I was locked between his body, his arms and the handlebar. At seven, I was really too old to travel in the child seat, but maybe he reckoned I would escape if I sat behind him on the luggage rack. Erwin followed on his own bike.

A few minutes later, we faced the blaze from the safety of the pavement opposite. My heartbeat roared in my ears like a locomotive. The fire was real in its frightful intensity. Thick smoke oozed through the roof and curled into grey spark-loaded columns.

Hot stink wafted in our faces.

"Smells like we're burning garbage," a woman with spectacles and wrinkly skin beside us remarked. People laughed; their laughter sounded eerie against the whine from the fire.

Many people had come to watch the house burn.

Onlookers stood in pairs and small groups, the men's faces muffled with shawls, the women's heads with headscarves, their hands in their pockets. They looked keen, smug, and not at all frightened.

My mouth was dry and tense; cold prickled on my skin, and I put my hand into my father's coat pocket to hold his hand. "I want to go home, Pa," I pleaded.

"Watch." He grabbed my shoulders and turned me towards the fire. "Watch and learn. Learn about what happens to garbage."

I tried hard not to look, but the glow drew and held me. I knew the house: A shop with a flat above, and a converted attic under a gabled roof. The facade looked thin and vulnerable. The upper windows contained dark emptiness and those on the ground floor screamed with orange heat. Everything looked black against this orange. The house reminded me of the lanterns we'd been making at school, black cardboard with rectangular cutouts, with brightly coloured translucent paper behind.

"Are they in there?" a young woman asked in a thin voice. She carried a small white dog in her arms and stroked it incessantly. She looked at my father. "The Mengers and the Arabs aren't still in there, are they?"

"I've only just arrived. I know nothing."

"If they were at home, they'd have come out by now, wouldn't they?"

When he gave no reply, she turned to the tall bespectacled woman. "The fire fighters are taking their time, aren't they?" She stepped from

145

one foot to the other, nervous, or cold. "They've been notified, haven't they?"

"Yes," the other woman said.

"Still, why…"

"I don't know anything, so don't ask." The older woman turned away, making it clear that questions were unwelcome. The young woman pressed her face into her dog's coat and stopped talking.

Not everyone was quiet, though. Erwin had met up with other boys from his class. They threw stones at the windows of the upper stories, smashing the panes the fire hadn't reached yet, chanting something about cleaning up the town. Their teacher stood by, and I expected him to call the boys to order, but he just watched, his hands folded behind his back.

Within moments, all the windows of the upstairs flat lit up at once like a garland of festive lights. Glass crackled and tinkled, a beautiful chiming sound, punctuated with poufs and bangs. The smoke grew darker and thicker, turning dirty brown and charcoal black.

Plaster blistered and peeled off the wall. Embers flew.

Wind blasted from the site and threw furious heat at us. My face felt like a roasting sausage, but when I averted it, the November night air was so icy it made my hair stand up.

Sirens howled, the dog yapped, and people made room on the pavement for a shiny police vehicle. Two uniformed policemen jumped out and shooed people back from the site, including the chanting boys. The space was clear. Then they stood, doing nothing, hypnotised like the rest of us.

Now smoke seeped from the small attic window, then it lit up as if someone had switched on a hundred lights behind a red curtain. A collective "Aah," rose from the crowd. A couple of people started to clap, but stopped when a policeman threw them a stern look.

I wasn't sure what it all meant. I couldn't believe that people were trapped inside this boiling heat. I looked for the woman with the white dog, but she had disappeared, so I asked the woman with the spectacles.

"Are there people in the fire? Are they burning?"

Fright must have shown in my eyes, because she soothed, "Of course not, dearie. See the sign in the shop window? 'Closed for holidays'. The Mengers have gone away. And even if there was someone in there, they wouldn't feel a thing. The smoke would get them first. So don't you fret." She fished in her coat pocket. "Here, have a sweet, dearie." I hesitated, because my parents warned me not to take sweets from strangers, but Pa had laughed with this woman, so maybe she wasn't a stranger.

"Come on, take it." She sounded impatient, and I feared my refusal might offend. I took the sweet and croaked a thank-you from my dry throat, but put it into my pocket.

Now a red fire engine pulled up with blue flaring lights. Dogs and sirens howled. While the fire fighters opened the hydrant and connected their thick limp hose, the burning house roared like an angry animal. The night sky now appeared deep blue, cool and clean.

I heard one fireman question a group of men. "Anyone still in there?"

"Don't think so. The Mengers are away on holiday."

"There won't be much left of their shop and their flat when they come back."

"They're insured."

In the meantime two fire fighters with helmets had rammed the door and gone in, but came out within moments, signalling.

147

The fireman standing near us translated. "The staircase is collapsed. Nothing we can do."

Flames leaped high in the air, glowing orange and yellow, red and lilac, and it was the most beautiful and most horrible sight I had ever beheld.

I heard screams in the midst of the tumult. People mumbled and shuffled their feet.

"It's the wood," someone said. "The fire has reached the ceiling beams." Another voice replied, "That's right. Old wood always sounds like that when it burns."

A fat dog howled and strained at its lead. But the people just stood, spellbound by the spectacle. The rumble and roar of the blaze absorbed any further cries. Huge billows of smoke and flame erupted when the roof burnt through and beams and timber collapsed with a crash.

A few moments later, the fire quietened, showing what was left of the building. The floor between the ground floor and the first storey still held. Above it, all was gone, apart from a few sagging fragments of walls, and the timbers on each corner which flamed like giant altar candles.

"This house is lost for good," the fireman said. "All we can do now is stop the fire from spreading."

The acid sting of wet ash got into my nose and into my throat where it scratched and tasted bitter. I protected my face as best I could with the knitted shawl. Ashes were everywhere in the air. They danced and showered us like confetti from a carnival float.

The darkness grew cold and silent as the fire withdrew further.

"Time to go home," Pa said to nobody in particular.

"The children are getting restless."

When we got home, I was shivering and I wanted to ask many

questions, but Mum packed me into bed and told me to be quiet and sleep.

All night I was plagued by images of fire and feared that I would burn. The bitter flavours of smoke and fear were stuck in my throat, and I heard the sounds of crackling fire. My heart hammered and my body was bathed in cold sweat. I touched the floor repeatedly, afraid that the storey below was burning. Any moment smoke and flames might burst through and engulf me in hellfire.

In the morning, I was still upset. My hair stank of nasty smoke, and my head burnt from the uneasy night.

Mum put her hand on my forehead while we sat at breakfast. "The girl has a fever. You shouldn't have taken her out in the cold."

Pa reacted with anger. "You've been too soft with the children. They have to become tougher." He lit a cigarette. Normally, he didn't smoke at breakfast.

The smoke curled and found its way into my nostrils.

While the others had bread with butter and homemade jam, Mum served up my cold sauerkraut. In our family, food wastage wasn't permitted and sickness was no excuse. I sniffed at the green-black mash and recoiled. Cold, it was even more repulsive than hot.

Mum sniffed too, but not at the food. "Jesus Christ, you stink. All three of you. The smoke is in your hair."

I tried to chew my way through blood-clotted sauerkraut while Erwin spread butter and thick blackberry jam on his bread. I looked at the picture of the red-cheeked, big-bellied, jolly musicians and decided it wasn't worth it. I hoped Pa would leave for work soon, and that Mum wouldn't punish me for refusing to eat.

The letterbox rattled, and a plop told us that the newspaper had arrived. Mum went to get it. She moved the bread-bowl to the side and spread the paper out on the kitchen table, opening it on the first page of local news.

I read the headline, one bold word after the other.

"Family Perish in Fire - Hoax Call Leads to Destruction of Shop and Homes."

Perish meant something like 'die'. But surely nobody had died. We'd been there, and everyone had said that the Mengers were away on holiday.

A large photo showed a smouldering ruin, a smaller one depicted fire fighters directing a blast from a hose.

From the state of the pictured remains, the photographer had arrived on the scene some time after we'd gone.

Erwin grabbed the paper and read aloud. "Four members of the Maqsoum family died in the fire. They were..."

He mumbled the names and ages of the victims.

So people had died. They had burnt like the martyrs in the most frightening stories of *The Children's Book of Saints*. But it couldn't be true. The saints had died in faraway countries a long, long time ago, not at the end of our road last night.

The report said that the local fire fighters had been called to a non-existent fire, which made them late to arrive at the site. It described how the charred remains had been found. The mother had cowered under a table while the father and the eight-year-old twin daughters had squeezed into a corner. The man's body was shielding the children with his own, apparently trying to hold off the flames from them until the last possible moment.

Nausea squeezed my throat again. These people had been awake and conscious. They hadn't passed out in the smoke, as the woman with the spectacles had tried to make me believe. With a pang of guilt I

150

remembered the sweet I had accepted from her. I resolved to smuggle it into the trash bin later when nobody was looking.

I realised that the Arabs had seen the flames coming, looked into the deadly orange, smelled that bitter, acid smoke. Perhaps they'd found the exit blocked, but kept hoping that someone would get them out, if only they could retreat from the fire until help arrived.

They'd withdrawn, shrunk into the corner, pursued by death. Even as the flames gnawed at them, as smoke clogged their nostrils and bit their throats, even as the flames started to devour their flesh, they continued to hope, even as the father sacrificed himself to gain a few more seconds for his girls...

And then they screamed. I had heard those screams of pain and despair and death.

"They suffered," Mum said. "Holy Mother of Jesus, they must have suffered. I thought they'd go without pain, from the smoke. It doesn't seem right. Even for Arabs, this can't be right."

Pa shifted on the corner seat. I thought he would say something to praise the Arab father's courage.

Instead he said, "Remember London - the 7th July bombings. That was people like them. Muslims. So don't waste your sympathy." He lit another cigarette. "I'd better be off in a moment."

Mum recovered and turned her attention to us. "Never play with matches," she lectured. "I've always told you so. Now you know what comes from being careless with fire."

Erwin also took a patronizing attitude. "They were only Arabs," he said, with the superiority of an eleven-year-old. "Dirty people. It was a dirty flat they lived in, full of clutter. I mean, just think of it. Four people in a one-bedroom flat. Decent people wouldn't live like that."

Although I didn't follow his reasoning, and couldn't understand

151

what Pa had said, I accepted that the deaths had been at least partly the Arabs' fault. The fire had happened because of the way they lived, and because they had probably been careless with matches.

I clutched my mug of hot milk.

Mum was still wondering. "Why didn't they get out?

They must have heard the fire, smelled something. They can't have been asleep at that time."

"Don't get involved," Pa said, took his coat, and left.

Because of my fever, Mum made me stay in bed all day and brought me chamomile tea and hot water bottles. I sweated in the heat.

I could almost feel the hot breath of fire on my arms and closed my eyes against the pain. In my mind, I crowded in the corner with the Arab family, trying to shield one another from the inevitable fire, the fear, the stinging leaps, the bites of the flames.

I thought of my own family. Strangely, I couldn't imagine Pa shielding us. I felt a yearning for the kind of love this Arab father had for his daughters.

In the evening, Mum made me sit at the kitchen table, perhaps because she thought my fever had gone, or perhaps because she didn't want to annoy Pa. I had hoped that I didn't have to, because of the sauerkraut, but she dished it up anyway.

I was saved when a visitor came: the old woman with the spectacles. Mum patted her hair as if to check that the waves were still in place, and swiftly removed the plate with the disgusting food. Instead, she gave me and the woman fresh plates and we ate bread and mustard like the others. Of course talk turned to the fire again.

Shame about the shop," the woman said. "I know Menger wants to move to larger premises, but it's still a huge loss."

Pa smiled. "They have insurance."

I didn't understand this grown-up talk, but had a vague idea that insurance prevented families from getting burnt. "Do we have insurance?" I asked.

"Well, not that kind. But we don't need it. We don't have Arabs living in our house."

The mention of the Arabs made me cry.

"The girl's upset," the woman said. "It's been too much for her. She's so young. How old are you, dearie?"

"Seven," I managed between sobs. Then I asked the question I had wanted to ask all day. "Are they saints now? Have the gone to heaven?"

"No, dear, they're Arabs. Arabs don't go to heaven."

I cried more. I wanted them to go to heaven. Mum tried to console me. "Maybe there's something like a lower heaven where Arabs can go, and other heathens, if they've been good." She patted my hand. "Remember when your cat died? Maybe she's in that heaven too."

Erwin giggled, and Pa made a snorting noise. "Don't talk rubbish. There's nothing in the Bible about that."

For a moment, all was quiet. Mum looked like she might cry, too.

The visitor spoke into the silence. "There's talk that if Menger isn't going to rebuild, this would be a good site for our new church."

"Oh, that would be good," Mum said, the relief in her voice audible. "Something good is coming out of this, then. We could use a new church." She placed her hands in her lap, folded them, and smiled.

Pa and the neighbour smiled, too, because everything was good and right.

"And what can I get for the two most important men in my life?"

The question mark had not even appeared at the end of the sentence yet, but the dread had already started flowing through my veins like a quick-acting poison. If only it had been poison.

"I'll take a coffee. Black. One fake sugar. And not one of those darn flavored coffees."

"I'll have a french vanilla cappuccino. And if they could stick in a small travel flask worth of an alcohol 100 proof or higher, it would be much appreciated."

"You two are pains in the ass."

My gorgeous (and I mean hotter than the equator) girlfriend kissed her father on the cheek, her boyfriend on the mouth and skirted away towards a nearby coffee/pastry shop. That left two. I put my hands in my pockets, sighed, and looked around for something to talk about. There weren't many conversation starters where we were standing.

"Look! A hot dog vendor!"

"Let's go for a walk, Nicklas."

I tried. It's hard to avoid an oncoming 18-wheeler if you're standing in an alleyway. That's how it felt when I was around my girlfriend's father. There was no beating around the bush with him, because he would beat through the bush. There was no BS-ing him, which was a problem for me, because that's my thing. And even worse, his daughter was just like him in that respect. Only hotter than the equator.

Charlie (the 'old man') and I sauntered down a stretch of interspersed maroon and pale violet bricks, outlined by white cobblestones, that led out to a wooden pier hanging over the ocean.

You could hear the greenish water ripple as we ambled along, and in the distance there were faint sounds of steel drums coming from a West Indies festival down the block. I did everything in my power to look at everything but Charlie. I glanced out at the dramatic background the New York City skyline was providing. I stared up at the white clouds, the gray clouds, the white-gray clouds, the clouds that looked like marshmallows and the clouds that looked like they were trouble. I closed my eyes and listened to the humming boat engines from the water and the roaring airplane engines overhead. I opened my eyes and watched people scattered around us, playing checkers, reading papers, enjoying the sun's rays, swallowing up the pier like a child swallows candy. And Charlie spoke.

"She's not ready yet."

Four words. Plenty of connotations. Plenty if you didn't know the situation. Charlie's eyes were focused on a speedboat rifting through the choppy waves. He could have been talking about that. But he wasn't. He was talking about her.

"I think she's getting closer."

Charlie snapped his eyes around and glared daggers so deep it felt like he was stabbing my corneas. He silently fixed his intimidating pupils on me as he rested an elbow on a metal railing overlooking the water. I glanced away for a moment. Then I stared back.

"What's that supposed to mean?" Charlie asked me.

"It means what it means," I replied as I turned and folded my arms on top of the railing and checked out the fish down below in the seedy water. "How many of these suckers you think are Yankee fans? And do they argue with the Red Sox fish?"

There was a heat radiating from Charlie's skin. He was always uncomfortable around me. I always had an answer. Always had a counter to every verbal volley he had. He could never quite get a read on me, and for an overprotective father with a daughter that he loved so much, that was difficult. You want your baby girl to be with someone you can trust. But how can you trust someone you can't read? If you can't put a finger on him, you wonder how your flesh and blood can, because you're both cut from the same genetic cloth, so you figure your flesh and blood can't either, and she is going to have her heart broken or her world screwed or her mind fucked because of it. And it'll be all your damn fault because you and her mother created her.

"It only happened a year ago. You only started dating six months ago. She's not ready yet."

"I'd say the Red Sox fish have plenty to flap their fins about these days. It's been a long year. In human years it's been a year, in real time it's been a year, but in her world it's been a heck of a lot longer, Mr. Tejada."

There it was. Another comeback. Met with a wall of uncertain, uneasy silence. What do you say to the man who knows everything? Not much if you think you know everything, but don't. The pause lasted B forever B ten seconds. I could actually hear the ticking of my watch over the sound of the water being sliced by the wooden support beams below.

"When the police came, when they knocked on our front door, their fists almost beating it down, I thought the worst thing they could tell me was that she was dead. That there was an accident and her car had flipped. That she had a seizure. That she had an overdose or something. So when they came and told us that she was ok, I felt relieved, because the worst hadn't happened. But the worst did happen. I just didn't realize it right away."

Little girls are always the apples of their daddies' eyes, even when the girls are 50-year-old grown women. This wasn't the case with Sadie. She was a 25-year old who demanded attention because of her looks and her confidence and her sense of humor and her sense of adventure and her laugh and her thoughtfulness and her spirit. But in her household she wasn't the apple of her daddy's eye. She was the backbone of the family and the trunk of the family tree. She was the motor that made the machine run. And because of that, Sadie was shed in a different light by her father. Not a spotlight. More like a white pristine light reserved for a President or a Pope. The family had revolved around her like planets revolve around the sun. And in a flash, the sun exploded, and all went dim.

"She told me everything, Mr. Tejada. Things that I didn't need, or want, to hear. But things I needed to know, and things she needed to tell me. She spread everything out in front of me, and she pretty much said that I could walk out the door and not look back and that she'd still respect me and like me. Man, that building over there must be 100 stories high!"

"She probably didn't tell you everything. She probably didn't tell me everything. Only her mother, God, and her know everything, I think."

"I'm staying, Mr. Tejada," I said as I watched a sailboat glide by an ocean liner traveling at turtle speed. "She sprayed her guts out on the table, but I'm staying."

"And you think this should be your damn reward?!"

The shrill in Charlie's voice vibrated through the spring sky. I swear the clouds turned into question marks. A child dropped his ice cream cone at the sound of Charlie's bellow. The fish stopped swimming. The air stopped circulating. The waves in the water crashed, leaving a flat sheet of aqua behind. A minute passed, another quarter went back into the machine which is the world, and everybody and everything began churning again.

"I'm not looking for a reward. I'm not looking for anything," I said as I dug into my pocket. I found a penny and blindly tossed it into the sea. Made a wish before it splashed. Called tails.

"I know you must be getting very anxious," Mr. Tejada started as he kept eyeballing me while I stared straight ahead. "It seems from the outside that you and Sadie have made a connection. Looks like you've found a way into that gigantic heart of hers. I don't know what feelings you have for my daughter, if they're genuine or not. But there is a chemistry there between you two that is undeniable."

"Then why make her deny it?"

The line I spewed would have made the normal man turn his head, turn away. Not Charlie. Not Mr. Tejada. He didn't pull his eyes off me. He kept his eyes on me and pushed them through me. I heard what sounded like coffee percolating. Turned out to be his blood. I noticed out of the corner of my eye that he was shaking, quaking like a ripe volcano. He was about to speak, and erupt, when I put a hand up.

"The fears have been faced. She's battled the demons for several months now, and for the first time, for the first fucking time . . .!

"Don't you swear in front of me!"

"Excuse me. For the first time fucking time she's ready to move on."

"You think this is something she can put behind her? You think this is something she can dismiss as 'part of the past?'" Charlie asked as he signed the quotation marks. "Something she can put in her deleted items or her recycle bin?"

"I know it'll always be a part of her, a part of who she is. Sadly," I replied calmly. "I'd be an idiot to think otherwise. I just think I can be a part of her, too."

"Yes, maybe you can serve as some sort of distraction," Charlie discounted, turning his back on me while he talked. "Sure, take her mind off things. That's what orgasms do, right? They relieve tension. Make you forget about what's going wrong in your life for a few seconds or a couple minutes, or several hours if you're into that Tantric Kama Sutra nonsense."

"I just . . ."

Charlie didn't let me finish my thought. He started walking away from me briskly, hands in his pockets, head down, like he was tuning me and the rest of the surrounding sound out. I began skipping behind him to catch up. He could hear me coming and spoke as soon as I drew within a few footsteps.

"She didn't want me to know about the bruising," Mr. Tejada led off. He didn't stop walking. I didn't stop following. He didn't stop talking. "One night a couple months later, when I said something inconsiderate about her getting on with her life, her mother took me aside and told me all about it, in great detail. Sadie didn't want me to know. She thought I might kill the bastard. She didn't want me to know about the pain, the scars. I haven't said anything inconsiderate to my daughter since. She's been through enough. She doesn't need me coming down on her like an anvil. This is why I've allowed her to deal with this how she wants to deal with it."

"No, you haven't."

The temper that had simmered for many months in the wake of the rape of Charlie's beautiful daughter was about to be turned around on the next man in line. I didn't have a force field or a bulletproof vest or a coat of wax or a plate of armor or a wall of invincibility around me to protect me from the onslaught. My mouth couldn't care less. It had

159

a mind of its own. And when it wanted to work, it worked well. Too well. From barroom dustups with strangers to spankings at the hands my father, my mouth always tossed me into trouble.

We were in a clearing of cobblestone. Suddenly no one was in the way. Nobody could be the witness or the audience. No people, steel drums, etc. The deafening quiet. That's all that was left. That and a breeze that snuck under my shirt and rippled though my ribs. The wind came out of my clothing and ruffled the patchy strands on Charlie's skull. He turned around, his eyes leading the way. They were watery and ripe apple red. And his eyebrows were cocked.

"You ambushed me," Charlie intimated, as if he had realized there was a twist in the plot. "You're coming to me after the fact, aren't you? You've strung me along. Always the last to know. That's what I've always been. You've been asking me a question when you already had the answer. The damn answer you wanted."

"She's ready."

"You're her shrink? Sounds like a conflict of interest. You know how confused that pretty little head of hers has been?"

"I'm telling you, she's ready."

"You come to me pretending you're seeking my approval. You don't need it. No, I don't mean you don't need it, because if you were a man you would have run this by me first, not pulled a cowardly run-around on me. No, you don't need it because you've already decided. Hell, you probably already asked!"

"I did. That's why I'm so sure she's ready."

"And you believe that the baggage is just going to disappear, don't you?" Charlie questioned. He looked down between my legs for a second before shifting his eyes back up. "When your one head rules the other, that's when you have to re-evaluate your life, son."

160

I sat on my tongue. Not because I wanted to. I could have reduced Charlie to a stuttering, stammering pile of tears. I could have been explicit and profane. I could have tortured him with verbal jabs and uppercuts until he bled to death out his ears. I could have launched a war where both combatants may have perished. But for the first time, possibly ever, I slipped my tongue in the back of my mouth and let it lie dormant. I wanted Charlie to get everything out of his system, to lay everything out on the table the same frantic, personal, honest way his daughter had.

Sweat streamed down Charlie's weathered face, only slowing when it rolled through the crevices in his cheeks and forehead that time had stamped. Charlie seemed calm to me. His breathing wasn't choppy. His face wasn't as flushed. His eyes were clearing up. He even cracked a weak smile. Charlie looked out at the water and sighed somewhat peacefully.

"So she told you she's ready, did she?" the father asked.

"Yes, sir. She did."

"Who brought up the subject?"

"It was mutually brought up."

Mr. Tejada blinked at me before putting his eyes back on the water. "Sure it was."

"It sure was."

"My baby. My baby girl. She may be 25, gaining fast on 30, but I can still call her that. She's my oldest, my wisest, arguably my best. But she's my baby. She's always been so innocent. Good. A young woman walking with a halo over her head. I know she's probably done some things I wouldn't be thrilled about. Probably experimented. That pure picture of her in my mind wasn't washed away the night she was violently violated, though. More like a memory was stolen from me. Her innocence was gone, lifted like a cat burglar stealing a jewel. Sadie didn't deserve that. She didn't ask for it. She didn't bring it on herself. It wasn't like she wasn't cautious enough. Wrong place, wrong time. Wrong man."

"You don't have to apologize for her to me."

Again, my mouth. I didn't think I was being disrespectful. I should have shut up. Twice in one day, though? That's difficult for someone wired like me. I thought I was just telling Charlie that I already knew it wasn't Sadie's fault, that I knew she didn't do anything wrong, didn't do anything to 'get herself raped' so to say. He took it another way.

"Wrong place. Wrong time." Mr. Charlie Tejada turned his head and eyes my way. I swear I heard an eyeball pop and a vein snap. This time his cheeks were pinker than an undercooked sirloin steak. "Wrong man."

Charlie grabbed me around the throat with his right hand. His meaty pointer finger and thumb curled as his tips dug into my windpipe, and he buried his palm into my chest. I couldn't yell for help because he was cutting off my air, and no one was in the nearby vicinity anyhow. No witnesses. No audience. Charlie squeezed, pinching the skin on my neck as he choked me. With one hand this middle-aged man was paralyzing me. I couldn't speak, move, breathe or defend.

"How does it feel to know no one is around to save you?" Charlie asked coldly as he flexed his surprising muscle. His head shook with every word he spoke, and his faded red lips came closer to me after every sentence. "Totally helpless. Totally alone. No safety net to catch you when you fall. No hook to pull you off the stage. Nothing. Nada!"

"What....are...you...doing?" I asked in separated spurts as I frantically tried to free my throat from this human vice.

162

"That was her that night. That was Sadie," Charlie said as he lowered his tone, though he maintained his grasp. "Even the smartest can be outwitted. Even the strongest can be overpowered. That was Sadie."

Charlie's inflection began to rise again. More importantly, though, he was using his force to push me closer to the railing. My body was leaning against the top rail, with the gray metal pressing into my hip.

"What do you think the man that raped my little girl was thinking that night, Nicklas?" Charlie asked. "You're a man. You're probably about his age. You find Sadie attractive the same way he probably did. What was he thinking, Nicklas? Do you think he was hard up and Sadie was the closest pussy he could find? Do you think he had been stalking her like a raving psychopath and had pictures of her that he wallpapered his bedroom with? Or do you think it was somebody, god forbid, that she actually knew? A co-worker, perhaps? Whaddya' think, Nicklas? I want an answer!"

Now my body was leaning over the railing, and Charlie was not letting go of or letting up on his death grip.

"I think...you better let...go...before I...fall into the water."

"Maybe he wasn't thinking," Charlie seethed, ignoring my last suggestion, pushing me enough to where from the waist up I was parallel to the water, hanging over the side of the dock. "Maybe it was like a stream of consciousness. Maybe he was mentally retarded. Maybe he was a minor who didn't know any better. Or maybe not."

Charlie leaned into it and turned up the volume. His fingers were like claws, crimping the nerve endings in my neck and throat. I could feel my hands going numb and my elbows tingle. I was coughing up words, not speaking them. I could feel the blood rush to my head because it couldn't travel farther south than my chin with how Charlie was choking me out. He held on for dear life and guided me down with his hand. My right foot came off the ground. I wrapped my arm around the railing to prevent myself from tumbling into the water as my face came closer to the green, fishy liquid below.

"I don't know what my little girl has done with the memories of that night," Charlie admitted as he forced my head down, causing me to wince and shut my eyes. "She may have locked them away in a box in her mind, buried them in the back of her brain. I know one thing, though. I'll be damned if I'm going to let you drudge up those memories for her again. And that's exactly what's going to happen if you carry out your plans!"

Charlie's voice was fading, like a song that was winding down. It was because I was losing consciousness. I could feel myself getting whiter. Life was being drawn right out of me. My right arm had turned into a strand of spaghetti, and it wasn't propping me up on the railing anymore. I was inches away from losing my balance and getting tossed overboard into the dirty shamrock-colored water, water filled with pollution, dangerous sea life and outboard motors. At the onset of the confrontation, once Charlie crossed the line and made it physical, I didn't want to fight back. Now I wanted to fight back, but couldn't. And as the sun felt cooler on my skin, the air bristled through less of my follicles and the surrounding sounds vanished into a vacuum, my eyes tightly closed.

"You're not going to get away with this."

I didn't say it. I thought it. Only I didn't realize that I didn't say it until the thought had already passed. Open, mouth. Open!

"She's not ready yet."

Four words. Plenty of connotations. But there was only one that made any sense to the two of us. The two men, that is.

"I am ready, Dad."

Four more words, followed by a splash of teaming black coffee (with one fake sugar) in the face and a string of expletives that could have turned the whole world blue. Charlie relinquished his grasp. I dropped down to one knee, brushing my cheek against the railing to add injury to insult. Sadie didn't even check to see how I was.

"You should have scared him off a couple days ago, Dad," Sadie scolded as her father lowered his head in shame while he wiped the coffee off his sullen face. "You're a little late."

"So I hear," Charlie whistled back dejectedly. I watched Mr. Tejada from my knees. His eyebrows raised, and the tops of his eyes peeked out from beneath his rippled forehead. He wore the look of a demon. Laser beams were shooting out of the whites of his eyes at me, but they did no damage. I knew I was safe. Even safer when Sadie dumped the rest of the coffee over her father's head. He shrieked either because he was surprised or because the hot beverage scalded his scalp. I pulled for the latter.

"I've been sending out signals for a while now, Dad. Mom was the only one receiving them, though. I guess your antenna wasn't up high enough," Sadie said with a frown as she finally came over and tended to me. She gently ran her fingers through my hair and over my ears, and instantly I felt better. She helped me to my feet, brushing sawdust off my corduroys. As I pulled myself together, Sadie pulled me into her and wrapped her delicate hands underneath my arm pits, hugging me for all I was worth. She rested her sensitive head and rounded chin on my shoulder and whispered, "I'm sorry for all this," into my ear.

"So touching," Charlie snidely remarked as he looked on helplessly at Sadie and I's lovefest. Sadie yanked herself out of my grasp and faced her father, stepping on her tippy toes to stare her dad square in the eyes.

"What were you planning on doing, Dad? Drowning him?" Sadie wondered aloud. "I've seen him swim. He does a mean doggy paddle. He would have survived."

"I wanted to protect you," Charlie returned, his voice wavering slightly. "Your life is finally getting back to normal. I didn't want that changing."

"Listen to what you just said. My life is getting back to normal. Yes, it is," Sadie stated clearly. "And what could be more normal than me having a boyfriend?"

"Having sex I guess."

Sadie could have recoiled, with the frank words of her father careening down her spinal column. She could have slapped him, rattling his teeth like that of an Eskimo walking with no snowshoes in a blizzard. Nah. Sadie was like her father. She knew how to control a conversation. She knew hot to raise the stakes, to put pressure on the other talker, to make the person she was speaking with make the decisions, to answer the questions. So as I watched with wonder from the background, with the scenery eating me up, Sadie swiftly, plainly, calmly and bluntly returned fire on her father.

"Yes, having sex, which is what Nicklas and I did last night. We had sex in almost every room, in almost every position, and when it was over, I wanted to do it again. And again. Over. And over. It made me feel alive, after years of feeling, well, dead. And you know what I was thinking when I was basking in my afterglow, puffing on a cigarette while laying my head on Nicky's chest, Dad? I wasn't thinking about the past. I wasn't thinking about the prick who raped me. I wasn't thinking about violation or violence. I wasn't thinking about the sex conjuring up horrific memories or opening up old wounds. No, I was

166

thinking about one thing only. I was thinking about how I couldn't wait to tell Mom I was back in the game again."

KISSING AND A-HUGGING WITH FRED

When I was a kid, Gran sang the songs to me my mum had loved when she was growing up. They were the kinds of songs that told stories. One was about this girl who was too embarrassed to come out of the water because she was wearing a bikini. Another was about a girl in love with this ordinary-looking guy just because of his weird clothes, especially his shoes.

The one I liked most was about two guys driving around with seven girls. The idea behind it is that the guy who's driving wants one of the girls to come and sit beside him but none of them will because they're all too busy kissing and hugging Fred in the back seat. The one driving is so keen for one of the girls to shift that he drives them all around the town and country to try and impress them with his car. He gets so desperate he even asks them how they like his triple carburetor. While a triple carburetor must have made his car fairly powerful, even I could see it wasn't the sort of thing that would impress girls.

I asked Gran what Fred had that made the girls like him so much but she didn't know. I felt sorry for the guy who was driving but I agreed with what he said in the last line of the song, that he wished he could be like Fred. I thought it would be nice having seven girls kissing and hugging me, liking me so much they'd rather be crowded into the back seat than have a full front seat all of their own.

I used to wonder how seven girls could actually fit into the back seat of a car but then I decided it must have been a van. I was learning the drums and what I came up with was that the two guys were in a band and Fred was the drummer and he had his drum-kit in the back with him and that's what the girls were attracted to. Mum told me when I started to learn, that girls always fell in love with drummers. She said she'd been madly in love with Ringo Starr, the Beatle's drummer, when she was a teenager and so had all her friends. So it seemed logical to me that was why the girls had gone for Fred rather than the guy driving them around.

Well, I kept on with the drums and eventually I was in a band. But by then I'd realized it would never be me sitting in the back seat kissing and hugging with a whole lot of girls. What alerted me to that fact was dancing with Davenport in the senior school dancing lessons.

I went to an all boys' school. It was where Dad went. I had to go there because it hadn't done him any harm and it wouldn't do me any either. It was the sort of school where you called the teachers sir, kept your socks up, set your sights on getting into the first fifteen and relinquished any claim to your first name.

The aim was to turn you into an all-rounder which actually meant mediocre at everything except sports. In the end, you got used to teachers shouting insults at you and being hauled out onto the sports field whether it was forty degrees or hailing. Anyway there was no choice. Dad had the idea the school would make a man of me. In a way it did.

By the fourth form the female world seemed removed and incomprehensible. Girls, other than Jan my sister who didn't count, had become some kind of weird other-species. Some of the guys bragged on about their girlfriends but not having one didn't bother me. I thought all that was ahead when I'd metamorphosed from the smelly, pimply being I was to the charismatic, stunningly handsome drummer I would surely be.

Then it was nearly the end of the sixth form and the senior dance was imminent. Pritchard, the Phys Ed teacher, was in charge. He read out the rules at assembly. The senior dance was compulsory. Every boy

169

must wear a dark suit, white shirt, black bow tie, black shoes. No variations and get a hair cut. No outside partners, the young ladies from St. Anne's would join us for the occasion. Every boy would behave like a gentleman or look out. No alcohol. Dancing lessons would be held during Mr. Pont's weekly music periods. Dancing lessons were compulsory.

So we turned up for dancing. Our school wouldn't let girls inside the hallowed halls so we had to team up together. Pritchard went round jabbing us with his finger and barking out, 'A B, A B'. For half the period boy A would take the girl's part, for the other half he'd take the boy's. Any questions?

"No sir."

"This week we'll do the waltz, next week the foxtrot, week three the gypsy tap, week four the gay gordons. Anyone stuffing around gets a detention. Do I make myself clear?"

"Yes sir."

"Right. In a circle. Face your partner. Boy A place your left hand on boy B's shoulder. Boy B place your left hand on boy A's waist. Clasp right hands, hold them at shoulder height. Right hand, I said, Timmons, you bloody idiot. When I say move, boy A steps backwards, boy B steps forward. One long step, two short ones. O-o-one two three, o-o-one two three, keep in the circle. Okay. Everyone move."

I was with Davenport. We gripped hands. I clutched his shoulder. He grabbed my waist. I lurched backwards. He followed.

O-one two three. O-one two three. We stumbled about to Poncy Pont's inept attempts on the piano at Strauss' s Most Popular Waltzes and Pritchard's anguished shouts.

"Bend your knees, Jenkins. Bradie and Sims, slow down, you look like a bloody pair of spastics. I said o-o-ne two three not one two thre-e-ee. Jeeez, what a hopeless mob of yobos."

Once I'd got used to keeping my feet out of Davenport's way I started to quite like the regular bounce of music - daa-ah da da, daa-ah da da -, the pace and the tricky, sliding motion. But then something bizarre started to happen. I was so close to Davenport I noticed how good-looking he was. His skin was so smooth and his eyelashes were thick and dark, curling around the edges of his eyes. Beneath my hand I felt the firm muscles in his shoulder tightening as he moved.

Something else started to happen. Stirrings. Down there. You know what I mean. For obvious reasons I had to get away before Davenport lurched against me again. I threw off his hands and backed away, reeling into Satherley and Frame. I pushed my way through the grey shirts and plodding feet

"Dunne! What the hell...."

Pritchard was staring at me. I clutched my lower abdomen.

"I'm sick, sir."

"Get back in the circle, Dunne. You're stuffing everything up."

I dashed past him, heading frantically for the door "No. I can't, sir. I can't. I'm going to be ...."

Pritchard turned and gazed at me with deep disgust.

"Go on then. Get out of my sight. You're a bloody pansy, Dunne."

I fled into the locker rooms. A bloody pansy. It was Pritchard's worst insult, hurled randomly at anyone that pissed him off. The worst thing was that in my case it might be accurate.

This wasn't my first experience of, what should I say?- arousal-related to my own gender. But before that I'd rationalized it. What I'd thought was because I didn't have much contact with girls and I was a normal, randy male teenager anything that moved would turn me on. But that feeling with Davenport- the way I'd wanted to kiss his neck and ram my body against him- seemed beyond even what I considered normal behaviour. I sat in the locker rooms shaking and sweating. I didn't want to be a bloody pansy. I wanted to be one of the guys. I wanted to be having it off with Sheilas in the back seat of the van I was saving up for with my paper-run money. I wanted to be Fred.

I biked home fast and headed straight for my room. I lay on my bed and stared at the ceiling. I thought about how just that morning I'd been there in that same position looking at that same ceiling. There was a crack near the centre and every time Dad painted it he tried to fix it and it never worked. I'd been in that room, looking up at that ceiling all my life. But now everything was different. Up until now, I'd thought I was perfectly normal, with a future like any other male kid. But I was queer, a gay, a poof, a fairy, a fag. I thought about Bentley. Bentley had a big round bum and giggled like a girl. Everyone at school treated him like shit. They wrote gayboy on his locker. He got shoved around, tripped up. When he walked past everyone yelled out, quick guys backs against the wall. I despised Bentley. I lay there staring up at that ceiling and I wanted to cry like I'd never cried before in my life. I wasn't Fred. I was Bentley.

What they told us at school when we were up against strong opposing rugby teams is that you always had to think of yourself as a winner. With the right attitude there was no way you could lose; strength of mind and sound tactics won every time. Quite frankly, I always thought that was bullshit especially since my team almost always got annihilated. But I started thinking that if I regarded this condition I'd been afflicted with as an opponent I wanted to wipe out, if I was fully into beating it, then I could.

The best tactic I could think of was to find a girl who'd cure me. I started going to parties. Every girl I met became my best friend. I got asked to school dances where I waltzed my partners sedately around the floor behaving like a total gentleman. I had no inclination to do otherwise. I never got that rush of blood to my dick like I'd got dancing with Davenport. At every opportunity I stared longingly at girls' breasts and legs, willing them to turn me on, searching for that goddess so sexy she'd make me want to tear off our clothes without even thinking about it. I knew she was there somewhere. She had to be.

But until she turned up it seemed I was stuck with perving and salivating over other guys. I couldn't help it. I was forced into it because school made us go to sports events to support our teams. Those cricket games where I got driven crazy by the bowlers rubbing the ball up and down on the fronts of their white pants. Rugby, with everyone dressed in tight shorts throwing each other around on the ground. Swimming sports, with nearly naked, tanned guys flexing every damn muscle in their bodies on top of diving boards. It made me nearly faint with lust.

While I was waiting for the goddess, I did a bit of surreptitious research in the local library. I looked up anything to do with homosexuality and sneaked into a dark corner with a pile of books, a mixture of terror and intense excitement churning in my belly. There were dozens of theories and heaps of random information. Homosexuality was something that could be fixed with willpower and therapy. Homosexuality was because of an unnaturally close tie with the patient's mother. It was inborn, the result of social conditioning, something missing in the genetic makeup, natural, an unnatural perversion. If you were homosexual you had no chance of getting a highly paid job. If you were homosexual you were more likely to have a penis shaped like a corkscrew. I scrutinized my dick in the bathroom mirror trying to work out how normal penises differed from corkscrews and if mine was more like a corkscrew than it should be.

I left school. The right girl hadn't turned up. Neither did she show up in lectures, tutorials, pubs or parties. Mum started whispering to Jan that her brother was shy and it was about time he had a girlfriend, what about taking him along with her to parties and introducing him to one of her nice friends? I went out with her and we eyed up the same guys.

Eventually I had to ditch the idea of the undiscovered goddess and admit to myself that willpower and tactics weren't going to work. I started hanging around gay bars. A double whiskey was a fairly effective antidote for terror. I met this older guy and he chatted me up. We went to a motel room. I thought I was in love. He went home to his wife and kids. I made a profound religious commitment vowing to be chaste and unsullied and dedicate my life to higher things. Then there was my one-night-stand, stud phase. Then I met Den.

Den used to come and listen to the band. I noticed him sitting near the front, this smallish, dark, edgy guy with the great smile. Sometimes he came on his own and sometimes he came in a group. I watched him over the top of the drums and he watched me back. Then I bought him a beer and we went out on a date. I did not know that love could be like negotiating a maze of unknown streets moving through pockets of radiance and shade.

For years and years, Jan's had boyfriends coming for Christmas. I'm twenty- seven and this is my first time. Taking Den home for Christmas meant I had to tell Mum and Dad. I suppose it seems surprising I hadn't told them before but at first I didn't want to believe it myself. After that, I thought I needed to protect them, then other things were in the way and it didn't seem the right time. Telling them was just too hard. It was easier to talk about work and the band. Anything, everything else.

174

I went home for the weekend, waited 'til Mum was by herself in the kitchen then I went in and pretended to be making coffee. I'd run over and over in my head, trying to work out the best way to tell her but I couldn't find the words. It was like I was a kid again and I'd done something wrong. I wanted to burrow my head into her body, have her stroke my hair and say everything was going to be okay. I stood there facing her, trying to make my voice work and then I just said it.

"I'm gay."

"I know", she said, "but I'm glad you've told me."

She was smiling but she had tears in her eyes.

"I've met someone. I want to bring him home."

"He's welcome," she said.

Dad was next. That was the hardest. He was in the garage working on the car. I helped him for a while, then we sat in the sun and had a beer.

We talked about how the cricket team was doing in Australia and the pros and cons of buying a European car. We talked about if Labour was likely to go in again. Then we both opened another can. I said I had something to tell him.

"I know what it is", he said. "You don't need to say it."

His voice was thick with pain.

"I don't know what to say to you," I said. "I can't say I'm sorry, Dad. It's the way I am."

"Yes," he said. "I understand that. But it's just that I'm frightened for you. I'm afraid."

"I know, Dad," I said. "I know."

We sat there staring into the garden. Then I felt his hand grip mine. I thought of all that he was facing. His boy not being what he expected and wanted. Not bringing home girls for him to chuckle over and assess. Not giving him grandchildren. I felt for him but there was nothing I could do. And I knew, as much as I loved him, if I could change I wouldn't do it. Not even for him. It'd been too hard becoming what I was.

So Den's coming for Christmas. The last person I have to tell is Gran. I'm going to go and see her. I've got what I'm going to say all worked out. First, I'm going to sing the song about Fred and the seven little girls and the guy who has to sit on his own. I'm going to remind her of how she used to sing that song to me, how much I loved it, and how we used to try to work out what was going on. Then I'm going to tell her the real story.

It is after the dance. The driver and Fred head off through the dark streets dropping the seven little girls, one by one, at their houses. Finally, the last girl gets out and they wait until they hear her call goodnight through the shadows. There's only the two of them now. Fred gets out of the back seat and sits alongside the driver who's been on his own all this time.

And then he's not alone.

HAROUN

Today, again, I caught sight of my image on plate glass, strolling back-projected through white goods, small appliances and plastic vegetables.

A young man followed at my shoulder. I gasped and turned. He did not see me and walked on, a stranger with his own thoughts. This happens much too often now, though it is not always a young man. Last week I saw the mother of my true love hesitate as she passed by a window where her glance snared on my reflection, then the thing itself.

I greeted her. She hardly knew if she should run or stay. Perhaps she thought I might know something she did not, for she halted and cried out to me in blame.

"He will send photographs to me, his mother! They will come!" she said.

Nodding to reassure herself, she pulled a purse out of her shopping bag, unclasping and clasping it, hoping to find keepsake likenesses that were not there. She glared at me defiantly as if anticipating the day she could stop me in the street and show me: Look, this is the eldest; she is named for me. And this, the baby boy. And here's the whitewashed pergola where they sit together, a well-made family sipping tea under the purple evening sky.

She walked a few more steps toward me, then saw her own image keeping pace across the window. She cast down her eyes and hurried to the far side of the street, where there are blank brick walls.

"How can you?" I once asked my love. "How can you live without a single mirror in the house?"

His family said the good life is only lived in constant prayerfulness, in duty to the holy presence. They said it would not do to catch sight of yourself while thinking prayerfully; you might mistake yourself for God.

"Then, when you ever do see reflections of yourself by accident, how do you know for sure it is you?" I asked.

His family said he does not need to know this, he only needs to be prepared for heaven at all times, for the quick sharp stop of breath.

Once, I ate at their table, sitting opposite his father. On the wall behind his head there hung an old framed photograph of a refrigerator tied down with stout ropes in the tray of a small truck. His father saw me looking at it.

"First of this machine in our street," he said. "My uncle gets this one for the keeping cold. He gets this for the electric to be put on."

I raised an eyebrow at my love. He shrugged; he does not know or care whether electricity ever reached the street in the country where the family used to live. He seemed more interested in seeing how I suck the dark flesh of an olive from its pit. When we had finished eating, his father leaned across the table to me.

"You do not understand that my son must keep the past to honour us," he said. I sat straight-backed and said to him. "How have you earnt this honour?" He said he did not have to answer me. At this, his wife stood up abruptly. With shaking hands, she cleared the empty dishes from the table and gathered up the corners of the stained white paper tablecloth that covered the brown oilcloth beneath. She wiped the oilcloth hard all over with a cloying, musky disinfectant, although I thought the cloth could not have been soiled. She took the white cloth from the room, and brought another, spotless, to replace it. She unfolded it and grasping one edge with both hands, flung it above the table to settle with a sigh of gathered air; though not before I'd caught

178

the shadow shapes of flowers and birds and tendrilled vines showing under the oilcloth.

Out of sight, below the tabletop, I raised the oilcloth edge with one fingertip and saw another cloth beneath, of brilliant silk embroidery, sensuous and brave.

"You shame my family in looking boldways at my son," his father said. "You shame your father too, he did not give you good ideas when you where growing to a woman. He did not keep ungodly thoughts from coming in his household. Now he must live with your bad wants and never can to say he have his daughter good and safe under his roof. He should be a rich man, for he must give big lots of money to get a man take you for wife. But not this for my son. He must go to his own country. He has a promise made there."

I do not bother to point out that his son was born here, in my country that is surely his, too.

"What?" my own father chuckles when I tell him this. "Pay to have you taken off our hands? Damn good idea! Let's drink to that." We do. My family prides itself on showing fine alacrity in every circumstance.

"Seriously though," they murmur, one by one. "Are you serious? Isn't this just a strong attraction? "

"Of course, I am," I say. "Of course, it is. Desire exults in earnestness, desire takes nothing lightly."

"Oh, well," they say. "Oh, well, if you must. We suppose . . . We dare say . . . We might as well accept . . . Make the best . . . At least he's clean. At least he works hard. Least he's got good skin. And those eyes. What would you call that colour? Green or hazel? Isn't that unusual for that part of the world - where his parents come from? He does have a nice proportion through the torso, and a good strong grip, though he doesn't always seem to know what to do next after shaking hands - He didn't stand when I came into the room. Didn't offer your great aunt his seat. Didn't use a fork to eat his cake. Didn't seem to realize that your uncle Reynold is an alcoholic who is never offered liquor in this house - Reyn would rather have a strong drink than be drawn into an exchange of views on the moral fibre of the West and how we might improve our odds of getting into heaven by staying off the piss. What do you talk about with him anyway? What can you have to say to one another? What we mean to say is, the conversation must be more than strings of compliments about that gorgeous golden skin."

And so it is. He and I talk about what we will do with one another when at last I no longer think he'll have his way and then put me behind him as a cabinet of curiosities that should be opened once, each object handled, marvelled at, held up to the light, remarked upon and finally replaced, locked behind a curved glass door in airless sanctity. Never used, never held again. I can't be sure this won't be how it is until he chooses to come back to me from whatever promises his family has made for him.

We talk of higher matters too. I speculate about the gods in all things, while he declares one God over all. I ask about the meetings that he goes to late at night which I must not know about; the letters that he gets that I may not ever see, (nor anybody else either, for he burns them after reading.)

He talks about the way my clothes fit close against my body. He holds up his hand with thumb and forefinger so close together that the whorls of patterns on his finger pads are almost touching, but not quite. "Look," he says. "There is only this much between our nakedness." Proximate, but sealed.

Once I took him to my home. I brought him to the room where blossoms of the coral tree outside the window tap against the glass with red curved petal claws, throwing flushes of rinsed blood around the walls, across the bed, and deep into the narrow cheval mirror. I moved the cheval mirror, tilting it just so, so we could be seen together in it.

"There," I said. "Aren't we a handsome pair?"

He smiled and leaned his cheek to mine and touched my breast. He slipped one forefinger, curled like a coral flower, inside around the neckline of my shirt and drew an arc of touch from collarbone to collarbone. I pushed his hand away.

"Not yet," I said. "You should see yourself alone in mirrors first. Look yourself dead in the eye and know that that is who you are."

He reached out to grasp my hips, one hand either side. I twirled out of his grasp.

He said, "I won't go if you say that you'll have me."

I said "But you must go; to find out for yourself that what your family says about their distant sweet-remembered world is all confection. To know that they did not take away true memories, but tracings of the outline of what shape life might be if it were perfect."

"What if they're right?" he said. "What if I find that heaven's there?"

"I'm sure they're wrong," I murmured, branding each word with the pressure of my mouth under the concave of his cheekbone.

So he went, to where the sun is always eight hours late.

Sometimes I think I see him there through his mother's eyes and hopes, on a dry, sunny hillside near a beehive and a lemon tree. He is looking down a path where a woman walks towards a well. She is wrapped in dusty drapery that swings with every step. It falls in folds that hide the tendrils of her hair, shades the flower that is her face and

181

those sweet fruits, her breasts. Her hands, like little birds, flutter eloquently. Her feet are bare; their naked soles show at each step. She leaves no mark along the way to tell where she has been.

I see him too, against my will, on some blue morning in a noisy street that smells of sweat and cumin. He waits. For what? A friend? A bus? A thought to crystallize. To keep the promise made for him to do what he is asked and not to question why? Perhaps he only waits in the wrong place at the wrong time and looks up in time to see an arm drawn back to throw. Perhaps it is his own hand that he sees, raised in simple greeting. Or to signal warning. Perhaps it is his own hand that holds the cruel petard.

His family said they do not need to know where he has gone and entered silence. They say he does not want the life I lead. They're sure that he's found paradise. Why else would he not have come back to them?

I know only this, I saw this; a photograph, an image from a new-made war zone of people fleeing, scrambling over rubble. They do not seem to notice something lying on the ground in one corner of a tumbled wall. Hand-sized you'd have to say if you saw it for yourself, and so like a coral blossom cluster brought down in a storm that it might be only that. See how the clawed petal-fingers curve into a palm? And there, a petal-thumb and forefinger hold tight together with no gap between; circle closed to end its course.

I have covered the cheval mirror with brown paper, pasted on. Still, its silver blazes. Still the blooming coral blossoms dance in it, capering under the hard glass skin.

I have draped the papered mirror with a rough grey blanket. Still, the mirror gleams beneath. Still, in some lights, a blushing pulse moves across the surface of the matted blanket wool.

Still the coral tree persists, throwing blossoms at the window, trying to get in, wanting to take back its likeness from the mirror.

Late in the drowsy afternoon I sometimes whisper to the shrouded looking-glass, my breath dislodging motes of dust caught on the fabric. I put my mouth so close and tender to it that I might be thought to kiss the weave; the warp and weft cross purposes that bind it into one whole piece.

"Haroun," I sigh. "Haroun."

THAT TEARS MIGHT FALL

There are times when I just want to flip over the cover of my notebook, toss it into a garbage bin and walk away. What good does it do, this writing down of other people's misery? This chronicling of injustice and rape and killing?

Take last night, on TV: a war photographer defended his pictures of bloodied children, of stricken men, of wailing women.

"I do it," he said, " so that they may have a voice through me."

Lying, unctuous bastard. He does it because one, it pays well and two, he gets a thrill out of it. I should know. I've covered four wars. It's wars that put my children through school, bought my wife a Nissan Infinity 4 by 4. That keep me in whiskey. That give me a thrill. Or used to - though in those early days, of course, I called it idealism: I was risking my life for a cause. Any cause that looked good on paper and you could take a picture of.

Take the old boy on the Gaza strip. Living in a cardboard lean-to on the beach. His corrugated tin shed had been bulldozed by the Israeli army because he'd erected it two metres the wrong side of some invisible line or other.

He came to me in his grubby djellabiya and said: " Write it down, what they did to us here so that it never happens again." So I wrote it down in my notebook and I wrote it down again, in different notebooks, in Rwanda, in Northern Ireland. In a township in South Africa. In Iraq. And the paper printed the story each time. The only thing they had to change was the date-line. Whereas I was changing the world. Making it a better place for the smiling, ragged orphans playing in a village in Laos ringed by anti-personnel mines. For the old women struggling to bring them up. For the South African girls who didn't even bother to report they'd been raped on the way to school because it was such a common occurrence. For the Zairean teenagers, robbed of their childhood and forced to carry guns by members of a jungle platoon themselves armed by some distant country they wouldn't even be able to locate on a map - that's if they had one.

Do I sound angry? No, I'm not. But Hettie is.

"You're just a supercilious cynic," she shouted at me last night. And because I'm fed-up taking the shit, I shouted back at her.

"If I'm a cynic, " I yelled, " what does that make you? You're happy enough with a four-bedroom house, your own car, a skiing holiday every year. You'd have none of those things if peace prevailed throughout the world. If people went around smiling and shaking hands instead of maiming and killing each other. You make me sick." And I stormed out into the kitchen to find a beer.

We made it up, of course. We always do.

"I think you provoke these rows," she said afterwards, in bed, "so that you can let off steam. It's all that tension building up."

"If I remember rightly," I said, "it was that gob-shite of a photographer on the television justifying his sleazy existence that started everything up."

She's right, of course. I am a cynic. But who wouldn't be after what I've seen? Done what I've done, cradling Bill's head as he died, his blood seeping through my shirt onto my skin. And as he died, I wondered when it would be my turn.

Once, trying to get some respite from the African heat, I stood at the doorway of the Jumbo bound for Khartoum, grounded in Cairo with some bomb scare or other, and looked at the metallic gleam of moonlight on the curved helmet of a soldier standing guard by a plane. And thought of his skull inside it: one shell inside another.

185

I can see my own death: my head crushed quietly, like a Christmas tree bauble, blood and thick white matter seeping from it into the sand.

People standing around. There are always people who want to do that. It's compulsive viewing, watching death for the first time.

But I'm hardened to it all. Death? Grief? I look away. And when I've got my story, I walk away.

"That's your trouble," Hettie said last night, at the height of our domestic battle. "You just turn away. You don't deal with pain. Not mine, not the children's. No-one's."

"Others have that job," I said. "The UN, the Red Cross. That's what they're paid for. Mine is to get the story out."

"That's all it is," she said, " a story."

"Look," I said later, for her words still pricked me, "if I took war personally, I'd never get out of bed. The snipers that killed Bill weren't aiming for anyone in particular. Nothing personal. The fact that he was a close friend of mine was neither here nor there."

"Oh, no, nothing personal," Hettie said. "Like rape." She turned over in bed abruptly and the conversation, if you could call it that, ended.

The trouble is, I'm right. I've seen snipers up in the hills around Sarajevo. Stood behind them as they pushed their Kalashnikovs through the small hole in a boarded-up window of some school or apartment they'd commandeered, waiting their moment and then firing at a figure beetling from one shelter to another. It was like lobbing pebbles at a column of ants.

They didn't care which one they got as long as they got someone.

Hettie and I never resolve these arguments and in the end, we call a cease fire. I go back to whatever war zone is currently in the news and while I'm away, she sees to the children, does the disco run, holds down her part-time job and puts up with my silences when I get back. And my rages.

This morning, she was cool, polite. Silent. Smiled at me over the coffee pot. After five minutes, I couldn't stand it.

"There's nothing I can do, you know," I said, more loudly that I meant to.

"I can't go in somewhere and get the two sides talking. I'm not a negotiator. I go in, set up the satellite phone, file my piece and get the hell out of it again chop-chop. Christ! Sometimes they don't want to talk. It's only when the required number of people have been killed on both sides that they're ready to even consider it. But the figures have to tally first - number of civilians killed against number of women raped against number of children orphaned. The scoreboard from hell."

"Oh, of course," she said and got up to carry her plate and mug to the sink.

"And don't be so bloody sanctimonious about all this," I shouted at her back.

She spun round: " That's what you think, is it? I'm sanctimonious? Well, you listen to me. I'm part of it too - whichever bloody war it is. You may think the only way to deal with something is to turn away but I'm tired of watching you turning away from your own children. There's no war here, yet you never listen to anything they say. They show you things they've done, tell you about what's happening in their lives. Hope for your attention. But you're operating on another level. You've cut yourself off from reality. If I could find some way of pinning you down, I would. Make you take on board what's happening around you. Force you to look. And listen."

But I'd had enough and I left the house, banging the door behind me.

As soon as I was outside, I wished I was inside again. I'd walked out into a cold December drizzle. I thought of going back. A kiss, a bunch of flowers, a few words would do it but I walked on, head down, till I came to a pub.

Women are too emotional. They just don't have the capacity to withdraw. Pin me down? Like a sniper picking out his target? She doesn't know what she's talking about. I'd like to see the man who could pin me down. But that's dangerous talk, of course. You can be caught unawares, like Bill. A bullet in the head while he set up his camera, his mind on something else.

I caught a taxi to a bar across town to meet Kwame Nbane's brother, Uchebe. I could have done without this interview, today of all days.

Uchebe was waiting for me at a table by the door, a glass of mineral water in his hand. I got myself a beer, took out my notebook and sat down. But of course, I already knew the story. Everyone did: his brother had been tried by the military regime back home - rigged, it was generally believed - accused of being a political activist, found guilty and hanged immediately - before the international community had a chance to protest. Then they'd thrown his body into a lime pit.

What shocked everyone was that Kwame was a poet - had been a poet - and poetry and hanging don't go together. Poetry is reflective, quiet, uplifting. inspiring. A poet is a harmless fellow. Probably a bit of a loony. Except that Kwame's poetry had charted the destruction of the land by the petroleum companies and his people sang it in the villages, beat their drums to it along the river banks. Danced to it in the compounds. Which is why he was hanged.

But the hanging had gone wrong. He was a tall man and first time they did the drop, his feet hit the ground. He had to be hauled up again, semi-conscious, and held there while the rope was adjusted. That part I didn't know. But Uchebe did and his eyes filled with tears as he told me.

"He was my oldest brother," he said. "I was next to him. Now I have to wear his shoes."

I looked away, first through the window at the wet pavements and the shops decked out with bright Christmas lights, then down at my glass of beer. I counted to ten - I'm used to these moments - and counted to ten again just to give him time. Through the window, I watched a woman go past pushing a baby buggy and dragging a large dog behind her on a lead. A man got out of a taxi wearing a long black coat, a red scarf wrapped round his neck and carrying a large camera case. My heart missed a beat: Bill? But of course it wasn't. Just someone with a red scarf like the one Bill used to wear. The man paid the taxi, pulled some gift-wrapped packages out from the back seat and ducked into the shop next door. I felt the tension drain from my body.

Three days to Christmas and I still hadn't got anything for the children. What does Hettie mean, anyway, that I turn away from them? I'm with them as much as I can but teenagers like their own space. I didn't want my father around when I was fifteen. Last thing I wanted.

I looked up at Uchebe. His eyes were still full of tears and it wasn't until I looked into them, and he held mine steady with his, so that I couldn't look away again, that the tears fell, bright and sharp as diamonds, leaving a trail of salt on his black face.

UNDOINGS OF A NESTING DOLL

Val made her entrance into the bright lights of the hospital maternity ward, shrieking and naked, at 12:04 am on February 14. Her mother, just 15 herself, grasped at the one fresh breath of romance that found its way into her polluted life, embraced it, and named her firstborn Valentine Saint. The last name that read in capital letters on the California birth certificate was that of Valentine's mother and her grandmother: Maureino.

It was a last name that, as Valentine had pondered over numerous times, had an entirely unbalanced vowel to consonant ratio.

As an elementary school child, she had felt a flush of pride when the pretty, perfect Alexis Penning had first swished her blonde ponytail at Val's grammar book, cornflower blue eyes studying it briefly, and then raised her pale, 8 year old arm to announce that Valentine Maureino had all of the vowels possible in her one name. She had then smiled, revealing a missing bottom tooth, and said two words that had stuck with Val for her entire third grade year: "That's neat."

At that point in her life, Valentine was attending Las Cruces Elementary School.

After a "turn of events," as her mother liked to call it, Valentine, her mother, and her mother's male friend of three weeks, picked up all of their belongings and moved into a one bedroom apartment in Mesilla, New Mexico.

Val remembered that one well. He had been the last decent one before the plague that became her mother's love life. Her mother brought him home exactly 3 hours after she had met him at the little green trailer converted into a pancake house that she waitressed at six days a week. Val liked him immediately. He came into the ranch style house that they had called home for four months, squatted down on his haunches, extended his hand to Val, and introduced himself as Bernie. He stayed less than an hour, despite her mother's invitation to stick around for dinner. As he walked out the door, he bowed slightly, kissed her mother's hand, and said that he

190

"bid farewell to Queen Teresa and her lovely Princess Valentine."

Over the next few days, Bernie dropped by in the evenings. He stayed considerably longer every day. Her bedtime was 9:00, consistent and unarguable, despite the conflicting style that Teresa applied to all other aspects of her daughter's upraising.

Some nights she would lay in her bed clutching her pale yellow elephant that she inexplicably referred to as *Dumpy*, and her heart would squeeze just a little bit when she heard the first closing of the door, indicating that Bernie had departed safely before the second closing of the door, which indicated that Marco was home from his second shift at Roadway.

So it went for three weeks, until one night, as Val laid on the carpet drawing a picture of a little grey house with lovely pink shingles, the front door swung open as a curtain pulls rapidly apart revealing the star actor in all of his spotlighted glory. Marco took four large, rowdy steps into the house, knocked into the small bookcase that held only the answering machine and a dirty, torn yellow phone book, and fell face first into the musty green throw rug that furnished the graying tile of the dining area.

Upon hearing the noise, Teresa ran out of the bedroom in only her underwear and an orange bra out of which the underwire poked through quite dangerously.

Following right on her heels was Bernie, wearing a pair of yellowing long john bottoms that Val still found odd considering their residence in southern California in the middle of August. In an almost comical fashion, both her mother and Bernie came to an abrupt stop in front of the entryway on which Marco was sprawled. Val still lay propped on her elbows three feet away on the living room floor. She held the pink crayon so tightly that, as Marco haphazardly jumped to his feet, she broke it right in half. The pink paper split not quite all the way through, creating a Crayola logo on a carnation pink hinge.

Marco stood up completely and seemed to be looking solely at Teresa, oblivious to the half naked stranger standing beside her. "I knew it, you know. I knew it. I

191

got into my truck early because I knew it." His words were sounding mashed
together, and spit was flying out at every syllable.

Her mother, glancing quickly at Bernie, spoke very calmly, *"Marco. Don't be
ridiculous. Don't take to your crazy ideas and go accusing everyone of things that
aren't even real. You and I both know how you get."*

In the next moment, the entire scene shifted from controlled to chaos.

"You lying, disgusting whore!" Marco screamed, spit flinging out and landing on
her mother's face just inches away. *"You WHORE! You ain't nothing but trash.
I let trash in my house!"*

"Don't you speak like that to me! Don't you dare." Her mother's voice sounded
indignant. Val sat solid as a stone against the ratty floral love seat, her honey brown
eyes peeled open like tea saucers.

"Don't speak to you like . . ." His fist flew in a forward arch, making no sound
at all as it made contact with Teresa's painted lips. She fell backward and Marco
lunged forward, past her mother, and into the narrow hallway that led to his and
Teresa's bedroom. Bernie stood motionless next to the front door.

"Mama?" Val remembered the first word spoken in the chaotic silence. Her
throat and chest felt so tiny, as though she couldn't even swallow her own saliva.
Her mother ran to pick her up, and held her head against her chest. The sound of
her mother's heartbeat felt like a drum against Val's temple.

"Its okay, mi querubin,*"* her mother breathed quietly, referring to her in the
pet name that she related to her daughter's angelic birth. *"Its okay. He will just
sleep it off. He will be fine when he . . ."*

The two gunshots hit the wall behind Teresa and Val. The sound of the bullets
tearing out of their steel womb rippled through Val, as her mother dropped her down
onto the love seat and screamed. *"You are crazy! Marco! Stop! Put that down!
Marco!*

You will go back to jail you sonofabitch!"

"Hell if I will," he spat out, and then fired the third bullet which traveled just

eight short feet before tearing into the abdomen of the little girl crouching on the couch.

As Val laid flat on the carpet, she was vaguely aware of the screams, but everything sounded the way it did when she went swimming at her friend Ginny's house down the street and they immersed themselves in an aquatic wonderland.

The room began to look like it was covered in a fuzziness. Val mused over the idea of thousands of dandelions blowing around the room, fuzzing it up and making the walls as soft as Dumpy's ears. She was thinking this as the room started to grow a little dimmer.

When the fourth shot rang out, and Marco dropped to the floor four feet away from her, she thought about how the mess that his brain made on the grey carpet was carnation pink.

* * *

I stood on the corner of Barker St. and Blueberry Lane. Blueberry Lane sounded like a quaint, country dirt road leading to cozy summer cottages, but in reality it's the same as Barker, Hurley, and every other pot hole plenty road in scummy Antioch, California. I threw my bookbag down and sat on the curb, carefully avoided the mural of gum decorating the cement.

Spring in California brings rain and windy days more than flowers and sun. I tucked my hands into the pockets of my windbreaker and waited for the bus to come. The smell of the wind on days like these always gave me my waiting feeling. I could be doing the most routine, everyday things, but one whiff of that wind and I had the strongest feeling that I was just waiting for some big, life changing event to happen. It never did, but I always watched myself on windy days all the same.

* * *

"How did your show and tell go?" I asked.

193

"Okay. Brian Watters brought in his blue truck and we raced in the sand and everyone said our trucks were cool."

Jonathan held my hand as we walked the block and a half to our house. His bus from Boone Elementary School brought him back to me everyday at 3:45. The bus stop was almost a mile away, and being that Jonathan had just turned six, I broke a sweat Monday through Friday running from the last bell to the bus stop in time to see him climb those four steps off the elementary bus.

"Think Mommy is home today?" He looked up at me, knowing the answer because every day he asked the same question as we reached the dingy house and started up the crumbling concrete steps. And everyday I said the same thing.

"Yup." We reached the door. "I got you something this morning on my way to school." I let go of his little hand and he smiled up at me, waiting for the surprise. I opened my book bag and pulled out a 64 count box of Crayola crayons. His long black eyelashes framed his dark green eyes as he smiled wider and hugged me tight.

"Sixty four! I never seen that many in a box! There's prolly so many colors I won't even get to use them all on one page! Thank you, Val! Oh, man! Thank you so much!" He hugged me tighter and I thought how it's wrong that a kid should be so grateful for something so small.

"You got it. Lets go inside and have a snack first and then maybe we can color in my room."

I opened the front door and the smell of home surrounded me. Our house was old, as was the almost identical houses flanking it, and all of the other houses on the same street. I imagine everyone's house has a smell to it that wafts directly towards them as soon as they enter. Ours was stale cigarette smoke and cat pee.

I looked on the shelf in the kitchen without having to open the cabinet door, because two weeks after we had moved in the door had fallen off and never been replaced. I set Jonathan up with a bowl of canned tomato soup, promised him that we would go food shopping tomorrow, and headed upstairs.

I climbed up the stairs thinking about how I couldn't wait to get into my room to take my shoes off. Jonathan and I both know that we do not take our shoes off anywhere but in my room because the fleas from the cats are in the carpeting everywhere else in the house. Right after we moved into this house, I spent an entire Sunday afternoon yanking up the nasty carpet from my eight by ten foot room. Underneath is a wood floor that, after I scrubbed it down, looks almost like the nice floors inside the courthouse. Plus, fleas don't like wood floors, so they stay pretty much out of my room, as do the cats.

I opened the door to my room and immediately noticed the disruption of my Russian nesting dolls. When I was in 6th grade, we went on a field trip to San Francisco to tour Alcatraz Island. I didn't like the prison because it was creepy and dirty and I hated that people had died there. But I loved when we got back to the wharf and divided into groups to shop on Pier 39.

Before I left, my mother gave me a rumpled five dollar bill and told me to use it to buy lunch and bring her back the change. There I was, walking into the little stores on the wharf, not touching anything because the shopkeepers watched anyone under the age of 21 as though they were going to stuff every piece of merchandise into their pockets and graffiti the walls and windows. Everyone was buying key chains that said San Francisco, and I really wanted to get one too, but I knew that if I spent the $3.27 I had leftover from lunch, my mother would be really angry. So I didn't even look at the key chains.

Instead, I wondered to the far end of the store, resisting the temptation of the souvenirs up front. There, in the back, is where I found the nesting dolls. They were painted bright reds, greens, yellows, and blues and laid out one next to the other, five in all.

I had to have them. They were beautiful. I stacked them one inside the other and carefully carried them up to the front.

"Excuse me? Ma'am?" I waited on the side of the register as the sales clerk talked on the phone.

"Hang on a sec, Marge." She covered the mouthpiece with her hand and looked at me like I was the biggest interruption ever to hit her urgent life.

"Hi. Yeah, I just wanted to know how much these dolls are."

She glanced quickly at the largest doll cradled in my hands. "$24.99." She put the phone back up to her face. "Go on. What did he do when he saw the stains?"

I wanted those dolls. "Excuse me?"

She gave an exaggerated sigh and said extra loudly, "Jesus, hang on a second, Marge. I have a customer." She turned and raised her eyebrows at me.

"Do you think that they will go on sale anytime soon?" I meant within the next 30 minutes.

She sighed loudly again. "No. This isn't K-mart, okay? The price is what the price is. Okay?" She turned her back to me and got back on the phone.

So I opened the zipper on my pink nylon fanny pack, set the dolls in carefully, and walked out of the store into the sunlight.

I waited to get caught, and when no one said anything to me, I felt so guilty that I walked back into the store, stuffed my three dollar bills into the plastic jar that said, "Save-A-Dog," and hauled my butt onto the yellow bus waiting outside.

Ever since then, I have kept any money that I manage to earn in the second to smallest doll, hidden well within the others. However, last week, and again today, the moron who broke into my dolls did not have the sense to put them back into one another correctly, so the middle one sat idly next to the others. I walked over and picked them up, opening the top one and finding just what I expected: a couple of singles and 27 cents in change. That made a total of $209 stolen in the last week. And it was really starting to piss me off.

"I'm all done. Can we color now?" Jonathan stood in my doorframe clutching a Batman coloring book to his chest.

"Yeah, Buddy. That sounds like a great idea. You sit here," I pulled my desk chair out and patted it, "and I'll sit on my bed and work on my English okay?"

He smiled that precious happy smile and plopped down at my desk. For the next three hours we sat like that, him happily lost in a paper world of superheroes, and me brooding over past participles and nesting dolls.

* * *

"Love you, Buddy." I kissed his cheek and smoothed his messy brown hair down.

"Love you, Val. Is my window locked?" I went through the motions of checking his bedroom window even though he and I both knew that I had locked it ten minutes before.

In the house that we lived in right before this one, the tenants next door were drug dealers who spent four months being staked out by the police. On the night that they made the move to bust them, one of the drug dealers ran out his back door, crawled into Jonathan's window and spent the next two hours threatening to shoot himself and Jonathan if anyone came near the window.

After an hour and a half of being locked in a room with a hysterical 3 year old, he made the fortunate mistake of letting Jonathan go to the bathroom, and the police eventually got him, but not before emptying six rounds into his torso.

So now we check twice before bedtime to make sure the windows are locked.

I turned off the lights and closed the door quietly.

"It's late for him to go to bed, isn't it?" My mother stood six inches from me in a ratty purple terrycloth robe, her hair held up in an orange banana clip leftover from what I was assuming was my first birthday.

"No, Ma, its only 8:30." I moved to the left and took a step farther down the hall.

"Did he eat today?"

"He eats everyday, Ma. That's the daily recommended dose for kids, ya know?" I reached the stairs and started down with her three steps behind me.

"Do your homework?" I could hear her slippers scuffing along behind me as I went into the kitchen.

"Yup."

"That's real good. I was thinking about maybe having a cake for when you get your diploma. You want that? It could be a nice cake with chocolate frosting. You like chocolate."

"I like strawberry."

I squeezed the soap bottle a couple of times, willing the air to push out the last couple of drops of dish soap so that I could clean up the soup bowl. It's funny how when you know that there is nothing left in a bottle of soap, or shampoo, or conditioner, you still squeeze it in that rhythmic way, thinking that if you just do it enough times more fluid will magically come out.

My mother opened the refrigerator and took out a yogurt and a can of beer. I gave up on the soap bottle and turned the water as hot as it would go before putting the dish under it. It's just tomato soup, right? How germy could it be?

She took a sip of beer and licked her lips. "Has Ernie been in?"

"I don't know, Ma. I've been in my room."

"The whole time? No, you came out. I heard you. You went in the bathroom."

"Okay." I dried the dish and put it in the cupboard that did have a door. "Yeah. I came out to go into the bathroom to put Jonathan in the bathtub."

"So was he?"

"Was he what, Mom?"

"Here, Valentine. Was he here?"

"No! I don't know. I didn't see him, but I didn't exactly send a search party around the house either. I don't know where he is at any given point during the day."

"Your hair is in your eyes. You should put barrettes in it. I have extra clips like the fine one I'm wearing. You should pull the hair out of your face. It's always in your face." She took another swallow of beer and shoveled a spoonful of yogurt between her lips.

"Are you going food shopping tomorrow?"

"Yeah. That sounds like a plan. I'll try to go tomorrow."

"You really have to go, Ma. There isn't anything left besides soup, beer, and yogurt."

She smiled and licked her spoon. "No more yogurt neither."

"So you'll go tomorrow."

"I'll try. Ernie said he is gonna bring me a paycheck made out just to me tomorrow. Kinda like a rent check. Good idea huh?" She finished off the beer and threw it at the garbage can, missed it by a good six inches, and watched as it clanged to the floor. From the little pocket in the side of her robe she took out a pack of cigarettes and used her lips to pull one out of the pack. She felt the outside of the pocket and then reached in to pull out a dark green Bic lighter. "He might be working at the post office now. That's a good job for someone, huh?"

I picked up the beer can and put it into the garbage pail. "I'm going to bed." I started to walk out of the kitchen.

"Tomorrow at the store, maybe we can get some of those jelly bean candies that you like so much. Just gotta wait for that check okay?"

I sighed. "Okay, Ma. That'd be nice."

She nodded absentmindedly and stared at something invisible in the middle of the table, taking a long drag on her cigarette and not even bothering to tilt her head upwards as she exhaled.

* * *

I waved and blew kisses to Jonathan as he looked out from the bus window. He smiled and gave a little wave before turning to talk to the boy sitting next to him. When he started first grade I was so relieved because now I can send him off in the morning and pick him up in the afternoon. Kindergarten was only half day, and Jonathan had the afternoon session, which meant that he was absent more days than he was there for simple lack of my mother waking up to put him on the bus.

I watched the bus turn the corner and then started walking the twelve blocks to my high school. I was late every single day of my senior year and today would be no exception. After the first seven weeks of walking in to homeroom 25 minutes after the flag salute and morning announcement, the principle had called me into her office and

200

had a little "sit down" as she called it.

"Valentine, Mrs. Tarcell has sent a final plea of disciplinary action to me this morning. Do you know why?"

Ms. Bloomfield was quite possibly the youngest principal ever to work within our entire school system. She looked no older than 25 years old, and she was a woman who clearly took care of herself. Her chestnut hair was always up to date with multi-faceted blonde highlights, and she dressed in beautiful pastel skirt suits that fit her slim body perfectly. As the west wing boys' locker room wall testified, Ms. Bloomfield was a "hotty with a body."

Fortunately, Ms. Bloomfield was also very diplomatic, and rarely punished without due cause. So there she was, French manicure tipped hands clasped in her lap, trying to figure out why a student who remained on Honor roll eight consecutive semesters, was acting Treasurer of student council, and never so much as had a hallway write up, would blow off school every morning of her senior year.

"Ms. Bloomfield, my little brother started first grade this year. His bus comes at 8:10 in the morning, and homeroom starts at 8:05." She looked at me as though I was saying two plus two now equals five. "I have to put him on the bus."

"Well, I'm sure one of your parents can put him on the bus. Getting to your own class on time is your responsibility, and your brother, although I'm sure you love him, is the responsibility of your parents."

That summed up the irritating thoughts that ran through my head every morning.

"Yeah, I know. But it doesn't really always work out like that. So if I don't put him on the bus, I won't know for sure if he actually goes to school that day."

She stared at me for a moment, her large green eyes under two well-applied coats of mascara. "Your parents don't ensure that he goes to school everyday?"

"Well, for one, it's just a mother. Not parents. And, yeah. I mean, no. No, if I don't get him on the bus, I can't ensure that he will go to school."

"This sounds like something that maybe we should consider calling someone about," she said gently. I knew what she was getting at.

"No, listen, I'm sorry, I will try really hard to not be as late. But I can't not be late at all." Basically I was telling her that I was going to be late and there was nothing she or I could do to make it different, short of me dropping out.

She knew this. "Okay. Well, I will talk to Mrs. Tarcell. This isn't something that is normally excusable, Val."

I nodded. "I know. Its just, he has to go to school. And I have to put him on the bus for him to do that. So?" The trail off said it all.

She nodded again and patted my hand. "Alright. Well, go back to class. I will speak to her personally. No more than half an hour late, okay? That's all that I can excuse on a daily basis." She stood up. "And Val, if I see a change in your grades or otherwise any other problems when you are here, I will need to make some phone calls to remedy this situation the way that it should be handled. Okay?"

I thanked her, and thought about hugging her. She smelled like lavender and chocolate, and she was so close. "Thanks Ms. Bloomfield. I really needed this."

"I know, sweetie." And before I could move a muscle she leaned in and wrapped me into a hug. "Hang in there, okay? Just hang in there. You're too bright with too much to lose."

I held tightly to her for a moment and breathed in the smell of her shampoo before letting go and walking out of the office.

So for the last six months, this morning being no exception, I slipped into my homeroom seat with an excused tardy, which, should be noted, displeased cranky Mrs. Tarcell to no end.

* * *

We stood on the front porch for a moment, and Jonathan looked up at me with wide, scared eyes. The screaming inside escalated to a dull roar, and Jonathan held tighter to my hand. I took a calming breath.

"It's okay, Buddy. No big deal. Let's scooch right up to my room, okay? We can have snacks up there today. Alright?"

He nodded and held onto my hand. I turned the knob and pushed the door open at the exact moment that something very breakable hit a solid surface and shattered to pieces. Jonathan spun into me and clutched my shirt, burying his face in my stomach. It was time to play the Tough Girl part.

"Oh for Christ's sake, this is ridiculous. Jonathan, come on. Let's go. Upstairs. Now! Come on." I held firmly to his hand and pulled him into the living room, towards the stairs. We were just four steps away from the upstairs landing when the lamp on the beat-up chrome end table was knocked off by two very drunk, very aggressive adults.

"Get out! Get your stuff and get out! I hate you! You hear? I hate you! Get out, you scumbag!" Jonathan began to cry at the sound of my mother's sloppy, strained voice.

I bent down and scooped him up, pressed his head to my chest, and used my one free hand to cover his other ear. "It's okay, Buddy. Up we go." I took another step up.

For a kid who hardly eats a single helping at any meal, he sure felt heavy clinging to me like a baby chimpanzee.

My mother's grayish pale face suddenly appeared as Ernie slammed

203

her body against the wall at the bottom of the stairwell. She scratched and smacked at him like a cornered animal. I took another step up.

"Don't you ever touch me again, you nasty bitch! I will kill you! I will kill you!"

He grabbed my mother's neck and slammed her against the wall again, and this time she yelled out in pain.

"Hey!" I screamed at the top of my lungs. Jonathan cried even harder into my already damp shirt. The sound of my voice momentarily pulled Ernie and my mother out of the inner world that they both dwelled in when they drank. Ernie paused with his hand on my mother's neck and turned a disgusted face towards the stairwell. "Get your hands off of her! I mean it! Right now, Ernie!"

He looked at me for a moment with eyes that couldn't focus, and then he shoved my mother over the back of the couch. "You, huh? You a big girl now, aren't you?" He grabbed onto the banister railing at the bottom, and my knuckles turned white holding onto my end on top. "You such a big girl now? Real pretty, like your mama. Real pretty, but you women all got the same problem. You can't keep your fucking mouths shut when they should be shut!" He placed one foot on the bottom step.

"Do not come up here, Ernie. You stay down there. I mean it. Stay down there!" I stood stock still on the top step, and I could feel Jonathan's hands on my leg. "Leave! Leave this house. Get out."

"Oh, get out, huh? Get out, Little Girl? You're gonna tell me what I do or ain't do? You know what your problem is? Real pretty, but its that fucking mouth. Just like that mother of yours. I think you need lessons on talkin' to men. I think you need 'em." I watched as he moved up two steps in only one motion.

I backed up. "I-I'll call the police, Ernie. Step back down. Ge-Get out! Now!"

He stepped up one more step, making the distance between us just two tiny feet. His eyes glazed and crazy looking, like someone ready to kill. Or worse.

At that moment, Jonathan jumped out from behind me with what I can only imagine must have been seven years of built up courage, and lobbed a huge wad of spit right into Ernie's deranged face.

Call it reflex, call it instinct, call it whatever you want, but I took that glorious moment of opportunity to kick Ernie square in the chest, knocking him right back down to the first level. He lay at the bottom, stunned and wasted. I grabbed Jonathan's hand and yanked him down the hall and into my bedroom, frantically turning first the doorknob lock and then the deadbolt that I had installed just six weeks before. We were both dead silent, listening for the thunder of footsteps we were in dread of. We only heard silence.

I turned and looked at Jonathan, who stood straight as a board, his forehead crinkled up and his arms pinned to his side.

"Okay. We're okay, Buddy." I kneeled down and held him tightly, and he wrapped his fingers in my hair and laid his head on my shoulder.

That night, I pulled out a milk crate that I stashed food in for just these very special occasions, and we dined on peanut butter and jelly on Ritz crackers, Fruit Roll Ups, and two Capri Suns a piece. Around 8:45 Jonathan apologetically confessed that he had to use the bathroom, and so we hustled across the hall and back into my room in record time, relocking the door behind us. I gave him one of my t-shirts to sleep in, and we crawled into my twin bed. He snuggled up close to me and wrapped his finger gently in my hair before dozing off within three minutes.

I laid awake long enough to hear my mother two doors down,

making up with Ernie, before falling into a restless, uncomfortable sleep.

The sun rose higher over the ocean, making the water sparkle into eternity. The beach was always empty at this time in the morning, save for the few dedicated runners who passed so quickly one could hardly know they were sharing the beach if they did not see the treaded prints of athletic shoes left in the damp sand. From the pier, a very old fisherman sat on the bench, looking out over the railing at the two figures skipping and twirling along the water's edge. The women would run and scoop the little girl up right before the tide could graze her feet, and the little girl would scream and laugh every time.

Occasionally they stopped, and looked at the sand, sometimes picking up and examining pieces of the beach.

Valentine held her mother's hand as they walked to where the sand bubbles from the remnants of the waves. She looked up at her mother's face, so beautiful and youthful, eyes narrowed as she looked out onto the ocean, and then down at the little girl beside her.

"What are you looking at?" Her mother asked playfully, "Do I have a boogie?"

Valentine burst out in a fit of laughter. "No! You're gross!" She grinned up at Teresa. "I was looking at your face. You look pretty."

Teresa stopped walking and knelt down in front of Val. She brushed her bangs off of her face and then kissed the little girl on the cheek. "Oh, sweetie, so do you. You look absolutely beautiful." Teresa kissed her cheek again, and then pressed her into a hug before standing up straight again.

They walked along another half mile before stopping at a place that held a sea of washed up shells. Valentine bent down to sift the shells through her fingers, looking for a seahorse, a sand dollar, or something equally holy.

"This one is the most beautiful one of all, don't you think?" Teresa held up a perfect pink conch shell. Not a single chip flawed the creamy, swirling pattern. Val made an 'Oooohhh' sound and reached out to touch it. "Let's save this one for home," her mother said, putting it in the beige cloth bag that hung from one arm.

"Mama, do you think that every one of these broken ones looked like that before it got broken?" Val used her bare toes to push the fragments of shell around in the sand.

"Oh yes, *mi querubin.* They are all just as magnificent as this one when they start out."

Val looked at the tiny, sharp pieces that she held in her hand. "What happens to them? Why do they get so broken?"

Teresa sat down on the sand and brought her knees against her chest. "They all start out so beautiful, Valentine, but the sea water and the rocks and the sand wear them down until they are nothing but shattered pieces. A sad, broken reminder of something that was gloriously beautiful at one point in time."

May brought summer. Whenever Northern California gives us an early summer, the last weeks of school feel like eternity. The air conditioning was broken for the third school year in a row, so the teachers resorted to swivel fans that they plugged into the corner of the rooms in hopes that some sort of air would be circulated. Basically, real teaching ended and the afternoons were spent 'reviewing' for finals which were three weeks away, and watching movies that were even slightly related to the subject matter.

I clicked my pen in and out as Mr. Brookes used the remote to turn up Forrest Gump, which he said would give us an idea of what the Vietnam War was like for soldiers. I thought about Jonathan, who was at home with the remains of the flu.

Thankfully, he had gotten sick on Friday afternoon, spent the entire weekend throwing up and feverish, and was practically well enough to go back to school by Sunday night. Practically. This morning he asked to stay home one more day because his tummy felt yucky still, so I had reluctantly went to school. All for a movie.

"Val," the only girl that I would consider my best friend, Angela, stage whispered across the aisle at me, "here. Take this." She held out a folded piece of notebook paper. I took it and glanced over at Mr. Brookes, who was watching the game highlights on his laptop, completely oblivious to everyone.

Inside the paper Angela had written, "Do you think we can go out after school? Mom said I can use the car now that Penelope has her fabulous new Jetta. We can just go shopping or something. Wanna?"

"Can't." I lifted half of my cheek into my sort-of smile.

She sighed and frowned over at me. "Fine."

Angela Scarpelli knew me better than anyone. We had met three years earlier when she had sat down next to me at lunch and shared with me that Justin White was the dirtiest, rudest, most obnoxious guy in the entire school district. I had raised my eyebrows at the emphasis on 'district' and she had promptly stated, "He dumped me yesterday."

For the rest of that day we met between classes to hand each other multiple-page notes that detailed the outlines of our most private lives. I kept it surface, of course. I did not detail the outlines of my most private life until nearly six months after we met, while we sat on the cool November grass behind the Maintenance building on school property.

The homecoming pep rally was going on at our football field, and I could vaguely make out the sounds of cheerleaders offering school

208

spirit by the mouthful. I pressed my hand against the stucco wall until I could feel and see the little hole imprints on my palm and the pads of my fingers.

Angela sat across from me, Indian style, the tips of her knees touching mine. She painted my finger nails with her one hand and held a Black and Mild with the other, bringing it up to her lips every few minutes as though it wasn't an action but simply a second thought. She hummed 'Amazing Grace', her choppy blackened brown hair blowing lightly in a somewhat messy manner, and when she paused to take a drag, smiling from her bare lips and her slate blue eyes simultaneously, I fell in love with her.

She flicked her thumb to ash the stick and, in the blatant manner that I had come to know as Angela, said, "So what the hell is wrong with your family, anyway? Your mom seemed totally out of it."

"Yeah. She is. She always is, sort of."

"Why?"

"Well, I mean she didn't always used to be like that. She used to take me on picnics and stuff, out on the water on these stupid little row boats, shit like that." I blew on my nails. Angela continued to paint.

"Man, I can't picture her on a picnic anywhere."

I thought about it for moment and then said, "Yeah." It was the only thing that came to mind.

"Oh yeah and ew. Who was that guy at the table? I swear to god he had pedo written all over him."

I pulled my hand away for a moment and looked at her. "What? You think so? Do you really?" My stomach tumbled over itself and I searched Angela's eyes for the truth I knew they'd smack me with.

She shrugged her bare shoulders and took another long drag. "Eh. He could just be your run of the mill perv. Who knows? Why was he in your house anyway?"

"It's my mother's boyfriend. Dino."

"Ew."

"Yeah."

"So then," she put the brush into the small bottle and turned it until it was tight, "how come your mom is so messed up now if she used to be like, you know, like you?"

"Her whole life, I guess. Her whole life has been, like it's like one thing after another with her. Her mom raised her by herself and then she had me when she was in 8th grade, and then she dropped out of school, and then she started dating these guys that were horrible, nasty men?" I stopped because tears were coming out of my eyes, slowly, but at a consistent pace that made me think of tiny streams running through a muddy ground.

Angela was silent sitting across from me. Her thin neck was bent slightly and her eyes were squinted just enough to let me know she was intently listening. I swiped the back of my hand across my cheek, holding my fingers apart so that I didn't smudge.

Anyway, yeah. So she just screwed up a couple times, and God probably hates her now and is like "That's it, no more chances for you." It wouldn't be so friggin' bad if she just didn't bring her scumbag boyfriends into my house.

"Do they hurt you?" She asked casually, quietly, and with the force of ten thousand warriors.

I laughed and lifted the corner of my shirt up three inches.

Angela reached her finger out and touched my skin, tracing the ragged edges of the scar. She said nothing with her mouth, just put the cigar to her lips and breathed in, and then handed it to me. I inhaled and held it until it burned my throat and gums and nostrils.

* * *

I walked into my kitchen to find my mother standing in front of the open freezer door, holding a bag of frozen baby carrots in one hand and a cigarette in the other. She turned quickly when she heard me.

"Valentine." She said my name like a discovery. I noticed the clarity in her voice, and, upon closer inspection, her eyes, too. She was sober. Completely sober.

"Hi." I looked at the carrots in her hand. "Are you making dinner?"

She also looked down at what she held and stared for a moment, as though deciding if she really wanted to cook carrots this evening. "Yes. No."

"Okayyy?" I walked towards the doorway that split the kitchen with the living room. My mother jumped.

"Valentine, wait! Just wait. Listen to me, baby, listen okay?" It could have been the fact that she called me baby, or the panic I saw flash across her face, but something made my lunch of tuna salad lurch dangerously towards my throat.

"What?"

"Now, let's just wait a minute, okay?" She looked around like she was waiting for that minute to reveal a way out.

"Mama, what is going on? Where's Jonathan?" It was the magic question.

"Val. There was a little accident, no biggie really?"

I didn't even hear her. I tore through the living room and took the steps two at a time, taking just enough time to turn the knob before flying through the doorway into his room. He bolted upright in his bed and I stopped in my tracks.

"Oh, my god. Oh, my god, Jonathan. Oh, my god." I knelt next to his bed.

211

"Hi." He put his arms around my neck and held onto me.

"Oh, god, I'm sorry, Jonathan. I'm sorry. Let me see you." He leaned away from me and I looked at his little face. His left eye was swollen shut, his eyelid and the soft skin around it was a nasty bruised mess. His bottom lip was extra plump, darkening in color, and I could make out a split where blood was crusting over. I stared at the face. I couldn't believe it was my little boy. "Buddy?"

"I'm okay, Val. I'm okay. Mama said the cold will make my eye feel better and I'll be good as new, she said."

I started to cry, and I tried not to sob loudly, even though I wanted to bury my head in the pillow and soak it right through. I didn't even bother wiping my face, I just held Jonathan's skinny body and thought about how I had finally made the biggest mistake ever.

"Valentine, don't cry, Val. I'm okay, look. Look at me, I'm okay."

I looked at his face and bit my lip. He started to smile, but it stretched the torn skin on his lip, and he winced. I'm pretty sure my heart broke right down the middle. "No, Buddy. No. Tell me. Just tell me what happened."

He looked down and picked at the edges of the tattered afghan blanket that we've had since I was little. "I said bad things to Ernie."

I smoothed his hair back away from his eyes. "What bad things, Jonathan?"

"The F-word."

My ears must have been deceiving me. I can count the times he has disagreed with me on one hand. And now he dropped the F-bomb on a 250 pound alcoholic on the one day he's alone in the house?

"Okay? Why did you say that?"

He glared down at the yarn strings. "He made me mad."

This was not my sweet boy. I closed my eyes for a moment and

212

took a breath.

"Jonathan, just tell me what happened, okay? I need you to tell me."

"It was just a little run-in. Stop being dramatic, Valentine." My mother's voice came from behind me, and I turned to see her holding the bag of frozen vegetables.

"Jonathan here was mouthing off, Ernie was in one of his moods. We can just chalk it up as a bad day." She eased Jonathan against his pillow and put the bag on his face.

I stared at what used to be my mother. Jonathan looked at me out of the good eye that was not yielding carrots. Something was about to blow up; I could practically smell it in the air.

"Don't touch him." I stood up and spoke evenly. "Don't touch him. Get away."

My mother looked baffled, like we were having a lovely day at the beach and I had just announced that I wanted to go home. She stood on one side of Jonathan's twin bed, and I stood on the other, facing her. "Valentine, what in God's good name?"

This, I thought to myself, must be what it feels like to have high blood pressure.

My temples felt like I had a very tiny but ambitious drummer boy doing his job oh too well. I swallowed hard before I screamed. "GET OUT! DON'T TOUCH HIM! LEAVE RIGHT NOW!" And with that, I leaned across the bed and shoved my own mother backwards. I actually pushed her. My own hands, the hands that I wouldn't have if it weren't for her, reached out and slammed into her shoulders.

She took two teetering steps backwards. "Valen?"

"Mama. Leave."

She reached down to take Jonathan's hand, but he yanked it away. He took the veggies off his face and then made a change of his very

213

own. "Don't touch me," he said, each word deliberate and leaden. "Leave me alone."

My mother held my stare for eternity, and then turned slowly and walked out of the room without a word. We sat silently there, me and Jonathan, until my palm started to get sweaty from the grip of his small hand.

* * *

I checked the red blinking numbers on the clock that sat on my dresser. 10:17. My purple duffel bag sat on my bed, chock full of? Well, of everything. My closet looked like a style-crazy thief had paid me a visit, leaving only the never-to-be-worn-again clothing on the floor below the wire hangers. I stripped my bed of all the linens and stuffed the sheets and as many blankets as I could find in two pillow cases. A mustard yellow suitcase sat next to my duffel bag, filled with all the contents of Jonathan's drawers, and the things I wanted to keep for us, like the few baby pictures that we had of him, his crayons and coloring books, and my freshly laminated diploma.

I passed by my dresser one last time and picked up the nesting dolls, laying them carefully inside Jonathan's suitcase before moving all of the bags into the hall, flicking the light switch downwards, and shutting my bedroom door.

I walked at a normal pace down the hall. My mother and Ernie had yet to come home from whatever bar they were at, and so I didn't even attempt to be quiet. I opened the door to my mother's bedroom and went right to the small top drawer of her night stand where she kept her lingerie and bags of potpourri. I slid it open and pulled out the small cedar box that was engraved with her name, a gift from Jonathan's father. It took me less than ten seconds to unlatch it and take the roll of money that sat nestled under some pearl jewelry, my

214

birth announcement, and a silver Zippo lighter embossed with a red rose.

Inside the box I placed the letter that was in my handwriting.

Mama, I love you so much. I wish we could have worked, I really do more than anything.

I'm taking him away from here, Mama. I'm taking him somewhere else, where he can have a real chance. No one should be hurt like this, Mama. I know that somewhere in you, you know this too. Do you remember when we snuck into the Holiday Inn when they were having breakfast time? Remember how we filled our backpacks with muffins and bagels and little boxes of Frosted Flakes, and you took me all along the sidewalks in Santa Cruz, and we passed out one or two things to the hobos who sat on benches or just the ground? When I asked why we were giving all of the food to strangers, you told me that sometimes people hurt so bad on the inside that they can't even help themselves get better. I think you're one of those people now, Mama. And I wish I could just hand you a blueberry muffin and make it all better, but I can't. So I'm doing what I know I can do. I'm taking him away.

I love you, Mama. I love you.

Love, your Valentine

ps I took the money out of here to help us. I took the car to get us out of here. I took Jonathan because I love him too much to keep him in this place. Please don't call the police about the car. If you do, I'm going to have to tell them about Ernie, and then they'll take Jonathan away from me and you both. I'm giving him a family now.

I shut the drawer and looked up to see Jonathan standing in blue cotton pajamas, holding his stuffed giraffe Lisa in one hand and his pillow under his other arm.

"All set, Buddy?"

He nodded.

"Okay then, let's do it." I pushed up against my knees and stood, went over to him and ruffled his hair. "Are you sure Lisa is the only thing you want to take? We can fit whatever you want."

"I'm sure."

"You can bring a couple other stuffed animals, if you want."

"No, its okay. They can stay with Mama in case she needs someone to snuggle at night in her bed."

I suddenly felt like I couldn't swallow. There was no time for second guessing now. "Well, okay then, Buddy. Let's go."

He followed me down the stairs, carrying one of the pillow cases, and I stepped outside the house into the perfect June night air. I shut the front door and put my key under the mat. It was just a spare now. We walked to the driveway and I opened the trunk of the nine year old white Mercury. I stuffed it all in, except for a red LunchMate cooler that held salami sandwiches on rolls, Doritos, Reese's Peanut Butter Cups, and some other favorites of Jonathan's.

I slammed the trunk shut and went to the driver?s seat. Jonathan was already seatbelted into the front seat, clutching Lisa. I turned the key and thanked someone that for as much as it looked like a piece of shit, it ran more than good.

"You be my navigator, okay?"

I saw a little bit of brightness in his eyes. "And you'll be the pilot?" He smiled.

"Yup."

"Does the navigator get to push the buttons on the radio?"

"Of course. What kind of navigator would you be if you didn't do that?"

He laughed. "Maybe a not good one."

"Nah, you're the best navigator probably in the whole world."

He grinned and shrugged, which made me laugh. I put the car in reverse and pulled out of the driveway, and Jonathan poked decisively at the buttons on the radio, pausing only slightly before settling on a song.

COCO DE MER

Even through the closed windows of the minivan we are bombarded with honks and yells. Small dogs, so thin they are almost the shadows of dogs, lick drops of water from roadside taps where little girls fill plastic buckets, their handles tied with string. An emaciated woman gulps beer on the grand plaza steps of the court house. Passer-bys give her wide berth, as if she is covered in sick. I glance away. I've dragged Sarah here for the lapis waters, the crystal beaches, the umbrella cocktails by the pool.

"We were first colonised by the Portuguese, then the French, then the English. We are close to Africa, yes, and the black people are descended from the slaves who planted the sugar," says Christophe in his funny accent.

I smile at this boy who is our tour guide, curious if he is aware of the irony of what he's saying. He is so white and so clearly European and yet it is all 'we' and 'them'. Sarah and I drop back into the conversation we've been having, off and on, since we left London.

"Sarah, all I've done is talk about myself and here we are, almost at the end of the trip, no further ahead and bored to tears!" I laugh ruefully. "Typical, isn't it?"

"Well, you know the kids will be fine. You're both great parents and that won't change, will it?" says Sarah, completely ignoring what I just said.

"Of course it will, Sarah! What about splitting family Christmases, juggling homes, penny pinching, Daddy gets a girlfriend, Mummy takes a holiday. This isn't what the children bargained for. It isn't what any of us bargained for!"

I break off as we pass houses that look as if dinosaurs have meandered by, taking a nip here and a bite there, leaving metal roofs with gaping holes. Windows are covered with tattered plastic sheeting; even concrete walls have chunks taken out. Suri Suri is one of those places that look like paradise in the pictures but now, driving through the interior, I can see how little, as tourists, we actually see of the country from our fancy white hotels.

"You know, Sarah, there's nothing new about this whole situation. It's the old saw—it's a cliché if it's happening to someone else, but it's fresh blood and guts if it's you."

"I still don't get it, though. He's a great guy and who's to say you could ever meet anyone else as good? You're 44. And he does love you," says Sarah, somehow again just missing my point.

"I love him, too. God, I've gone through this a million times. The problem isn't him. It's me."

"Jeannie, I'm your best friend, right? Listen to me; I really think you need to stick it out. It kills me to think of you rattling around in some little flat, eating meals-for-one."

"You just don't want to come save me when I'm old and I fall down in the shower!"

Christophe breaks in and we look at him guiltily: "Ladies, I am sorry to interrupt but this is the market and we will disembark for several small minutes so you can purchase some of the touristic goods and view the native fishes and fruits. There is also the government supermarket across the street where you can buy the Western foods."

I skid as we enter the market, my skimpy sandals sliding in blood and scales. Fish cover the wooden tables: an enormous grey suede shark smiles at us; red snappers, arranged in schools, fly over the splintery waves; long eels glare from boxes of damp sea weed. And everywhere are sea gulls, their malevolent yellow eyes glinting, as they snap at bits of fish.

"Madam, Madam would you like some fish today?"

"Buy from me, Lady! Fresh from the boat, Lady!"

We smile at the fish sellers and snap pictures and grimace at each other about the battalions of flies crawling over the fish we could be eating for supper that night.

"Lovely! Come to sunny Suri Suri and eat scrumptious food covered with fly shit," I joke, hoping to relieve some of the tension that has been building all week.

"Oh do shut up and stop being such a girl!" Sarah snaps at me. She has always been much heartier than I. Something as natural as fly shit wouldn't bother her.

"Maybe the problem is that I just find him boring? He never reads and he doesn't appreciate me, and when he kisses me, I don't feel anything."

"Oh God, Jean, can we leave off and enjoy the sights?"

"Sorry…"

"Ladies, you are with me? We have four varieties of banana here," boasts Christophe, leading us into the fruit section of the market. He breaks off a banana, small and plastic-looking like a child's toy, peels it, gives each of us a smidgen, and hands the stall owner a tiny copper coin.

"Oh wow! Delicious." I enthuse, reverting to being a jolly tourist.

Sarah rolls her eyes at me. I am not going to get upset with her. I know that I am looking for a level of understanding that is impossible. I do realize that it really is my problem and not Jeremy's. But, sometimes I can't help wonder if I had married someone different… Sarah escapes to the supermarket for some biscuits and bottles of water.

"Oh, yes. I will take one biscuit, thank you," said Christophe, back on the minivan. "I have had such trouble with the food here. I have lost much weight—maybe 10 kilograms. You can see—here they have only fish and fruit and I do not have the monnaie for the supermarket. There is no meat, especially no sausage, no potatoes. I am Belgique," he said, as if that explained everything. "I have been sick very many times since I have been here. Each winter I have been in the hospital for one month, maybe two months."

I think of the hotel buffet. We joke we are eating 2,000 calories a meal, not a day, and that we will have to be rolled onto the plane. Christophe reaches for another biscuit and eats it hungrily. It probably isn't the fish and fruit, I think, it's the flies. I wonder why in the world a normal-looking Belgian kid would stay on this island starving to death and so ill he has a bed with his name on it at the one crummy hospital?

"Ladies, now to the botanical garden to see the rare palm tree, the Coco-de-Mer," says Christophe. "It may sound how you say, exagere, all this talk of the Coco-de-Mer. Before I saw it, I thought, it is only a tree, what is so special?"

We putt along in the bus, out of the town traffic now. Since we arrived, we had heard about the Coco-de-Mer. In fact from the time we read the guide book, it was Coco-de-Mer this, Coco-de-Mer that. Esmeralda, the heaviest land tortoise in the world and the Coco-de-Mer each had their own individual photos in the Rough Guide to Suri Suri.

"What are you doing here?" Sarah breaks into the silence like a shark fin in the calm sea around the island.

"Chris…" she repeats, "what are you doing here?"

"Well, you know, I am a tour guide. Before I was an accountant for a multi- national. But I was always sick. The tour work, it is how do you say? Sporadique? So, I can do it, because you can see, I am too

221

weak. Also, in the company I had a big problem. You know in the Suri Suri we work on Saturday and in my church, we worship on the Saturday, so I could not continue."

He turns, as if he has explained everything, and speaks haltingly in Creole to the driver. Sarah shrugs, puzzled, and we stare out the windows at sugar fields waving willow green. Giant cultivators crouch over the cane protectively. In the middle of the fields are mountains of withered cane, dirt and rocks.

Christophe explains, "Those were made by the slaves when they were clearing the fields."

It is hard to believe the piles have lasted all these years. Everything else on the island, even the hotel, looks as if it is dissolving: mildew and rot melting even solid concrete and yet these rubbish mountains look as neat as loaves of banana bread fresh from the oven.

"Chris, I still don't understand. Why do you live here?"

Implicit in this, of course, is why is he on this God-forsaken island where a pack of biscuits and a shark cost the same?

"OK! I understand!" he smiles, happily, "You want to know why I live here in Suri Suri?"

"Yea, exactly."

"One moment," he says as we enter the botanical gardens.

"To be continued…" I quip to Sarah. A nattily dressed black man in a uniform struts over as we struggle out of the bus, our thighs sticking to the plastic seats. How could it be worth giving up a glorious day at the beach to check out a couple of palm trees?

"Allo, Christophe, 'ow are you?" the guard smiles, giving Christophe the light finger tipping hand shake I notice the waiters using in the hotel.

Specks of grass sparkle in the air like fairy confetti and dragonflies dart from one patch of shade to another. Frangipani blossoms litter the lawns like tiny stars. Enormous tortoises, with their giant penis-shaped heads thrust forward, lumber across the lawns. We saunter through the gardens, our hips swinging sloppily and our flip-flop feet splayed.

"Sarah, do you remember Nick?"

"Nick?"

"Nick Richards. You know, BBC Natural History Presenter. World Famous Naturalist. Best-selling Author. MBE, OBE, blah blah blah. Yes, Nick, the guy I lived with before I got married? Remember him?" I find my voice getting shrieky.

"Don't tell me you're back with Nick! After all these years. How could you?"

"No! No! Calm down! I'm not having an affair. Don't be ridiculous. Then it really would be as trite and clichéd as I said."

"Oh God, what is it then?"

"You remember that whole thing with his wife, Elizabeth?"

I thought about when I saw the TV documentary where Elizabeth had revealed she had an incestuous affair with her father while she was at university. I had been watching in bed with Jeremy and I was so stunned I almost missed the next bit of the film when she paraded about nude and emaciated and talked about how she had starved herself while she was pregnant.

"Of course I remember, there's no one in England who wasn't disgusted by that!" said Sarah.

We were brought back by Christophe, "Ladies, please pay attention! This is Esmeralda, the giant tortoise. She is our national celebrity—you know, like Madonna!"

"You're some material girl, Esmeralda!" As I patted her warm brown shell, I thought about how Nick had been my Big Passion. The summer before we were to get married, he had left to make a documentary in Brazil and while he was there he had hooked up with Elizabeth, his series producer. We followed Christophe across the gardens.

"Would you like a Pepsi, ladies? There is a nice place to relax for a few small minutes."

"Thanks, Chris. That'd be lovely," said Sarah.

"Go on!" she says as he hands us the thick cold bottles.

"God, don't get your knickers in a twist!"

"Yes...," her voice is impatient.

"Well, you know, I hadn't seen him in almost twenty years," I hesitate, "only what everybody else has on TV-- crawling around in the Amazon and the pictures in the papers going to premiers and things. And then I was in Waterstones and I heard a voice..." I paused. I had heard a voice that had felt so familiar it was like a cup of tea.

"So you started an affair? I can't believe you would go back to that shit after he dumped you, after all these years!"

"Sarah! I'm not having an affair. I only spoke to him for a few minutes. It's what he said."

"What he said?"

"Uh huh, he said something like, 'So what have you done with yourself all these years, Jeannie? I keep expecting to read in the newspaper that you've done something great—I never knew anyone with so much potential.' And he sounded so excited to know, as if I actually could have done something amazing and great."

"So? Did you tell him about your job and Jeremy and the boys?"

"Yes, yes, of course."

Sarah searched my face.

"Jean, did you tell him that you run the biggest medical research charity in the UK? That you bake your own bread? That your friends call you Saint Jean?"

I dropped my eyes. "Don't be sarcastic! No, of course not! I just said something like, 'Nothing, Nick, nothing, I haven't done anything much at all.' And he smiled and said, 'Oh well, you look well on it, Jeannie.' And he left. Can you believe he still called me Jeannie?"

"I can't believe I'm hearing this. Why would that want to make you leave Jeremy?"

By this time Chris is describing the various plants and pointing out the French-style governor's mansion. We meander after him. How could I explain it to Sarah?

"Sarah, you know the thing he said about The Potential?" I said it like that, with a capital T and a capital P.

"Well, that's what everybody said all my life! I always thought I would do something, you know, be something…And until Nick said that I hadn't really noticed when people stopped saying it. After law school? After I left The City? Was it when I was thirty and married? Was it when we moved out of London? When I had the children? I just can't stand the fact that I had it one day and then it was gone and now what am I? Nothing."

Sarah is silent and I try to remember exactly when I had gone from being filled with that magical quality to being drained, bereft of potential. How had that happened? Potential wasn't like beauty or even like youth, which however you used it at least you had once had it. No, potential was one of those things, like breast milk and talent, that if never used, simply dissipates and there is absolutely no sign it was ever there.

Sarah stops short and faces me, her face twisted and angry. "Oh come on now Jean, don't condescend to me! 'When did people stop telling me I was amazing?' You with your fucking potential! Have you forgotten about me or Daniel or Jeremy?" She shakes her finger. "We were all the same—white hot with smouldering potential. The glow of our potential lit every room we entered. You know what? It was youth. You're not special."

I try to explain but she cuts me off.

"What did you expect? To be Darwin? To be fucking Amelia Earhart?" She continues, "You're lucky enough to get paid for what you do. I slog my guts out and I barely make enough to pay the bloody mortgage. So just shut up about all this potential."

Her face is a furious red, much redder than just from the heat.

"You're completely self indulgent and I'm sick to death hearing about you and your problems. You want to leave Jeremy because you haven't lived up to your Goddamn Potential? What good does that do? Potential!"

Christophe tries to interrupt, touching Sarah lightly on the arm. "Ladies, would you like to follow me to see the Coco-de-Mer?"

He looks completely upset when Sarah shakes him off.

"Chris, I'm sorry!" I gesture toward Sarah who is stalking away. "I think we need a minute."

I run to catch up. Finally, breathing heavily, we both rest against a tree, neither of us looking at the other. Sweat trickles between my breasts.

"Sarah, that's exactly my point! Why is it that you and Daniel and Jeremy can just plough on each day and enjoy your lives? Why am I so bogged down? I know I'm not special! If I were I would have done something. But I'm not and I haven't and that's why Nick left me and I feel, I feel, I don't know …"

Sarah interrupts, "See that's even worse, because you are special, you twit! And you've done so much and if you don't value what you've done, then it means that what I've done—what everybody's done is useless. And his wife? She's totally messed up. You wouldn't want to be like her, even if she is some famous film maker-performance artist, weird freaky whatever she is."

Tears join the sweat dribbling down my nose.

Sarah hands me a tissue and says, "Ok, ok, I'm sorry. I shouldn't have yelled at you. Let's go see this precious palm tree."

"You are all right?" Chris asks. "Do you want to return to the hotel?"

"No, no, we're fine. Let's go on with the show!" I sing out, smiling bravely at Sarah, who looks back grateful that I have pulled myself together.

"Ok!" Christophe exclaims, gesturing upwards, "I told you it is magic—the tree you have bumped into is the Coco-de-Mer that you have come to Suri Suri to see."

We look up at the smooth grey trunk, the glorious crown of green fronds, the enormous coconuts dangling high above.

"It is a very special tree because there is one male and one female and they must be near to each other to make the baby. The fruit, it only comes once every ten years and it has a very interesting shape, no?"

Chris picks up an enormous nut from the base of the tree. It looks like an immense Siamese twin coconut, but as we move closer we see its contours, the sides curving like a woman's hips, the cleft a deep V.

"Has this been carved?" Sarah asks, "It looks like a Henry Moore."

She runs her finger the length of the curve.

"No, no, they are all like this. 'The beautiful lady' is what she is called here. You can see why the Coco-de-Mer so special, no? This is the only place on earth where she grows. That is why we call ourselves the Garden of Eden. It is the meaning of life, no? The man and the woman and the babies? Everybody here, they want a piece of the Coco-de-Mer, it is like the horn of the rhino. The people come to touch the Coco-de-Mer for luck."

Sarah and I stroke the warm brown torso, each perhaps hoping that we will absorb its talismanic qualities through our skin.

Finally Sarah says, "It is lovely, isn't it? But my God, they certainly give it mythic properties, don't they?"

"Well, I guess that when you don't even have cinema, watching palm trees mate can be pretty exciting!"

We burst out laughing, tears still running down my nose. Christophe looks on, astonished.

Sarah takes my arm as we walk toward the bus and wraps it around her waist. It is hot and soon we are stuck to each other, our hips fused through the thin cotton of our skirts.

When we reach the bus, I hiss to Sarah, "Let's not talk about all my rubbish!" I gesture sharply at Chris.

After we are settled, Sarah turns to Christophe. "So Chris, back to you. Why are you here?"

She has always been the one to fly into anything—and always got away with it. Somehow the combination of her curviness and Minnie Mouse voice disarms even the most recalcitrant. I slump against the seat, drained.

"Well, it's complicated..."

"Go on!"

"When I was a teenager, my life was meaningless. So I joined a church. My parents, they were very unhappy. At first they thought it was like football, you know? I would be crazy about it for a while, but then I would become interested in something else. But no, I have the faith."

He points out the small town we are driving through. "This is my village where I live!"

We look at the rough huts, each hunched in its little patch of dirt, a tall paw paw tree an ineffective parasol overhead.

"Well, the church had only a few dozen people in Belgium. At first I was on the streets, trying to convert other young people. But, I was not very good!"

We dodge chickens and dogs and small children as they dart across the road. A sign painted on the side of a house directs us to: 'Clothing Outlet—Turn Left' with a huge blue arrow pointing to fields of sugar cane.

"Well, there were no girls in our church in Belgium for me to marry, so our leader, he wrote to all of our other churches until he finds a girl for me."

There is a definite lapse in the conversation as we absorb this—in fact, there is a giant gulp.

"So what, he arranged a marriage for you?" asks Sarah, surprisingly hesitant for her.

"Well, I would not call it that. We did not have to marry if we did not want. We exchanged the photograph and the letters and then we decided to get married."

"Just a sec! I'm missing something. Start again. Where was this girl from?" I am getting agitated and it isn't even my life.

"Well she is from here. She is from Suri Suri and that was a problem at the beginning because you know she does not speak French and I did not speak Creole, so it was very difficult for us to communicate. I would write the letter and then my leader, he would translate it into English and then her leader would translate it to her and we would exchange like that."

"So how long 'til you decided to marry?"

"Oh it was not long; I knew she was the one."

He interrupts himself, "That is where I live with her and her family!" He points to a tin-roofed hut with banana trees slumped messily in front.

"But it was many monthses before we could see each other because we had no money for the aeroplane. The Church had to raise the money and it took much time."

"Did your parents come to the wedding?" I asked.

"How soon after you saw her did you marry?"

"Was it weird?"

Christophe shrugged, "No, no my parents did not come. They were very disappointed. You see, I was an excellent student and I was a top chess player in my area. I had a very promising future, you know, with a good job and a salary and a house and the cars and all of the things the parents, they think are important. No, I do not think I will see them again."

He lowers his head, but soon perks up, "We were married the week I arrived here! It was wonderful! We saw each other several times and then we were married. You know, it is natural a man and a woman to be together."

We sit silent, a vacuum of sound, a halcyon of thought. This boy is like us, like our husbands were, like our sons will be.

"My wife's mother, she works in the hotel in housekeeping. That is how I got this job. Her name is Regina. You have seen her?" Christophe asks.

We shake our heads, no we are ashamed to say, we haven't even really looked at any of the ladies in their starched pink and white striped uniforms. Certainly we haven't noticed a name or a face. We drive on, the sunlight pouring in competing with the blasting air conditioning.

Christophe turns to me and says, "You are all right? You have had a big day today. You have learned many new truths, it is not the case?"

I smile and nod. Yes, yes, I am fine. Thank you.

After a silence, Christophe asks, "You would like to see a photograph?" He pulls out a wallet, smooth and shiny from wear. He proffers a childish face: white teeth glistening, puffy braids in colourful plastic baubles.

"She's so pretty!" exclaims Sarah. And she is pretty—gorgeous really, like a young kudu, all delicate flared nostrils and wide dark eyes.

"So young! How old is she?" I ask.

"She is 18 almost 19."

"But, I thought you had been here three winters—three years?"

"Yes, that is right. We have been married for three years!"

And then we are back, the sun just below the horizon, the sky still a bright delft blue. Christophe unloads our straw shopping baskets, filled with the shell necklaces and embroidered hankies we'd bought that we'll give to Oxfam in a few weeks. I whisper to Sarah and pull out the contents of my wallet: coin and bill, whatever and hand it to Chris.

"Good luck, Christophe! Good luck! Thank you so much! It was really a great tour. It was a great day!" I am desperate to thank him, to be grateful, to show we are not just spoiled English woman. That we are different, that this is different, that we don't do this all the time.

"Oh la!" exclaims Chris, "That is very kind! It will be so helpful for the baby. You know, I will be a father very soon."

"How lovely!"

"Yes, I am very lucky! Goodbye! It has been a pleasure. Have a good trip back to England!"

He is off, strolling down the long black drive on a rickety old bicycle.

***

"Ladies would you like to sit next to the pool? This evening we have an island feast—all of the fish, our chef, he bought it fresh at the market today."

The concierge leads us to a table lit by fairy lights twinkling on the overhanging palm tree.

"See I told you we'd be eating those fly-shitty fish for dinner!" I laugh.

After we serve ourselves, neither of us, in fact, avoiding the fish, we jump immediately into a discussion of Christophe.

"Can you believe she was only 16 when they married?" Sarah asks.

"Can you believe they barely knew each other?"

"That they live in that tiny hut with her whole family?"

"It just seems impossible he would choose to live this way. I just can't imagine it." I say.

"I know, but when I think about it, what really makes us happy? Is it being able to go to films and plays or send our kids to ballet class or have a nice car?"

"God Sarah, I wish I knew. I wouldn't have dragged you all the way here to help me figure out whether to leave Jeremy." I respond. "But, the wonderful thing is, Christophe seems happy."

I am relieved Sarah isn't asking me about Nick and the whole potential thing. But finally, I leap back into it, scraping my chocolate mousse from the plate.

"You know what we were talking about before the Coco-de-Mer?"

She nods, gazing out at the beach.

"I guess that what really struck me when I saw that crazy documentary, was how much Nick cherishes and respects her, even though she's clearly a nightmare, and how being married to the right person can allow you to become who you are, what you want to be. And how being married to the wrong person can just mire you down, through no fault of yours or theirs."

I hesitate before I say, "So maybe if Jeremy and I had married other people we could have each done more, been better, strived for a greater greatness, you know what I mean?"

"I'm not sure," she replies, "I don't know if I had married someone else, I would have done more. Do you think if you had married Nick you would have won the Nobel Prize? Just do what you want, Jean. It's you who needs to do it. Did you think that just because you were smart and pretty you'd automatically grow up and be something?" Her tone is calm, the heat of earlier in the day dissipated. "Come on! What's wrong with being happy with what you've got?" she asks.

"I know, I know. It's not exactly that—look at Christophe and his girl, what was her name? It's clear he treasures her. I just think if you have something like that..." I trail off, knowing how silly I sound.

For I do know. I know that had I married Nick I still probably wouldn't have painted a great painting or written a best seller or come up with a cure for diabetes. That's the problem, isn't it?

***

Next morning, as I sip the strong black coffee, dipping my croissant and flicking crumbs to the sparrows hopping on the tables, one of the cleaning ladies approaches.

"Excuse me Madame, you are Miss Jean?"

"Yes?"

233

"Christophe, he is my daughter's husband. He give me this for you." She hands me something wooden, like a peach pit.

I look at it closely and see it is a piece of Coco-de-Mer, carved exactly like the big ones. A tiny little charm.

"Thank you! Please tell him thank you." I look at Regina and search for her young daughter in her lined face. Her paper cap is pinned to stiff gray curls and her feet are cracked in broken flip flops.

Her face lights up, "No problem, Madam, Christophe said to me he thinks you need it more than him."

I turn it over in my hand, studying the variegation in the wood. I stroke it and feel how light it feels, light yet strong, and I rise to go pack for my trip home.

THE SILENCE OF THE VOLUNTEER

Scenes from Baghdad dance across the screen, columns of smoke ascending from the husks of blackened cars, men in green flak jackets and heavy boots running into dusty lanes, worried residents gathering near the the car where the bomb exploded, their faces asking, Will I be next?

My widescreen Quasar television carries me there every day. The remote control flicks back and forth between two channels; the smooth sentences of Al Jazira, the Arab channel, to the sturdy English of CNN. It is all so familiar. It brings to my nostrils the pungent memory of burning gasoline and the strong iron smell of burning cars.

Once, American soldiers roamed my neighborhood, here in Beirut, just as these warriors advance into Iraqi ones. Their fingers were tense on metal triggers, backs pressed against limestone walls, groping their way down Lenbi Street, rifles thrust menacingly before them. It was a time when all Beirutis hid in their homes, and listened to the crashing sounds of war.

The same thing always happens. My thoughts drift back to Kendra. Kendra. An American girl with brown hair. A girl of average height and average aspirations. A girl upon whom the great problems of the world seemed to barely have made an impression. A girl who once told me she never read the newspaper because it was 'depressing.'

At the time, there were hundreds being killed in El Salvador, Britain went to war with Argentina, Poles marched for freedom and the Israelis invaded Beirut. Kendra took as little notice as possible.

She came to Beirut the way the Israelis came to Beirut, up along the coast road from Tel Aviv. She traveled with other volunteers, on their way to clothe our orphans and comfort our grieving widows. When

Kendra spoke of that trip, her eyes looked inward, and her voice took on that low, hushed tone which she also used to speak of her mother and anything to do with the Catholic religion.

She had never known scenery like that. She was a child of New Jersey, a child of weary, smog-filled cities and busy people in busy cars. She was not accustomed to the quiet hills of Lebanon. She described the ancient olive trees and steep cliffs, small beaches around every bend, and Arab peasants hurrying along with their donkeys.

"Kendra," I said, "they were running from the war."

At the time, I found it curious that she did not mention the tanks and armored personnel carriers and jeeps and troop trucks the group had surely encountered along the way.

"Maybe just one or two trucks," she said lightly. She took off her earring and played with it in the palm of her hand.

Neri brought Kendra to me, as he has brought me so many things. Neri, my oldest son. He had stopped at the hospital near Shatila and suddenly bombs had landed someplace quite nearby. Patients were screaming and crying and running in all directions. He had seen this brown-haired girl, standing in a window, clutching the sill, sobbing uncontrollably. He had pulled her away from the window and calmed her. He brought her to dinner at our house.

We had lamb, French wine, and tomatoes from the garden of a neighbor who was leaving the war by boat, to Cyprus. A good table. But she ate very little.

We took our coffee in the courtyard, and I noticed her staring at me. "Where do you come from, Kendra?" I asked.

"New Jersey," she said, and I thought she would fall silent again, but words came pouring out, as if she'd waited for years for this night to tell her story.

She was twenty-two years old and Catholic, she said, looking at us nervously, as though she expected us to disapprove. From Trenton, New Jersey. Her parents were not rich, but not poor, either. They got along okay. The family had raised four sons and then an only daughter. The family was devout to the Roman Catholic religion and went to Mass on Sundays and all appropriate holy days, the reward for which was huge meals prepared by mother and grandmothers and aunts and Sister Bonita, who was also an aunt. (At this point the conversation was halted to explain to my daughter-in-law Mali what 'sisters' were.) Kendra burst on; yes, and can you imagine, she still wears her habit, not like some modern nuns, and she even cooks in that habit, yes, she brings an apron on Sundays and rolls up her sleeves. She sweats terribly.

Kendra laughed.

Mali looked confused.

Can you imagine, said Kendra, staring at Neri as if she really expected him to imagine it, that her family had pushed her to become a nun like Sister Bonita? And that she had almost done it? (Here she giggled.) All that stopped her, when the time came to really decide, was the thought of spending her Sundays sweating in her habit.

So she had become a nurse. St. Jude's School of Nursing, she said as though we'd heard of it. At first her mother had been terribly opposed, but had eventually decided that it would be okay since she could now marry a rich doctor.

She worked at Princeton Hospital, she said. Princeton Hospital, according to the story, was a wonderful place, full of wonderful doctors and wonderful nurses. Even the patients were wonderful. She described it in such glowing terms, the flower gardens, the murals on the walls, the fun in the staff cafeteria--that it was hard to imagine

237

anyone bursting a gall bladder or bleeding internally or dying from acute myocarditis there.

Neri was tapping his fingers against his wine glass as the dialogue of Princeton Hospital rolled on. I think he felt an implied criticism of the less-than-perfect medical facilities of Beirut.

I don't think that was what she intended. She was merely providing a counterpoint for her life. She was trying to get straight in her own mind why it was that she had left the wonderfulness of Princeton for the uncertainty of Beirut. On this particular day, she did not seem to understand it.

Why did you come? Neri asked, and Kendra answered quickly, To do good.

That night there was bombing, and the servants climbed to the roof of the house to watch. They were fascinated by the explosions. Small slices of West Beirut would light up suddenly, from tracer bullets, followed by the crash and light of the bombs. They were thrilled when a stray shellcasing or rocket landed in our neighborhood. I lay on my bed, face to the wall, and thought of the people the bombs struck, and how their real cries would sound.

I could hear the servants' voices: "The port's been hit!" "That one hit Hamra Street!" "Look at that explosion, it must have been where they were hiding ammunition."

The war the Israelis brought to us that summer was more like entertainment than any of our other crises.

The next day Aran brought Kendra to tea. Aran is a very young man of twenty who likes to defy me, and had beer. Kendra, it turned out, had withdrawn from the hospice of the volunteers, and gone to work at Aran's hospital. There was little she could do for women with small children and no homes. But she knew how to bandage and stitch and ease a broken bone, so she'd done those things, as frantic doctors triaged all around her. She said she had done many things that were really against regulations (by this she meant the regulations of Princeton Hospital) but that the supervisor had not stopped her.

"There was this woman who had been hit in the stomach with a piece of metal, and she was pregnant. The baby was destroyed. We had to take it all out. Anyway the woman died."

Kendra twisted her earring, then sipped her tea.

"I saw the bombs fall last night, did you? We went to the roof of our apartment building. It was like the Fourth of July, there were so many explosions."

I said that I hadn't slept, that the bombing had been too frightening.

"Oh, we don't have to be afraid," she said matter-of-factly. "The doctors told me that this side of Beirut is safe. The Israelis will never hit us. They know exactly which targets of the P.L.O. to hit. Especially, we may be sure that they know where the volunteer workers sleep."

"Kendra," I said, "the Palestinians shoot back."

She twisted her earring and looked away.

Trenton, New Jersey, Kendra told us, was the most wonderful city in the United States.

Since none of the others had been to New Jersey, it was left to me to ponder the veracity of that statement.

It had colorful ethnic neighborhoods, including her own Irish-Catholic one. At first, around the turn of the century, she thought, there had been some fighting between the various groups. Czechs arguing with Germans, Poles who didn't know their place, Slovak children raised up to throw stones at Jewish children in schoolyards.

239

"You know, they call America the 'melting pot'?" she told us. "Because eventually everyone melts. Melts together."

She was unclear as to what exactly ignited this process. In her mind it seemed to be a specific quality of the region, as if the ability to get along with each other was a chemical that could be found in the Trenton citizens' drinking water.

The men worked in paint factories and lumber yards and steel mills, and after work went to bars and had beer. The women worked in shops or daycare centers (daycare centers had to be explained to Mali, who had never heard of such a thing), and at night they cooked and waited for the men.

The Jews, it turned out, had moved away. To the other side of town, where they prospered.

I think that I was the only one at the table who understood that implied in all this was the idea that since the parishioners of St. Peter's and Paul's had been able to get along without resorting to bombing or guerrilla war, we of Beirut surely should be able to do the same.

The naïveté of the comparison made me chuckle, and I felt the disapproval of both Mali and my wife.

"Why did the Jews move away?" Aran asked.

"Well," said Kendra, playing with a glass of water, "the reason was, there was no room in our neighborhood for the Temple."

Oh.

We rarely ventured beyond the walls of our house, that summer. Lilacs and jacynths grew in the garden. My wife struggled to keep good meals on the table. We ran through various shortages of food and supplies. The phones did not work.

When Kendra had been in Beirut for one month, she showed up at our gate early one evening, and did not wait as usual for the servant to announce her, but walked slowly to the garden, and, not finding me, let herself into my study. I was startled. Both her forearms were wrapped with bandages, and there were two small bandages on her cheek.

"Hello!" I said. "What happened?"

She dropped herself into a chair, wincing as she lowered her forearms. Her eyes were dull and colorless.

"Sometimes," she said. Her voice trailed off. I waited.

"Do you have a cup of tea?" she asked.

Tea was brought, and many moments of silence passed. To fill the void, I talked of my own project, the building of a country club for the bankers of Jordan. I don't think Kendra heard me. After awhile there was a loud explosion in the distance, and the sounds of gunfire.

"It never stops, does it," she said.

"It will stop when the Israelis have chased out the P.L.O. Soon, I think."

"Not soon enough," said Kendra.

There'd been an accident, she said. A house was blown up. Just outside Shatila, just beyond the hospital. She'd been walking there, and seen it.

"But I wasn't able to do anything," she said in a low voice. "What could I do? I tried. But everyone died. They all died. I tried to help, I really did. I can never seem to help enough."

I made no comment.

The idea that one American girl could feel responsible for people killed in a city of war appalled me.

"It just goes on and on," she said.

Maybe it was time to go back to Princeton Hospital, I suggested.

"You must be kidding," she said. "Back there? What good could I do there?"

241

"Why do you have to do good at all? Just go."

"I have to do something."

We got the real story of Kendra's 'accident' that night at dinner, from Aran. The building was blazing, he said. As he watched, Kendra ran out with a child under each arm, ran back in, carried out a young woman, went back in again and got another. Kendra, after scrubbing at the hospital, was found to be suffering from large cuts down both arms, and a cut beneath her eye that required nine stitches.

"There were more people in that building," said she miserably. "I couldn't get back in. I tried, but there were too many flames. I couldn't see the door."

Kendra stood up. "Aran, take me to the hospital."

"No," said Neri. He was close to the Gemayels and he seemed to know a lot about what was going on in Beirut that summer. "Not into West Beirut at night."

"I wouldn't go anyway," said Aran huffily.

Kendra looked at her bandaged arms. That night she slept in the small guest room in the children's wing of our house.

For one week, she worked only light chores, to give her arms time to heal. She spent those afternoons sunning herself in our garden, sometimes talking to Mali and her children, sometimes by herself.

I looked out from my study one day and was surprised to see her there, sitting on a low wall amidst the roses. Her back rested against a wooden post, her knees were drawn up to her chest, her poor bandaged arms on the knees.

She looked to me like one of those scrawny kittens the children bring home. In those cases, we pet the kittens and feed them. Inevitably, something unfortunate happens, the kitten scratches, or disappears, or trots out in the street and is run under the wheels of a car. But that particular analogy to her life was not in my mind at that moment.

It was not long after this that Kendra met the Israelis and made the trip to Broumanna.

It was inevitable that she would meet them. We are all together here, in this neighborhood of Baabda. My house, the apartments of the volunteers, the Israeli headquarters.

Kendra passed the headquarters on one of her walks. The soldiers spoke to her in English, which she liked, and she was quite well along in discussion with some of the officers before she realized that they were Israelis. She shrugged. Soldiers were soldiers. Kendra made no distinction. For instance she was not sure which side were the Moslems and which were the Christians, nor who the Phalange were, nor how the Palestinians came to be living in our city. Rather basic, one would think, to the make-up of someone who wanted to help in Beirut.

She knew a lot about severed arteries and compound fractures and general anesthesia and various infections caused by poor hygiene. Beyond that, soldiers were soldiers.

Broumanna is a separate city from Beirut, high up a mountain road. It was sheltered from the war; its elegant buildings and neon lights stand proudly untouched. Music from discotheques blasts in the street, young men line up with their coins at pinball. The cars are Jaguars and Mercedes. Women wear silk dresses and have diamond straps on their high heels.

Neri went through a Broumanna period, and sometimes still goes. Aran does not go, but that is because Aran fancies himself a gambler and likes to go to the casino at Juniyeh and pretend he has money.

At any rate.

Kendra and the Israelis were served on a flower-filled terrace overlooking Beirut, by a tuxedoed waiter who brought shrimp and French champagne. The restaurants of Broumanna were inconvenienced by the war that summer only to the extent that their wine lists were sometimes limited, and the supply of Iranian caviar was totally cut off.

Kendra went several times, danced at the discos, drank good wine. She went up with the Israelis in their jeeps, and they left their Uzis and M16s on the table when they danced. Once a gun had fallen across a waiter's foot, causing him to drop the veaux l'orange on the terrace. At one of the discos there was for decoration a Jaguar automobile, spliced in half, and one of the Israelis had suggested that all the automobiles spliced in half on the streets of Beirut should be used to open discos.

Kendra's perception of how things were in Lebanon was not helped by Broumanna. Already she thought of it as a sort of play war, full of toy soldiers, toy bombs, toy crumbling buildings. The injured and the dying were real, but that was her job. She did not perceive in Beirut that summer any real threat to herself.

They want me to take a day off, said Kendra miserably.

We sat in the garden on a hot July day. Kendra was drinking iced orange juice, or rather, had a glass of iced orange juice in her hand. As my wife had pointed out, Kendra never really drank, or ate, anything, in the usual sense. She played with things. Today she was sucking the ice and spitting it back in the glass. One hand reached up to twist the gold earring.

I said a day off sounded like a good idea.

"But what will I do?"

"Sleep. Relax."

"I don't want to sleep and relax. I want to do something."

There was not much by way of sights that one could safely see in Lebanon that summer.

"Write letters. To your family."

"You sound like my mother," said Kendra. Since I do not sound at all like Kendra's mother, I could only conclude that she did not wish to write letters.

She had received letters, though. My servant's sister reported that three letters addressed to her sat on the night table in Kendra's room.

Moreover, the U.S. embassy courier had come by only that day, bringing me letters from Houston. He had shown me a postcard addressed to Kendra Johnson. On the front was a rather sterile-looking white building titled Princeton Hospital. On the back was one sentence which read--"Why didn't you tell me you were going to Beirut?" and signed, Adam.

"Why don't you write to Adam?" I asked.

"I left him," said Kendra. "He doesn't understand me."

"Does he know he's been left?"

"He'll get the message. I mean, I'm not there, am I."

"You wanted to travel," I suggested.

"Not particularly." In fact Kendra had gotten the address of the volunteer project from a friend, had stopped in that day and now found herself in Beirut.

I wondered if a different address obtained from a different friend might not have landed her a job treating flood victims in Mississippi. I mentioned this to her but the possibility did not seem to interest her. Kendra was not a great believer in fate.

Her mother had told her she would be happy if she went every Sunday to Mass. Her mother had told her she would be happy if she would do good.

Well, here she was.

You must know that I am hypothesizing here. These are not the things Kendra said to me, that afternoon in July. These are her thoughts as I think she would have put them together. Should have put them together.

At that time there was one major idea that Kendra had not yet grasped.

Her mother was wrong.

***

"Hassan is dead, Ishram is dead, Jihad is dead, Moses is dead ..."

"Moses?" asked Neri. "There was a Palestinian named Moses?"

Kendra consulted her notebook. She was reading to us from a list she kept of people who had died at Shatila Hospital. "Yes, Moses. Moses was a prophet, and now he's a Palestinian."

"Well," I said, "Moses was from a time when there were no Palestinians, nor Christians, nor Jews. Actually, Moses is very respected in Moslem history. Moses is one thing everybody has in common."

"How about Abraham?" asked Neri.

"Ibrahim," said Kendra. "It's the same thing. It's a very popular Palestinian name. Two Ibrahims. One came in with no left arm, the other with a head wound. It's a very bloody name."

"Why do you bother taking the names of the dead?" I asked irritably.

"Sort of like an address book," Neri said. "Some girls keep phone numbers. Kendra keeps lists of dead people."

"It's just a notebook," said Kendra calmly. She read a few more names. "Gada, Ramar, Aboud, Paul. Just some things I'm trying to remember."

***

August was finally silent. The bombing stopped.

Aran spent two days in the mountains, with friends.

The phones began to work.

Kendra reported fewer injured at the hospital.

Neri reported that he had seen Kendra playing soccer with Palestinian children.

An agreement was worked out whereby the P.L.O. fighters would leave Beirut.

All of this was good news.

In fact there was only one small flaw on the horizon, and that was Kendra. She came by less frequently, and when she did come, was quieter. One morning I heard my servant's sister grumble that Kendra was untidy; she spent the night writing letters but never mailed them, leaving the pages strewn about the floor.

That was a day when I was very busy with the Saudis. I was showing them the plans for that part of Beirut they could buy cheaply now, while the Israelis were here, and rebuild profitably later, when the Israelis left. If the Syrians left and the P.L.O. left, the profits would be even higher, and we were contemplating this when Mali entered. She approached with her head bowed, like a proper Arab girl.

"Kendra is here," she whispered.

I was annoyed. Surely Mali of all people had the sense not to interrupt my business for this announcement. I shook my head and waved her away.

When I saw my Saudi visitors out, many hours later, Kendra was sitting sullenly in the hall.

"You wouldn't see me," she said accusingly. I don't think she even saw the Saudis.

"A minute, Kendra," I said sternly, and continued speaking in

Arabic.

Kendra interrupted me again, this time grabbing my arm. "You wouldn't see me, and I depended on you! You wouldn't see me, and I have nowhere else to go!"

"Kendra!" I said, and shook off her hand. The Saudis were extremely embarrassed. They moved away from me in that little hallway. Their flowing robes distracted everyone. Kendra ran into the garden.

I made what apologies I could. I was furious.

I went to the garden, where Kendra stood.

"What's the matter with you?" I yelled angrily, "interrupting me like that with my guests? You are a guest in this house too, and you have no right! I have extended the hospitality of this house to you for three months and I never expected it to be abused in such a manner! You have the manners of a goat!"

"I'm not a goat! I have nowhere else to go, and you wouldn't see me!"

"What is it then? What's so damned important?"

"You won't understand, now. You won't understand."

"Kendra. I have always understood before. What is it now? What's happened? Are you hurt? Are you in danger?"

She sat down and clutched at her stomach. Her voice quavered. "Forty people died," she said. "I was there at the port and I saw it. They were celebrating. We had to fill up all the ambulances. The men were leaving. They were riding in trucks. They killed their own families. By accident. Because they were happy. Don't you understand?"

I understood only too well. Neri had called hours before with the news. The Palestinian fighters, who felt themselves to be victors and to be leaving Beirut with dignity, had fired their guns constantly into the air all morning. One could have started another war with all the bullets they let off, Neri said.

Bullets shot into the air may have a certain energizing effect that denotes celebration and victory and possibly the release of tension. Randomly fired bullets also have a tendency to be fired accidentally into buildings or into people, but the fools hadn't thought of that, that morning.

When Neri told me, I had been disgusted. I was doubly so now.

"Kendra," I began, "you are one American girl. Just who is it that you think you are? Do you think you can change Beirut? Change us? Change the Palestinians? Yes, you do," I said, because she was shaking her head in objection. "You have some misguided sense of mission that makes you believe that your presence here is somehow going to change things for the better. Well, forget it."

"It's not that!" she cried. "I just don't want them to kill each other!"

"How are you going to stop them? You are nobody. You are a nurse who works with blood and bones and that should be enough for you. You can't change Beirut, you can't change the way things are, and you can't come screaming into my house as if you blame me for this situation!"

I went into my study and slammed the door. The house fell into its silence.

***

The next day we heard from Aran that Kendra had not come to work. She sent a message, saying she was sick. My wife made a gift of flowers and sweet rolls and some local cures and took them to the apartment. She reported that Kendra seemed more tired than ill, that

249

she had lain in bed and held my wife's hand, and cried, real tears, when my wife left.

I was disturbed with myself and disturbed with Beirut. There was a tremor of uncertainty in the ground. Then, my servants reported two Israeli jeeps at the front gate, and Kendra came to see me for the last time.

I opened the door myself that day. A form of apology. I wanted to show her that she really was welcome here. Anytime.

"I'm leaving," she said. She said it in a strong voice, and she took my hand in a strong clasp.

I was startled. "Why?" I asked.

Kendra laughed. "You've been telling me to leave for the past two months!"

"You never listened before!"

"I know." She laughed again. "I just decided."

"We'll miss you," I said.

She left so quickly. She got in one of the jeeps, and they rumbled off down the road. Only then did I realize that she would be riding all the way down the coast, all through Lebanon, with the Israelis. Only then did I wish she hadn't gone, had waited for the hospital or me to arrange a ride with a neutral party.

The two jeeps were stopped first in my neighborhood by an American peacekeeping force of Marines. That they were detained for an hour while a superior officer was sought and permission granted to leave the neighborhood.

From there the group proceeded to a Lebanese army checkpoint, where their papers were checked for another hour.

After this, they were stopped by the Israelis. It seemed that since Kendra had come in with the volunteers but was not leaving with them, the Israeli officer thought she did not have the proper permission to pass back across the border.

They were detained another hour while the proper form and the proper officer to sign it were found.

At this station, Kendra was reported to be angry, to have met some officers she knew from her Broumanna days and told them they were messing up her life, that she had to get going, that time was running out.

The small group started out again, back through the Lebanese army, back through the Israelis, were in fact only twenty minutes down the road when they were stopped by a roadblock of Arabs.

It must have appeared to the group to be a Lebanese Army checkpoint. But it was not. I think I know what group it was, but considering the number of factions in Lebanon, it is not worth mentioning. It would confuse Kendra's story.

They stopped. There was some business of asking for Kendra's passport, which she angrily threw out. The passport was studied carefully, most likely by an Arab who wouldn't have understood its English prose.

Kendra repeated again and again that she was a volunteer. She held up her volunteer papers.

There was a long delay.

Kendra gestured to the Arabs to move the damn roadblock and let them get on the way. The Arab standing next to the jeep laughed at her. Kendra shoved him.

Everyone opened fire on everyone else. The dead: two Arabs, two Israelis, one American volunteer.

I cannot get her out of my mind.

New dwellings have blossomed on Beirut's formerly cratered

streets, and our scattered diaspora have jubilantly returned home. Mali's children are grown, and will soon have their own children. And I sit at night in a darkened room, staring at an open eye that stares unblinking back. It shows me a wavering sea of distress and the unlined faces of young American men. One of them could have been Kendra's husband. They look very much like her.

COLLATERAL DAMAGE

I gripped the sheet of paper in both hands to prevent it shaking. I looked at the name again, hoping I had read it wrong. It stared up, mocking me with intimacy, haunting me with double-barrelled familiarity. I shifted from one foot to the other trying to correct the wobble in my knees. The blood drained from my face. I hoped no one noticed.

They were all listening to Hartnett. He had come from Belfast on a morale-boosting visit. For good measure he was orchestrating a purge of three men, the known local wing of the splinter group that had split the movement.

"We take them at four tomorrow morning." Hartnett paused. "All three to be rounded up and brought directly to Noone's Field. Any questions?"

Noone's Field—No-One's Field as locals jokingly called it. My skin went clammy; my head felt light. Prisoners were interrogated there before their bodies were dumped.

At dismissal I avoided friends and enemies alike and walked quickly to the back of the farmhouse where I locked myself into the toilet. I leaned against the wall—to prevent it closing in around me—and studied the list again.

It was an everyday name, Luke, chosen for brevity to sit alongside Mulraney-Murphy. One followed the other in a natural and harmonious way—the plain in synchronicity with the convoluted. If only life were as simple. I balled the sheet and looked into the bowl. Someone had been here before me. I threw the names onto the conical heap and flushed it around the bend into pipes and drains up all over an ugly, stinking world. I needed a place and a time to think. When the crumpled-up list had disappeared, and the turbulence of the flush had ceased, I put the lid down and sat on it.

Two hours later, a young man peered into an alleyway. Something feral scooted behind a skip. I whispered that syllable again, almost cooing it like I used to long ago. The breeze carried it to his ears. He stepped forward until my shadow moved. He froze.

"Hello, Luke," I stepped from behind a stack of bins, hands in pockets trying to look casual.

"What do you want?"

I thought I detected spittle sailing straight at me. "They're on to you, Luke. They'll come for you tomorrow morning. You've got …"

"They'll come for me? You mean you'll come for me. You're one of them, you prick."

Wafts of old arguments slithered down the alley. This was no time for a reprise of a long simmering feud. "There's going to be raids in the morning, Luke. I don't know why you're on the list but …"

"Of course you know why."

"We've no time for a wee chat." The alley walls reminded me of that toilet cubicle, the way they hemmed me in. "You've got to get out of here."

"I'm going nowhere."

"Aye, well then I've got to arrest you."

He stared at me like a dumb fish, which was understandable considering I had just blown my cover.

I started to lift my right hand out of my coat when he did the unthinkable. The metal of the handcuffs were peeping from my pocket when he reached into his jacket and pulled out a gun. I must have done my own impression of incredulity as he raised it. "Luke …" I tried to show that I only had cuffs—how could I ever have carried, let alone raised, a gun to him? Taking my hand further out was my second, almost fatal, mistake.

In the moment he pointed the muzzle, time slowed. Memories swooped from places long ago. Ghosts of long-dead ravens winged through the alley, flocks of them, swirling and diving around my head, none as fast as the lean bullet cutting through their feathers, its trajectory scattering them, obliterating all memories as it tore into my arm.

No past tense then, only present. My mind blanked save for surprise, disbelief, shock. No pain, only a picture of Luke wheeling away.

To my astonishment two Police Service uniforms jumped him at the head of the alley. All three fell to the ground. The gun discharged again, pinging its load harmlessly off the pavement into the thick wintry air of a grimy Ulster day. The uniforms had him, one yelling into his lapel for backup. Then the pain came. Seconds later I heard the wail of sirens before slumping to the ground, a useless pair of cuffs tangled around my blood-stained fingers as I tried to stem the flow.

From my hospital bed next morning I replayed over and over the memories that had flashed at me in the alley: kite-flying in the park, fishing in the stream, the joy of seeing him stay on his bike that Christmas long ago. I saw then his angular face—the way his neck muscles strained in a police arm-lock as he spat me his last farewell, an accusing look that screamed: 'what kind of father shops his own son?' I stared at the ceiling, trying to get to grips with a son who shoots his own father. How was he to know that I hadn't set up those two uniforms to jump him? 'Bit of a coincidence,' he might add in his Queen's University accent, that they happened to be passing by the alley and heard the commotion.

Another uniform stood outside my ward to protect me from Hartnett and his cronies who were doubtless itching to get even with a traitor. This third uniform held the door open for a decorated officer to step inside. I nearly needed to ring the bell for a bedpan when I saw who it was. The pretty young assistant by his side carried a suitcase that looked disturbingly familiar.

"Well, Murphy, I believe the bullet went clean through?" The Assistant Chief Constable offered me his hand, nodding at my arm.

I was so surprised by his chummy tone that I couldn't speak, but returned his nod and warm handshake.

He was smiling. He turned to his assistant who hefted the case up onto the wheelie tray over the foot of the bed.

"Here are a few wee tokens of our gratitude. Some are from HQ, others from the officers at the local station."

I watched dumbfounded as the lady officer took out a bottle of single malt (Sixteen Year Old), a box of liqueur chocs, a get-well card and an official-looking envelope. As she placed them on the bedside locker, the Assistant Chief pulled up a chair. "Normally," he began, "we have no time for maverick, one-man operations. We try to discourage impulsive actions on the part of our officers, and our … other agents. But given the record of the man who shot you, and that he was your son, and that you were trying to make a citizen's arrest, we …"

I could hardly believe my ears. Luke's attempt to kill me, plus the cuffs in my bloodstained hand, had made me a hero in the eyes of the Service.

"Of course," the officer droned on, "there were witnesses on the street. Dozens of people saw you being taken away by ambulance. The other side may now be aware that you've been working for us all along. They'll be after you. That leaves one option. We took some items from your flat this morning—clothing, footwear, the suitcase. These things, plus the money in the envelope, should tide you over for a month or so. The hospital says you'll be discharged tomorrow. In the morning we'll escort you to the mainland. The process of permanent relocation may take a few weeks. There's a lot of paperwork involved: a new passport, credit cards, a new identity."

His words washed over me. I looked beyond his distinguished rank to walls of sickly green. Those walls had me surrounded; tilting over, top-heavy with the guilt of what I had been: snitch, mole, or the dread-word spoken in hushed tones by my own people, my ex-own people, informer. The colour of the walls mocked me, not with the vomit of what I had been, but with what I had become: a snake in the supergrass, and what I would soon be: exiled, banished, Sinn Féiner no longer. A true Me Féiner—Myself Alone, in every sense.

* **

Three weeks later my request to visit was sanctioned. Such an odd term, sanctioned—its cold sound made a perfect bedfellow for the wintry snap that had descended on the whole country. The word rhymed with the hollow sound of clanging gates. It echoed the essence of leather soles on polished corridors. The final sharp metallic clink stays with me always. It brought us face to face. His look matched the word 'sanctioned'.

"Thanks for seeing me, Luke. I know it's not easy. There are things I need to explain … things you should know."

I found myself wishing for a glass of water. There was so much to be said but already my prepared speech was in smithereens. One look at his face morphing from adult to teenage to wain made my brain tumble through fifteen years to a day when rumours had flown across Luke's schoolyard that a man had died in the local factory. After he had ran home, mum told him that, yes, a man had died but not to worry, it wasn't dad. Later that night, she had joked with me about how worried young Luke had looked. That had been in the days when I was the Best Dad in the World. Back then things had righted themselves instantly for a nine-year old. How I wished for simple solutions now. His face was adult again, glacial.

"Have they fixed you up with a new life yet?"

He was staring at me so severely I struggled to meet his gaze. "Aye," I said.

"Where are you staying? England?"

I nodded.

"Devon? Cornwall?"

"You know I can't answer that."

"Did they escort you here?"

"They offered but I made my own way. I took the long way around via a bus from Dublin. Less chance of being spotted than at the main points of entry up here." I tried to make it sound like an everyday thing.

"Did you switch to a local bus once you crossed the border?"

"Aye." I swallowed. Something about his chatty demeanor did not ring true.

"I thought so. Will you go back the same way?"

"Maybe." I felt I was whistling on a mountaintop as magma coiled itself in the ground beneath my feet. "Listen, Lu ..."

"The beard won't help. They'll expect that—and the dyed hair. Where will they send you permanently? Down under? New Zealand?"

"Luke, I ..."

"You fucking bastard!" He was up off his seat, eyes bulging so close to the glass his breath clouded over the snarl on his mouth. He tried to punch me through the panel—I reeled back in shock. In the instant his fist bounced off thick glass his expression changed from anger to pain. For a moment he was my small boy again, hurt from a very cruel game of make-believe.

I held my hand up to indicate to closed circuit that I could handle it. "I saved your life and what thanks did I get? You shot your own father!" I hoped that deep down I could draw the bitterness and resentment from him. A faint hope. He stood with his back to me, hunching over his bruised fist.

"Hartnett was going to round you up, you and two others. They would've tortured and shot you. I had only a few hours to figure out what to do. I tried to get you to run but you wouldn't! The only way I could save you was by turning you in. Did you really think I was taking out a gun? Those were handcuffs in my pocket, not a ..."

As he began to turn, I heard again the shrill lament of a referee's final whistle. He had wheeled around that day when Cliftonville beat Linfield. Of all his friends he had chosen me for his embrace. I saw again his teenager's shiny joy, and in an instant relived all the empty terraces I've stood on since, my Saturdays at Solitude, my head everywhere but on the Reds.

"Where did you get the cuffs?" he snorted, completing his turn. "The local station or do you use them for bondage with that whore?"

That startled me. Politics was bad enough without bringing her up. "That's not fair. I'm sorry things didn't work out between your mother and I. We all make mistakes."

"Mistakes? You betrayed my mother. Then you betrayed your country. And all you can say is: 'we all make mistakes'? Some mistakes. You're only a cunt."

"Shut up and listen, Luke. It wasn't as simple as that. Your mother and I had our difficulties. Things were tough. The work in the factory didn't pay well. There was all kinds of pressures. The estate was full of shootings and beatings. We saved up to get you out of it, to keep them from poisoning you as well! But sending you to university—aye, now there's a mistake! They sought you out for recruitment. You became their number one target …" My voice broke at what he had turned his education to, how he had swallowed their rhetoric, turning his technical expertise to carry out their orders.

"Will you be bringing her with you?" His callous eyes made me look at the hard floor. "Answer me one thing before you go," he said coldly. "When did you go over to the Brits?"

"I couldn't stand it any more, Luke. I did my bit for years; this and that, digging a hole for myself until it was so deep I couldn't climb out and walk away, a hole so deep it trapped you and your mother. I went over shortly after your mother and I divorced, around the time I realised what use you would put your education to. That really put the hat on it." I studied him hard but he didn't react. "One day I just had enough. I rang the confidential hotline. And didn't I do the right thing? Didn't I what! Aye, three weeks ago they expected me to sacrifice you! Maybe involving me in that was some kind of mistake. Maybe they didn't twig that the Murphy part of your name is mine, but I doubt it. If anything has convinced me that I was right to do what I did three years ago, it was that." I paused and drew breath. "The police set up a meeting. They gave me more money than the factory ever paid. As for the woman you called a whore," I looked at him directly. "She and I split up a year ago. I have no one now. You're all I've got."

It was a plea that drew one last accusing glare. I knew then that he was right—it was time to go. There was nothing left, and nothing left to say. All the years of rearing him had come to this. This time he had no gun to pull so I took something from my pocket again. I held up a piece of paper and showed him the lines written on it. I gave him a wee minute to memorize them.

I went back the way I came. Had he got word out, they might have got me before I left Ireland for the last time.

I stepped out of the bus onto the streets of Dublin and turned up my collar against the cold. A drab woolly hat blended me into the background. It also made it harder for anyone to recognize me. I sniggered at that: whether they got me or not didn't seem to matter any more. I walked the streets, shoulder-rubbing Southerners who felt safe—for the moment—behind the façade of their busy economy.

I admired their neons and glittering window-displays, I heard their silly ring-tones but my eyes and ears existed only for the looks and words of Luke. I saw and heard all he had done and said in all the years of growing, and wondered how the trust and love had ebbed so quietly away that I never noticed it was gone until it was too late. I told myself there could never be reconciliation—he had called his father a cunt, after all. I hoped that maybe, just maybe, he had aimed deliberately for my arm.

It was time for the flight to my temporary safe-house in England. As the plane taxied to the runway I looked out at shades of green slipping by beyond the wings.

When he is released, through breakout or under the terms of whatever new agreement there may be, I know he will seek me out. They say there is no more determined and dangerous freedom fighter than an educated one. They are right. I ought to know.

As he sits alone in his prison cell, with these fields of green falling far away from me, I hope he remembers the address in Fuengirola, Spain, that I held up to the glass panel for him to memorize, and that he will regard it as the calling card I intended it to be. And whether he

reads it as Come to me, Luke or Come and get me, Luke I will leave
entirely up to him.

WIRES ON A PLANE

It's about the time the matronly security guard is in the throes of publicly molesting me when I realize my flight has been delayed. Again. "Crap." I mutter. The guard glances up at me momentarily before continuing her search of my body with her sausage-like fingers, looking for what I presume is contraband. Like hair gel stashed in my bra or a bomb in my undies.

"You can go." She turns as I gather my shoes and purse and I want to say something like "hope it was good for you" or "aren't you at least going to tip me?" but I manage to refrain from smart-assery.

I pick up my copy of "Freakonomics" and move on through the terminal. I bought the book online for 16 dollars specifically for this trip. It's number six on the New York Times Best Seller list and is quote "a must read" according to one review. I really hadn't intended on reading it at all. I just wanted to look smart while at the airport in case someone famous or rich saw me.

I plod over to Starbucks and in an attempt to waste a few minutes and because I want to get a bit of free caffeine, flirt with the dorky barista behind the counter. I decide that he must be gay because despite my sweetest smile and charming demeanor I still end up paying $4.75 for a latte.

Hello, buddy? Did you not see these boobs?

The hour and a half before my flight seems to endlessly trickle by. I decide to take my boredom into my own hands and head to the bathroom to check my face. Yep. Still cute. I'd totally do me.

I people watch, arguably the best sport there is. I stare in awe as crowds of poorly dressed people file by. What happened in these people's childhoods to make them think that wearing socks and sandals in public was appropriate? And mullets? Really? People still wear those? It looks like a dead squirrel accidentally landed on their heads and instead of cleaning it off, they just let it be, chalking it up to fate.

I drink. Martinis. Several delicious, chilled martinis.

After a while, I begin to scrutinize the people I am about to travel with. Woman, two children. Two loud children. Two very loud spoiled children who are interfering with my martini buzz. Two super irritating children whose mother is reading a magazine and completely ignoring the fact they are driving everyone in the terminal crazy. I mentally make a note to send a thank you card to the person who invented birth control. It's a shame that lady didn't use any.

My gaze lands on several business type men scanning smart looking newspapers (think the Wall Street Journal) who are also shooting irritated glances at the two obnoxiously loud children, who, for the record, are seriously grating on my nerves at this point. I need another martini just to drown out the sound of the two children screeching about Spongebob and Dora.

A couple of quiet families sit around as well as a scattering of what look like mid-twenties worker bees like me and a couple of college kids. I wonder who I will be sitting next to and if they're going to be any fun. I am hoping that I will arrive at my seat and see someone hot in the seat next to me. I am currently vying for the cute young looking businessy type guy in a pinstripe suit (is that Armani?) sitting near the gate but wouldn't be too upset if the hottie boy wearing the Northwestern T-shirt ended up sharing airspace with me. I am certain both of them will love me.

I'm hovering on the bar stool, still amusing myself with people watching (check out the fanny pack!), when boarding is called for my flight.

A dull and angry looking man mumbles into the microphone, something like flight blah blah from O'Hare to Dulles, first class and rules and line. I tune him out and wonder why all airport workers are so grouchy. They're worse than postal workers. I decide that martinis just may well be the answer for their little crabbiness problem because I have had two or three or something like that and right now I feel great! I don't even notice those stupid loud kids anymore. I down the last of my drink, mumble "martinis, I love you" into the glass and pay my tab.

It is not until I am on the plane before I bother look to see what seat I've been assigned. "Valerie Simmons, flight 3089, seat 13A" the boarding pass reads.

"Hi there. Welcome. Hi. You have a great flight. Hi, how are you?" I plod into the plane and am greeted by the perky delicate features of one of the flight attendants. "13A? right down this aisle" she purrs.

"Word." I respond, feeling cheeky.

I make my way down the plane toward my seat. This takes roughly forever since everyone on the plane seems to have packed up their life's possessions, declared them carry-ons, and is now searching for an empty overhead bin.

I arrive at good old 13A. I look down and see a man in 13B, which also happens to be the aisle seat. "I'm 13A." He wordlessly gets up to let me in, scowling slightly. He is not cute, he is not friendly and I am not happy to have to be squished in next to him for the next few hours. He does, however, look Middle Eastern. Great, I think, I'm stuck next to a freaking terrorist. I plop in my seat, make myself as small as possible so as not to touch him and pretend to read my book. In actuality, I am pouting (I was really hoping for one of the cute guys) and truth be told, because of recent events, I mull over the fact that the guy next to me might actually be a terrorist.

I'm not a racist (I swear. I watch Oprah.) but this man next to me looks like one of the terrorists that hijacked the planes on 9-11 (Mohammad something) and as I realize this, a little ball of dread is beginning to grow in my belly. We're about to fly to DC… where the President lives! What if he's going to try and kill the President? Or attack the Pentagon again? This evil killer is just glaring at the back of the seat in front of him with a huge backpack at his feet.

I spend a few minutes trying to decide if I want to be scared. I try my various thoughts on for size and after a considerable internal debate; I decide yes, I do in fact want to be scared.

I decide that this man is going to blow up the plane. The sudden realization that I'm going to die at 29 washes over me, giving me chills. I mean, I wanted my own Lifetime movie of the week but I didn't want to go out this way!

I take a deep breath and reprimand myself. I repeat the mantra "not all brown people are terrorists" to try and calm myself.

I just need to keep a close eye on him and if I have to, I think I can take him out. I did take a self-defense class after all. I make a mental note that if I make it out alive, I need to thank my mother for making me take "Master Ken's Self protection class for ladies" last summer. I begin to make a mental checklist of places to hit first. Nose, check. Gouge out eyes, check. Elbow to the throat, check.

I sneak a sidelong glance at the crazed killer and HE'S STILL STARING STRAIGHT AHEAD. No movement whatsoever. Not even as we taxi the runway and take off – nothing!

I have one hour and 48 minutes to try and survive this flight.

The plane levels out and the drink carts are brought out. Psycho next to me refuses the offering with a gruff "no." I consider buying a mini bottle of vodka but decide that if I am to fight this man successfully, I should probably be sober.

I have a diet coke instead. No need in dying fat.

My new terrorist friend leans down to extract something from his backpack. I watch as intently as I can, my eyeballs straining as I try to be subtle. His narrow shoulders hunch over and I can see his shoulder blades work as he digs in his bag. I see wires. I SEE WIRES AND A BOTTLE. IS THAT CONTACT SOLUTION? I was right. I knew it. I'm the only one on this plane that knows we're all going to die and there's a terrorist who's going to kill us and it's up to me to stop him.

I try to calm myself. "Val, it's up to you to save all these people. You can't let the terrorists win. Do it for America. Protect our freedom"

I decide to take action. "Excuse me. I... have to use the restroom." He lets me out and I head to the cramped bathroom for one last pep talk. Locking the door behind me, I look in the mirror. I am flushed and looking rather sexy-- I think. Apparently being a hero agrees with me.

I exit and make a bee-line for the first flight attendant I see. Her bright smile falters slightly as I grab her hand and speak quietly and quickly.

"Don't panic but the man in the seat next to me is planning to hijack this plane. I saw wires and contact solution."

Her eyes widen and she exhales "Contact Solution? But how did he...?"

"I don't know," I interrupt. "And we don't have time. Is there a Homeland Security Guy or someone with a gun on the plane so we can take him down?"

"Yes... Oh God. Are we going to die?" Tears well up in her eyes. Her name tag says Debbi.

"Debbi, I think we will if we don't hurry." She grasps my hand tightly and nods. I am feeling super brave right now.

"Follow me." We walk into first class (Jeeeeze. Those seats are huge! Is that a foot rest?) and Debbi bends down, whispering into the ear of a man who looks suspiciously like David Cross.

This is who is going to help me save this plane? David Cross is the Homeland Security guy charged with keeping us safe? Great. Not only do I not get to sit by a cute guy, I don't even get a cute Homeland Security agent. The defender of freedom and the American way of life looks like David Cross? More importantly, what kind of Lifetime movie is this going to make if I'm the only attractive character? I suddenly lose a little bit of the faith I had that I might survive this.

He stands. "I'm Michael."

"Valerie," I reply.

"Tell me what you know, Valerie."

I tell him what I know. "I'm sitting in 13A and the guy next to me is Arabic and has been totally mean looking and grouchy. Super suspicious. I think he's going to try and kill us because I saw him digging in his bag and I saw wires and contact solution."

"Contact Solution?" He exhales, his bushy eyebrows rising above his glasses. "We better act fast." He purses his lips. "I'm gonna need your help. You up for it?"

I nod. Am I up for it? I've been planning it for the last hour.

"OK. You go back to the seat and when he gets up, I'll come from behind and arrest him but I'll need you to grab the bag to make sure he can't set it off. OK?"

"Yes." I am solemn. I am no longer doing this for me, or for my Lifetime movie of the week. I am doing this for America.

He turns to Debbi. "You keep the passengers calm, OK?" She nods, wide eyed.

"Let's roll," he says.

I am a little peeved about this. Hello? It's already been said. How insensitive! Something like "America Rocks!" would have been a little better I think. Whatever. I have a country to save. I have freedom to protect.

We head down the aisle back to coach, Michael far in front, me trailing a bit behind him and Debbi following me.

Seat 13A. Go time.

"'Scuze me." I say again, nervously.

He gets up, waiting for me to get back into my seat.

This is when Michael pounces, screaming "I AM A HOMELAND SECURITY AGENT AND YOU ARE UNDER ARREST FOR SUSPICION OF TERRORISM. DO NOT MOVE!"

The terrorist freezes as Michael grabs him, putting on handcuffs. "What…" the terrorist begins, trailing off. He looks confused. What an actor.

The heads of everyone on the plane whip around to see the commotion. Someone screams.

I reach down, grab the backpack and place it behind me. Before I can help myself I shout "You Arabic bastard, you thought you were going to kill us, you terrorist! We're American, we're smarter than you! Screw your Jihad buddy!"

Michael is dragging him to the back of the plane. He looks so confused I almost doubt myself. "Arabic? Terrorism? WHAT IS WRONG WITH YOU PEOPLE? I'M MEXICAN! I WAS BORN IN OHIO! I'M NOT A TERRORIST!!!!"

"Oh yeah?" I scoff. "Then why did you have contact solution in your bag?"

The plane lets out a collective gasp.

"I wear contacts, that's why." He huffs and strains to turn his head toward Michael. "I'm not really under arrest, am I?"

Michael slams him against the side wall of the plane. "You bet your sweet ass you are."

"You people are crazy! You're all crazy! I didn't even do anything." He mumbles into the wall.

A voice pops up from the front of the plane from a short balding fellow. "Is this even legal? I, mean, what proof do we have he even planned to do anything?"

I glare at him, clapping my hands together as I say each syllable. "Con–tact So-lu-tion. You're not allowed to have it."

He continues, despite my brilliant retort. "This is still America right? Innocent until proven guilty? Have you even opened the bag to see what he had inside?"

"Too dangerous." Michael shouts from the back of the plane where he's hovering over the terrorist who's been placed in the empty back row. The terrorist looks defeated, his shoulders slumped, eyes glazed. "Could be a trap." Michael calls. "I'll get it and bring it back here with me."

"I'm moving to Canada." The short guy mumbles as he turns back around and sits with a thump.

Michael moves to get the backpack from where I've placed it on the floor. He claps a hand on my shoulder, his face inches from mine. Good Lord his glasses are thick. I can't even see his eyes. "You did good."

"Thanks." I sigh, suddenly tired as I slump into my seat. I pick up my book and blink several times. Everyone on the plane is just kind of looking around as if they're waiting for something else to happen.

I sit silent, staring blankly, soaking in the events of the last 10 minutes. As is customary when I do anything rash, doubt begins to creep in, making me wonder if what I did was really just and best for America. It has to be, right? I did it for freedom. Better safe than sorry I try to tell myself. I can't shake the feeling though as if I've done something wrong, as if I'm the bad little puppy who piddled in the corner, and although he's cute and he means well; you're still going to beat him.

Thoughts are racing through my head at the speed of light – could I go to jail for this? Am I a racist? Oh god. I don't think I am. I mean, I don't use the 'n' word or hate people for no reason (except when they're stupid. I just really hate dumb people.) and I'm just trying to be patriotic and do the right thing and save the world and I recycle and everything. I just really thought he was going to kill us all and I didn't want to die just yet, (I don't think I'll ever want to die to tell the truth) but I just feel guilty for feeling proud of myself and I'm sure I've got to be smarter than those people who flip over every little thing and are paranoid freaks…

"Excuse me." The woman across the aisle leans over, breaking my train of thought.

"Yes." I am slightly dazed at the moment but not too dazed because I immediately notice she is currently wearing a knitted sweater with a cat on it. She moves in to the seat next to me and grabs my arm. I sure hope bad fashion sense isn't catching.

"Thank you. What you did was really brave. I really appreciate it, you know, saving our lives and all. Will you tell me what happened, from the beginning?"

"Maybe a little bit later. I just need a minute right now."

"Of course." She says, looking disappointed. She pauses, and then

271

her face lights up. "If enough people heard about you, you could probably go on Oprah and tell your story, you know."

Oprah? My ears perk up.

The person in the seat in front of us turns around. "Thank you for what you did." The person next to him leans in and says "Yes, thank you."

I nod as the cat lady leaves to return to her seat. Halfway there she pauses, turns around and looks at me. "You're a real American Hero."

I swell with pride and barely hear the snort coming from the front of the plane (no doubt that short dork).

A real American Hero.

Yes.

I most certainly am.

DISCARDING

"I'll show you around, Harry," she chirps. "You don't mind if I call you 'Harry?'"

I shake my head. I do mind. I'd like her to call me "Mr." Shows respect. But I don't make an issue of it.

"First stop is lunch," she smiles cheerily. She takes me to the dining room. We sit down for lunch. Macaroni and cheese, lettuce salad, and ice-cream. The food is hot and fairly tasty. But the room is quiet.

"The inmates don't talk much, do they?" I say.

"We don't refer to them as 'inmates,' Harry. All our guests are 'residents." She smiles as she corrects me. Doesn't want me to take offense.

"Well, they don't talk much," I repeat. I think that no one says much because whatever is said is overheard by the twenty-odd people sitting at adjacent tables. There's no privacy.

When lunch is over she leads me down the hall. I go slowly, pushing my walker. The walker requires that I lean forward over it in order to keep my balance. I'd rather stand up straight, like I always did when I was young, but pushing a walker makes it hard.

She shows me the room I will occupy, with its hospital bed, its 10' X 10' sitting area, its desk and two-person sofa. She points out my bathroom; the shower stall has a bench in it.

"We want you to sit on the bench under the spray when you shower so you don't slip and fall," she says. "And one of our staff will help you."

"Scrub my back too?"

She misses my sarcasm. "Of course." She smiles brightly. "All our staff is anxious to help you."

273

Each room has strategically-placed pull-cords hanging on the wall. "Just pull the cord to summon help, if you ever have an emergency," she instructs me.

Next she leads me past a lounge area. Five people, four women and one man, sit grouped around a forty-inch TV. Two are slumped in sleep. One of the other three looks up at us standing in the doorway.

"This is our TV room," she announces. "Hello, John, how are you today?" she asks, smiling warmly at the man staring at us.

"Fine," he reports, without enthusiasm.

"That's good," she smiles at him.

She explains that all this will cost me in excess of $3500 per month.

Petronius, I remember, had "opened his veins." According to the novel Quo Vadis, he was sentenced to death by the Roman Emperor Nero. Rather than submit to the humiliation of public execution, he summoned his friends to a banquet. When the eating and drinking was finished, his slave mistress brought him a razor and a bowl. He cut his wrist and bled into the bowl until he died.

Not a bad way to go, I think. Surrounded by friends; assisted by a beautiful young woman; being the death of the party. Better than years of boring diminishment in these compartments.

But I don't have any razor blades. I shave with an electric shaver. If I decide to imitate Petronius, I'm going to have buy some.

The staff lady shows me the library. "We have computer access here," she says, "either in your room or in our library, and high-speed internet."

"I don't know how to work a computer," I reply, irritably.

"You really ought to learn," she urges. "It's a great way, an easy way, to stay in contact with your friends and relatives. And there is another advantage: you can change the size of the print on the screen,

274

enlarge it to make it more readable."

"There's nobody to teach me how," I object.

"Oh, we run classes here. We think it is really important."

"I suppose that costs extra," I mutter.

"Well, yes, it does. We charge $15 for group instruction and $65 for individual help."

"Don't think I can afford that," I say.

"Some people ask their grandchildren to help them. The kids, a lot of them, really know computers. Many of them are quite expert."

***

"Hey, Deanna, over here!" I yell.

The girl standing by the bus spots me. She's tall; spiked orange hair; face marked with acne. Her eyebrows are plucked thin. My granddaughter.

She grins, waves, picks up her suitcase, and heads toward me.

"Hi, Grandpa," she calls.

I spread my arms. She sets her suitcase on the platform and leans over my walker. We hug each other.

"I'm so glad your Mom let you come," I say.

"Grandpa!" she protests. "I'm over sixteen! I can go anywhere I want!"

I cock my graying head. "You telling me she didn't give you permission to come?"

Deanna shrugs. "She didn't want me to skip school for a week." She glances up, shy but aggressive. "But this was more important. So I decided to do it anyway."

I frown. "Does she know you're here?"

"By now she does, I guess."

"What does that mean?"

"When I didn't come down for breakfast, I guess she knew then."
I sigh. "I guess we'll have to call her when we get home so she won't worry."

"She deserves to worry a little bit," she says darkly.

"It's been bad since their divorce?"

She nods.

"Well, don't be too hard on her. She's had a tough time since my son left her."

"She drove him away!" Deanna mutters.

"Maybe." I hesitate. "But it takes two to tango."

She frowns.

"Even if he is my son," I continue, "I think he probably did things, or said things, that made her 'drive him away', as you say. Probably they both did things to hurt each other."

I start moving toward the door.

"C'mon, we have to get a taxi. Don't forget your suitcase."

"Grandpa!" she protests.

"Sorry. I forgot that you are all grown up." We exchange grins.

"I had to give up my driver's license last year," I tell her. "Couldn't pass the eye exam—even with my glasses."

"I didn't know," she says.

"No, I haven't spread it around. Bad enough being ninety without adding people's pity to it."

Deanna hesitates, then reaches out and touches my hand. "I'm sorry, Grandpa."

"Well," I sigh, "I guess being old is better than being dead. Though I'm not so sure."

We get ourselves a taxi and head for home.

"It's not really much of a home anymore," I explain. "I've sold or given away a lot of the stuff that was in it. It looks pretty bare."

"How about Grandma's pictures, the ones she got from her father?"

"They're still there, hanging on the wall where she told me to hang them—maybe thirty years ago! I've got some wall space in the retirement place I'm going to, so I can take them along."

"I like that one with the storm clouds."

"You do? I'd love to give it to you. You know, give it to somebody who remembers her, my wife, I mean. You want it?"

Deanna hesitates. "I don't want to take stuff that you still want. But I remember that picture. Especially the storm clouds."

"OK. It's yours," I say.

I turn to face her and change the subject.

"So, Granddaughter, you think that you can teach me to use a computer? This place I'm moving to, this assisted living place, they think I should learn to use the internet so I can send you messages. And they said sometimes old people get their grandchildren to teach them how. That's why I called you. And because you came, I guess you think you can teach me?"

"I'm pretty good with computers," she admits. Then, with a grin, "Are you a pretty good student?"

"I used to be," I smile back. "Not so sure about that anymore. It's harder to understand new stuff. And my memory for new stuff is getting weaker."

She looks away. "I'm not a good student," she says. "Mom says I've got a bad attitude."

"Do you?"

"Probably. But I've tried to change it and it just seems like I can't do it. It changes for a while but then pretty soon it comes right back."

I reach out and pat her shoulder. "Dee, I've got a bad attitude about moving into this retirement center."

She looks at me.

"And I've tried to change it, but it keeps coming right back to me."
I pause. "Maybe we can work on our attitudes together."

"Maybe," she says.

The cab stops.

We get out, Deanna fluidly, me stiffly. She hands me my walker.
We shuffle up the snow-drifted side walk. She takes my arm and hugs
it.

"Thank you," I say.

"Don't want you to slip and fall," she says.

I fumble with my key-ring, select the house key, unlock the door,
and open it.

We go in.

The living room carpets are gone. As are the curtains. The sofa is
gone. Only two chairs and an old scoop-shade lamp remain.

My heavy old-fashioned mahogany table still dominates the dining
room. But it's supporting cast of drapes and carpet have disappeared.

"I've kept a bed for guests upstairs. Hoping somebody might visit
me, you know."

She hangs our coats in the hall closet.

I push my walker into the kitchen.

"You want a coke?" I ask. "I'm going to have some tea."

"Yes, thanks," she replies.

She sits down at the kitchen table. I get the two remaining glasses
from the cupboard, add ice, take a coke out of the refrigerator, and set
them in front of her. I put some water in the teakettle, set the kettle on
the stove, and turn on the burner.

"Grandpa," she says tentatively, "You turned on the wrong burner."

"Oh shit," I say. "Sorry. Excuse the French."

"Not the first time I've heard it," she grins.

"Is that right?" I smile back.

"Right."

We laugh together.

"I don't see as well as I used to." I sigh. "That's one reason I'm moving. I'm not safe here alone."

She pours the Coke into her glass. I pour my tea.

"See this roll-away island?" I ask her. "I built it. When your grandmother and I were living in married-student housing. At the university. Out of four old wine boxes and the top of a Sear's portable dishwasher.

"You know, Dee, all my life I've gotten this huge kick out of rescuing junk and making it into something either useful or pretty—or both."

"You take stuff that's ugly and make it pretty?" she asks.

"I try," I chuckle. "Once I found an old ice-cream churner on the burn pile at my folk's summer place. I stripped off its old blue paint, sanded it, stained it mahogany, and painted its steel bands black."

I chuckle again. "It made a lousy wastebasket because it's so heavy. Takes two hands to empty it. But I love it. It's different, it's interesting, it's even attractive, at least to my eyes."

"I've still got it upstairs. I'll show it to you if you like." I look away. "I know I should have gotten rid of it but I just couldn't toss it. It was too much like throwing a part of my self away."

"I think it's neat," she says. "I'd like to see it."

I believe her.

So I continue. "I sometimes wonder if these junk things are kind of stand-ins for myself—like when I was rescuing this junk I was really

279

trying to rescue myself."

She is staring into her Coke glass.

"Well, enough of an old man's reminisces. What do you say we call it a day and start the lessons tomorrow?"

Deanna retrieves her laptop from her suitcase and opens it on the table. "We'll have to sit side-by-side," she says, moving her chair to my side of the table.

"Well, to begin," she says, "This is the mouse. You stick this plug in this space here. It's called a 'port.' Now we're going to turn it on. See this button? Push it."

I tentatively put my index finger on the indicated button.

"Push it," she encourages. "Don't be afraid. You won't break it."

I push.

Together we bend our heads toward the glowing screen.

"Welcome, Grandpa Harry," it says. "You and I are going to enjoy each other's company."

"What th…?"

"I programmed it to say that," Dee laughs. "I thought you might get a kick out of it."

"'Kick' is the right word," I say. "Kind of a shock, actually."

"Now," she says, pointing, "when you move this mouse on this pad, it moves the cursor around the screen. See that little arrow? That's the cursor."

"Now move the cursor up to File."

I do so.

"Now left click on New."

"Left click?" I ask.

She shows me how to do a left click and warns me not to do a right click.

Finally we get a blank screen, which she calls a new file. "Now, you type something," she orders.

I start to type. I make a mistake. She points out the delete key. I type some more.

We go on for some time. Her sweater gets caught on the edge of the keyboard. She absent-mindedly shrugs her sleeve up to get it out of the way.

"Now," she says, "we want to save what you wrote. Put the cursor on File." She guides me through the Save As function and Exit.

I am not paying attention.

"What's that?" I ask, pointing to the gauze bandage on her wrist.

She reddens.

"Oh, I cut myself."

I stare at her wrist.

"Bad?"

"Not too bad. Took a couple of stitches."

"How did you cut yourself there?"

She says nothing. I wait.

"You don't have to tell me if you don't want to," I say finally. "It's none of my business, I guess."

"Yeah, let's go back to the computer," she says.

We continue the lesson.

The next day she teaches me some more things. She makes me practice. The day after we do the same.

She's teaching me how to get on the internet when suddenly she again pulls up her sweater sleeve.

"You asked me about this." She points to the bandage.

"Yes," I say carefully.

"Have you ever heard of 'cutters?'"

"No, not really." I have some vague ideas about the word but nothing very clear.

"Cutters are girls who slash their wrists on purpose," she says.

"Oh," I say.

"I'm a cutter. I cut myself. This isn't the only one." She pulls up her other sleeve. A gauze pad is taped to that arm too.

"Jeez, Dee," I say. "How come?"

She stares at the wall. "Because I'm ugly. And lonely."

"You're not ugly!" I protest.

"My mother says I am. And the kids at school think I am. There's nobody that likes me and sometimes I'm so fucking lonely I just want to die!"

"So what lonely?"

"Oh, sorry. Just so awful lonely."

"No, no, the word you used."

She hesitates. "Fucking? I'm sorry. I know it's a bad word."

"But 'fucking' means 'love-making,'" I persist. "So you are so 'love-making lonely' that you want to die?"

She frowns.

"I'm fucking lonely too," I tell her. "Ever since Emily died eight years ago." I shake my head. "Love-making lonely. You know, Dee, I've not cut myself. But I think a lot about suicide."

I tell her about Petronius.

"But you shouldn't want to die!" she bursts out. "You've got all your life to look back on, all the things you've accomplished, all the people who like you"—she pauses—"who love you"—she pauses again—"like me. Me—I got nothing to be proud of, nothing to look back on."

"OK, we're different, you and me," I admit. "I've got a past--but

282

you've got a future." I grin. "So which is worse?"

She says nothing.

"What do your parents say?" I ask.

"My Mom doesn't want to talk about it. And neither does my Dad, when I see him. All they say is, 'How could you? You have so much to live for! You've got your whole life ahead of you!" She snorts. "A whole life? Like theirs? Big deal!"

"Tell you what, Granddaughter," I say. "You've been teaching me some things about the computer. How about me teaching you some things about being lonely?"

She shrugs.

"Uh, are you a good student?" I ask, grinning.

"Never have been," she grins back. "But there's always a first time!"

I tap the table.

"Now this table we're sitting at, for instance. This table is about loneliness.

"It belonged to my great-grandfather and great-grandmother. Their children—my grandfather and his sisters and brother—sat at it when they were kids. One of those sisters, my great-great Aunt Joan, inherited it. She was a maiden lady and I guess she was lonely. Her dining companions were her two cats!"

I laugh.

"Each cat had its own place-mat and saucer. The maid would pour milk in the saucers and the cats would sit on the table and lap it up while the rest of us chewed our meat and potatoes."

"My dad sat at it," I continue, "when my grandfather took the family back to the family homestead for Christmas holidays. Me and Emily, we sat at it with our parents when they came to visit. And we ate almost every meal with our children—your mother and her brothers—at it. And then you and our other grandchildren, we all ate at it and talked around it on holidays.

"And so when I eat at it, and there is nobody else eating with me, and I remember all the family that has eaten at it, I see how alone I am.

"And now it's going to somebody—I don't know who—who doesn't know anything about all those memories. I'm breaking the tradition. Breaking the chain."

My throat is tight.

"Kiddo, it's really hard! To be a traitor, I mean. That's a special kind of loneliness."

Tears come.

"Aw, Gramps!" she sympathizes.

"Everything I've sold or given away has been full of memories. And when the things go, it seems like they take the memories with them."

My voice subsides into a hoarse whisper. "Seems like my memory bank is getting emptier and emptier. The few memories left are all alone.

"Time for supper," I say. "Where would you like to go?"

"Go?" she asks.

"Yes, to a restaurant. What do you like to eat?"

"Well, any place is OK with me. Except, I don't eat meat."

"Any restaurant, except one that serves meat, huh?"

She laughs. "Yeah, that isn't really 'anyplace', is it?"

I smile. "But I know a place that serves good fish and has a good salad bar. I don't eat much meat anymore, either. I'm missing a few teeth and so I don't chew very well. Fish is softer, easier."

The hostess seats us and hands us menus.

"I'd offer you a drink but I know you're underage," I say.

"Grandpa," she protests, "I've been drinking beer, and sometimes hard stuff, since I was fourteen!"

"OK", I say, "but that's not the point. The law says 'Eighteen.' Unless I've got a very good reason, I obey the law." I try to gentle my criticism. "I'm going to have my usual martini. I won't insult you by offering you a 'kiddy cocktail'. But is there anything else you'd like?"

"No thanks," she says. "It's OK."

We eat and are nice to each other. But it's a little cool. So going home, I tell the cabby to stop in front of a liquor store.

"What kind of beer do you like?" I ask her.

"You gonna' buy me beer?" she asks, incredulous.

"Yeah…if you tell me what kind."

"But that's against the law, you said."

"No, Dee, it's against the law for a restaurant or a package store to sell alcohol to a minor. But I'm not going to sell it to you, I'm going to give it to you. Besides," I smile, "even though your birth certificate says sixteen, the way you act, I believe you are at least eighteen."

She blushes a little.

"What kind?" I repeat.

She tells me.

"Wait for me," I instruct the cab driver.

"Dee, would you give me a hand going up these stairs? My arthritis is hurting a little."

"In your legs?" she asked.

"Legs, back, shoulders—all over," I say.

Together we climb the stairs, one step at a time, hanging on to the rail. When we reach the top, I walk into my room and sit down on the bed. I stare at the dressing table against the wall. Dee slouches in the doorway.

"That's your grandmother's dressing table," I say, pointing.

"I remember," Dee says.

"The drawers are all empty now."

I roll my shoulders.

"Grandpa, would you like me to give you a back-rub?" Dee asks. "Would that make your arthritis feel better?"

"Well, yes, I would like that."

"Take off your shirt, then, and lie down," she says.

I take off my shirt and lay face down on the bed. She sits down beside me and begins to run her fingertips lightly across my old skin.

"That tickles," I laugh.

She laughs too and switches to kneading my shoulder and neck muscles, gently, firmly.

"Grandpa," she says, "sometimes when boys look at me, it's like they're taking my clothes off, like they're looking at me bare." She pauses. "Grandpa, did you do that, I mean, look at girls like that, when you, when you...."

"When I was young?" I smile sheepishly. "Yes, Honey, I guess I did. We all did. Young men are like that."

She rubs some more.

"Did you like doing that?" she continues.

"Yes, I gotta' admit, I enjoyed that. Why do you ask?"

"I just wondered." She pauses. "I don't like it when boys look at me. It's embarrassing and makes me mad. Mostly they say I'm ugly. They make fun of my nose. And my chest. And my skin. My pimples."

Her hands move up and down my spine.

"That's when I cut myself," she says. "When I'm feeling ugly. Then, when I start to bleed, I don't feel ugly anymore. My blood seems beautiful. My outside maybe is ugly, but what's inside me is beautiful. And I like my inside stuff."

I am listening hard.

"When I cut myself, I hurt on the outside but then I don't notice the hurt on the inside. You know what I mean?"

"I guess I know what a hurt on the inside is like."

"When I cut myself," she says, "the blood comes and then I put a bandage on the cut. I take care of myself. I treat my cut skin gently. And I feel good when I'm bandaging up my hurt, when I'm trying to heal myself."

"Trying to heal your insides by bandaging your outsides?" I said.

"Sort of."

She massages my neck and shoulders.

"Grandpa, do you think I'm ugly?"

"No, Deanna. No. I think you're lovely."

She stops rubbing, thinking.

She stands up. "Turn over," she says.

I roll over on my side.

"Look at me," she commands. She begins unbuttoning her shirt.

"What are you doing, Dee?" I stammer.

"I'm taking off my shirt."

"But..."

She opens her blouse. I stare at the valley between her breasts, the curves rising gently on each side.

"But you shouldn't do that!"

"I shouldn't? Grandpa, I've taken my blouse off for boys I didn't even like. Why shouldn't I take it off for my grandfather—who I love?"

She shrugs out of one sleeve.

"No, this isn't right!" I struggle to sit up.

Her blouse falls to the floor. She leans over me, her breasts pressing over the top of her bra. She pushes me gently back against the pillows.

"It's not your call, Grandpa," she says, defiantly. "I'm a grown woman and I can take my clothes off whenever and wherever I choose."

She flashes a wicked grin.

"The only thing you can do is decide whether to shut your eyes or keep them open."

She slips her bra-strap off her shoulder. The top of her bra cup peels down.

"Deanna…"

She unhooks her bra and lets it fall. She hooks her hands behind her head.

I don't close my eyes.

"Do you think I'm pretty?"

"Yes. Yes," I breathe.

As we prepare breakfast the next morning, I take the storm-cloud picture down off the wall.

"Here you are, kid. Enjoy."

"Thanks," she says. "What's going to happen to the rest of this stuff?"

"The auctioneer is going to come and pick it up after I'm gone." I reach into the refrigerator for the last of the orange juice. "I decided it would be easier if I left it, instead of it leaving me."

"Like it's that hard?"

"Yeah. Getting rid of these things, and moving from this house, it's like my life is over. Most of my past will be gone and most of my future will be empty. Not much to live for."

We are quiet. Then, staring down at her plate, she says, "Grandpa,

I'm going to throw away my razorblades."

I nod. "Good."

I think a moment.

"Tell you what. If you're going to get rid of your blades, Dee, then I won't get any for myself!" My grin feels a bit twisted. "To hell with old Petronius!"

"Then can I come back again and give you another lesson?"

You bet!" I enthuse. "But look, uh, next time, uh, I think we better skip the finale of the back rub."

"Didn't you like it?" she teases.

"I loved it, but, well, I think it was a one-time thing. It would sort of cheapen it to try to repeat it."

"OK," she grins. "Next time I'll keep my shirt on."

CONFUSIONS OF A TROGLODYTE

Back in October of 2003, I was in Karachi for one day on way to my niece Kathaja's wedding in Islamabad. I stayed with Zahid, an old high-school buddy. The Karachi of my time, 1950's and the Karachi of 2003 were two different cities. Karachi of my youth was small, clean, and orderly. There was two-way traffic on Bunder Road, trams going to Bolton Market, Sader Bazaar to Gandhi Garden, the city zoo, and picnics on Sundays at Monora Island, Sandspit, Clifton, and Paradise Point. There was roaming around Elphinstone Street, Bohri Bazaar in the evenings. The days were blistering hot, but after sunset, a breeze blew in from the sea to cool the nights. Now the tramway was long gone and Karachi sprawled over seven million people. The evening breeze no longer seemed to blow. The humidity, heat and dust were oppressive, but I was with Zahid, Anwer and Kazi, friends of my high school days, and the weather was irrelevant.

When we were in high school, Zahid, Anwer, Kazi, and I went to Thatta, an old city a little over sixty miles north of Karachi. Mr. Hanifi, Zahid's uncle, who was a doctor of homeopathy, was our chaperon. Dr. Hanifi was very thin, very dark, and wore a thin moustache and very thick eyeglasses. Thatta had been the capital of the Sindh Province for about three centuries under the Moguls (1475-1737). Makli Hill, two miles northwest, is a silent city of a million graves scattered over an area of six square miles. Some of the tombs offered excellent specimens of architecture, stone carving and tile coloring. But our mission to Thatta was much more basic, ancient and primitive.

It was all Kazi's idea. There we were, four boys of seventeen, traveling to become four young men. It was a well-thought-out, well-planned trip in terms of time, money and purpose. We had saved

290

up for it for quite a while.

We stayed in a large room with five cots above a restaurant and shared a bathroom with a couple of other rooms. "Early to bed and early to rise, makes a man healthy, wealthy and wise," was Dr. Hanifi's motto, and so that night, we all went to bed promptly at nine o'clock. Our plan was simple: Once Dr. Hanifi fell asleep, we would get up and sneak out for our rendezvous.

The next thing I knew, it was early morning, Dr. Hanifi was up, and all my comrades were still asleep. Sitting on my cot, I wondered if Kazi, Anwer and Zahid, like me, had fallen asleep, or unlike me, had gotten up and gone about the rendezvous as planned. Before going down for breakfast and while Dr. Hanifi was in the bathroom, I asked them one by one. Zahid and Anwer confessed sheepishly that they had fallen asleep. So did Kazi, but there was a certain smile on his face and a look of satisfaction that was telling. Zahid, Anwer and I did not believe him. We knew that Kazi was now a man. As was our plan for the second day, we went eleven miles north to Kalri Lake, just off the national highway, where people went for fishing, boating, swimming and relaxation.

Forty-plus years later, during this trip to Karachi, sitting in Zahid's living room with Anwer and Kazi, with a ceiling fan swirling the smoke from Kazi's cigarette, I thought of that trip and asked him again. "On that night in Thatta, while every one slept, did you or did you not go out and have sexual intercourse with a Jezebel?"

"You guys chickened out. I had to. I didn't have a girl friend and I'd never had intercourse before."

"Who had?" asked Anwer sharply.

"There is no known prostitution in Pakistan now," Kazi informed. Zahid looked at me briefly scratching his head. "Tomorrow you

291

leave for Islamabad and who knows when I'll see you again? I don't know how to say this." He paused and looked back at me, his dark eyes wise. "The world of our youth and the world we live in now are not the same. Not only the innocence is gone, it has become dangerous. There is a street version of radical Islam that permeates certain youth culture, where Osama bin Laden is a hero, George Bush and Israel are evil and the French are hated because they want to ban Muslim head scarves in schools."

"Neither Osama bin Laden nor George Bush is my hero," I told Zahid. "They both are acting like military men."

"I don't know what your point is," said Zahid. "What I'm trying to say is very simple. People like you, Pakistani-Americans, who feel at home here because they speak the language, know the people and the culture, sometimes become easy targets of kidnapping or other violence. So, dear friend, be extra careful."

"Welcome home," said Anwer. "How does it feel to be living overseas?"

The day after my reunion with my friends, I left for Islamabad. My nephew Mazher picked me up from the airport. He drove fast and recklessly, overtaking bicycles, motor rickshaws and delivery vans, pressing on the horn rather than the brakes. I had asked my sister Shamim, Kathtaja's mother, to please make arrangements for my stay in a hotel. I wanted to be comfortable. Mazher informed me that they had made arrangements for my stay at a guesthouse less than half a mile from their home. I had dinner with Shamim and her family and visited with other relatives, a side benefit of traveling to funerals and weddings.

It was past midnight when I asked Mazher to take me to my accommodation. On the way, Mazher told me that he had made reservations under his name because his mother, my sister, wanted to

292

pay for my stay. "I have told the management that my uncle from Karachi will stay for four nights," Mazher informed. He advised me to tell no one at the guesthouse that I was living in America or that I was an American citizen. "Just tell them that you are from Karachi."

I was not very comfortable with his request. "Mamonjan, Kabul is a stone's throw from Islamabad," he explained, "and ever since the U.S. offensive in Afghanistan that ousted the Taliban, there are daily raids. Every day there are killings of suspected Taliban leaders. Also the Eastern Kunar Province and the Korengal Valley, near the Pakistani border, holds hundreds of Afghan, Pakistani, Saudi Arabian and Chechnya rebels. And now, since March of this year, the war in Iraq makes this a dangerous part of the world." He looked directly into my eyes.

I said nothing. My sister wants me to be from Karachi, so she can pay the room rates for Pakistanis, which are much cheaper than what they charge Americans. I convinced myself that safety, concern for my well being, and economic savings for my sister were worth it. I ccould live with that.

The guesthouse was a large, magnificent mansion painted yellow, fortified with a ten-foot concrete wall topped with broken glass. A man in a black turban and a rifle in hand stood guard at the front iron-grilled gate. Mazher pulled into the carport, and with my suitcase and bag in hand, approached the gate. Mazher flashed the key to my room, number 11, at the guard and told him that he was dropping off his uncle from Karachi. The guard was a tall man with a thick grey mustache, the ends waxed and pointing upward. "Salaam, Sir," he said in a commanding voice. He opened the side door of the gate and let us in.

The guesthouse was more like a small hotel, with a large carpeted lobby, a check-in counter, fifteen air-conditioned rooms, and sixteen-hour room service offering Chinese, Mughlai and Continental cuisine. There was also a large dining room, open for breakfast, lunch and dinner. But at this hour everything was closed and quiet. My room was furnished in dark teakwood with pleasantly colored furnishings and cable TV. It was on the first floor, facing a large garden in the enclosed back yard. The deck offered a magnificent view of the surrounding mountains and valley.

Before leaving my room, Mazher removed the address tags from my suitcase and carry-on bag and put them in his pocket, "You don't need these right now," he said. He also told me not to walk the half-mile or so to his mother's house but to call them; someone would come and pick me up. "That guard at the gate is private security; they work to protect. They are fighting a private war. The situation around here is chaotic. The environment is dangerous, unchecked, out-of-control cowboys and Indians. I mean the Pakistanis, and there is no green zone."

I was ready to say good night when he asked me if I knew that forty private bodyguards from an American company had kept President Hamid Karzai of Afghanistan alive since 2002. I didn't and I told him so. "Private Security is big business in Iraq, Afghanistan and even in Pakistan," he informed me.

The following morning I woke up after nine o'clock, flipped on the TV and walked to the bathroom. When I returned, CNN news was on. Four Marines had died in Iraq, another in Afghanistan. A member of the Pakistan Assembly died in Islamabad, his convoy ambushed on his way to Parliament. A grenade exploded, buildings shook, mortars crashed, windows shattered, large fragments cracked from building walls, vehicles were ripped apart, and his car was consumed in flames.

A few days earlier, I recalled, President Musharraf's convoy had been ambushed, but he had escaped unhurt. I turned off the TV and called Mazher to please pick me up.

The next day during Rasem-e-Henna (a ceremony in which the groom's family brings henna to the bride's home), I met a Pakistani journalist, Mr. Shervani. Mr. Shervani was a friend of the groom's father. He knew that I lived in America, and he thought I was the bride's mother's younger brother. I am the older brother, but I did not correct him.

In the living room, the women sang wedding songs accompanied on a dholic, a double-sided Indian drum, while a young woman painted my niece's hands with henna. Mr. Shervani and I sat in an adjoining room along with a few other men. He turned toward me and said, "America exploited the sentiments of the Islamic world in Afghanistan by training and arming the rebels and Mujahadin to fight the Soviet occupation. For ten years the US, Saudi Arabia, Iran and Pakistan, funneled money along with Stinger missiles to take down Soviet helicopter gun ships. But as soon as Soviets left, you abandoned Afghanistan. Now, you have a new enemy, the Mujahadin that you trained and armed to fight the pro-Soviet coup and Soviet invasion."

I live in America. I wanted to tell him that I was not responsible for her foreign policy. I said nothing.

In the distance, there was the call for Isha, the night prayer. Allah-o-Akbar. Allah-o-Akbar. God is Great. God is Great. We call our God often, at least five times a day. It is something that keeps one in touch with the haves and haves not, good and bad, what's there and what is lost.

After the call for prayer was concluded, Mr. Shervani continued, "The war in Iraq was started with selected intelligence and the exaggeration of truth. What I want to know is, was the intelligence intentionally misused or did Bush intentionally go to war without proper information?

"What the American forces have destroyed in Iraq will take much longer to rebuild than you think, and that will cause even more frustration and resentment among Iraqis. And what's worse, there's no exit plan."

In certain situations, I found it better to listen than to talk, and this was one of them.

A servant in a white uniform served us chai in teacups with saucers, sugar and milk already added. Mr. Shervani took a sip of his tea, pursed his lips and swallowed. "I've always welcomed and admired American values and ideals until recent times, when they became mandatory for all nations—by force or other means. In the name of fighting terror you are terrorizing the world. Your leaders misled you, but who misled your leaders?"

Drinking my tea, I half-listened to the Mr. Shervani's unsolicited monologue.

"I don't have a grain of doubt that the Israeli-Palestinian problem lies at the heart of terrorism in the Middle East and beyond."

I stared in silence and focused my attention on the joyous music, the songs of the women singing, filtering in from the adjoining room.

Mazher dropped me off at the guesthouse well past midnight. "Shab ba-khar," I said.

"And a safe night to you as well," Mazher replied. I got out of the car.

The same guard with his rifle and black turban was on duty again. Mazher waited until I got inside. Then the guard, whose name I had learned was Darya Khan, followed me through the gate and padlocked it from inside. "Am I the reason you were waiting outside?" I asked.

"At night, we wait until all the registered guests are back before we lock up. We have security cameras that monitor both the inside and outside of the building."

"Thank you," I told him sincerely. I wished him good night and walked to my room.

On my last night in Islamabad, I attended Rukhsati, the reception given by the bride's family, during which traditionally the bride and groom meet for the first time, after the wedding rites are completed. Although, my niece's marriage had been arranged by her parents, bride and groom had actually met earlier in the presence of a chaperone and had given their consent to the union. On this night, they sat on a stage under a large shamiana, a colorful domed tent that stretched from one side of the street to the other for half a block. The guests were fed kabobs, korma, nan, biryani, palak bhaji, and sweetmeats. Before the end of the evening, the bride and groom were shyly feeding sweetmeats to each other.

I got back to the guesthouse at about 1:30 a.m. Darya Khan was waiting. He walked in with me after padlocking the gate. "Are you enjoying your stay in Islamabad?" he asked. He had a kind face. He reminded me of my high-school coach, Mr. Saddiq, who always asked me to look up, walk straight, and be truthful. Darya Khan was the same age as Mr. Saddiq had been then, in his mid-fifties. And so was I, now, come to think of it. All that had been more than thirty-five years earlier.

"It has been a pleasure," I told Darya Khan. I was feeling nostalgic, not knowing if or when I would see these people again.

"Where do you live in Karachi, sir?" asked Darya Khan.

Last time I was in my father's house was more than fifteen years ago. I spent five days in his room in Karachi, cleaning out his closet, looking at his papers, the awards and certificates: Drawing Master of Merit, Artist of Distinction, his membership in the Royal Drawing Society of London, yellowed invitations to high teas with dukes, banquets with shahs. I felt a swelling of pride and admiration: this was a grand man, my old man, my dead old man.

One week after the death of my father, I packed for the return trip. Into my carry-on bag I put the portrait of my mother that Baba had painted when she was a young woman and an unfinished self-portrait. I also took two of his books, a biography of Mohammed and the poetry of Ghalib, his silver betel tin and his diary from 1930 to 1937, a thick, black leather-bound notebook, with his name engraved in fading gold capital letters. My nonstop flight to Amsterdam made an emergency stop in Cairo to fix a plumbing problem, the toilets wouldn't flush. In Amsterdam, I missed my connecting flight to Chicago. There wouldn't be another until the next day. I didn't care; there was no rush, my father was no longer dying. From the airport I booked a room at the Museum Hotel. I had stayed there before, great location, a quiet street, two blocks from the Rijksmuseum. In a night's journey I had traveled from 118 degrees Fahrenheit in Karachi to 54 degrees Fahrenheit in Amsterdam, not counting the temperature at the Cairo airport.

At my hotel I closed an adjoining hallway door on the index finger of my right hand. After absorbing the initial excruciating pain, I examined it under a lamp. The skin was not punctured, blood was not gushing out, but there was a Rorschach pattern spreading under the nail and a purple swelling, a blister, on the fingertip. Unlike my mother, who had long thin fingers, I had my father's hands with short stubby fingers. Hands-- I regretfully reminded myself, remembering my boyhood fantasy-- that would never bowl for a national team in a test

298

cricket match nor pitch for the New York Yankees. I asked for a band-aid at the front desk. They directed me to the hotel bar. The Dutch are so practical, I reflected, cradling my sore finger in my left hand as though it were a small, crippled bird. Antiseptic and mood-elevator both available in one convenient location.

Behind the bar stood a stunning maid, spellbinding enough to make me forget my throbbing finger and move the throbbing to a different location. She wore tight, black jeans and a loose-fitting black silk blouse. Around her waist was a short red cotton apron. She was watching world soccer-- Holland verses West Germany-- on a television mounted on a pole. There was nobody at the bar. With her dark, curly hair, large brown eyes and tanned skin, she reminded me of an old girlfriend, Tara Khan. I ask her for a band-aid.

"Are you Indian?" she asked, handing a plastic strip across the bar.

"No," I answered soberly. "Actually, I'm a cowboy."

She ignored my attempt at humor, her eyes on the soccer game.

I sat down on a bar stool across from her, watching the game in the mirror behind her.

"My grandfather was Indian. A sailor," she volunteered. "He jumped ship in Holland when he was nineteen and married my grandmother when he was twenty-one."

"Until last night, I was in Wonderland," I said. "Now, I'm only Alice."

"What was that?" she asked.

"Nothing," I said. "That was a private conversation."

On the TV, the game stopped; someone had committed a foul.

Looking at me for the first time, she said, "My name is Rita. Can I get you anything?" Her smile completely did me in. She had full, red lips, and even, dazzlingly white teeth.

Anything I want is a generous offer, I wanted to say. I wanted to bury my face in her bosom, spill out my life story. I became conscious of my finger throbbing again. "A shot of Bokoma and a St. Pauli Girl, dark," I said, smiling back.

"My grandpa took me to India once, Bijnor," she continued, pouring my drink. "I was four or five; he was an old man. All I remember now are spices, shades of yellow, green and red and animated conversations in languages I couldn't understand. He died a few years later. We never went back."

I had just missed my father's funeral. I said nothing. The soccer game on TV started back again. We both watched.

"I play soccer," she said. "I love the game."

I looked at her standing in front of me and I saw her in the mirror. She was slim and petite; she had a perfect body for the game. I pictured her in knickers and knee socks, kicking the ball and I was ready to tell her that I was captain of my high school cricket team when another man walked in, someone she seemed to know well. I sat watching soccer, sipping my drink and listening to Rita and the other man talk. Apparently, he was an Englishman, a captain on a cruise boat, and he had an apartment in the city. I responded only briefly when they tried to draw me into their conversation. Before I finished my drink, he asked Rita if she would join him for dinner when her shift was over.

I had planned to ask her out to dinner myself! I wanted to scream. Lovely Rita looked away from the TV toward me for a brief moment before she consented. I finished my drink and looked at the cruise ship captain sitting a few stools away. I rubbed my thumb over the band-aid. I thanked Rita and left.

"Where do you live in Karachi, Sir?" asked Darya Khan again.

It was my sixth day in Pakistan, and to my amazement, I was wide awake. It was twelve in the afternoon in Chicago. I turned back to Darya Khan. We were the same age. He could have been my old classmate, my friend, but we inhabited separate worlds. His world was a difficult one. This man had been looking out for me the last three nights, waiting each evening for me to safely walk into the guesthouse. The least I could do was to give him two minutes of my undivided attention. "My father built a house in Gulberg, Federal B Area in 1972," I replied. That had been twelve years after I left Karachi to study in America, and I had never gone back to live in my father's house. A writer has to be careful with the truth, I told myself. I needed to be creative. "I grew up in an apartment building on Hospital Road not too far from Civil Hospital." I added.

"Do you have children?" He didn't ask if I had a wife.

"I've two sons at home, one in eighth grade and one in college," I told him, without saying where home was. Home is where the heart is. When I die, bury my body wherever, but bury my heart at home. "How about you?" I sat down on an overstuffed chair in the lobby and gestured to Darya Khan to join me in an adjacent chair. It was easier to ask questions than to provide answers. "Do you have a family?"

Darya Khan looked at me with sad eyes. He looked too warm in his army-green uniform. "I lost my only son, Sakendher, fighting in Afghanistan against the Soviet occupation. He was only twenty."

What does one say in response to that kind of loss?

"I'm a soldier," Darya Khan continued. "I joined the army when I was seventeen. My father was a soldier in both the British and Pakistani armies. My grandfather was sixteen when he left his village in Afghanistan and crossed the Derah Pass into India. He became a rifleman in the British Army. I was thirty-seven years old in 1980, two years after the pro-Soviet coup and Soviet invasion, when I went back

301

to Afghanistan to train and arm the rebels and fight with the Mujahadin. The war against the Soviet occupation and the subsequent civil war and the devastation from the earthquake drove over three-and-a-half million Afghans to flee their homes, about a million and a half to Iran and more than two million to Pakistan. Millions of them are still living in tents and mud huts in sprawling camps after more than twenty years."

"In Karachi," I told him, "I have seen plenty of Afghan refugees."

"More than a million Afghans and over 15,000 Soviets died between 1979 and 1989, when the Soviets finally withdrew," Darya Khan told me, laying his rifle across his lap.

"The way of the world is nothing but war," I said. "My family fled from our home in India to Karachi in 1947."

Darya Khan nodded. "With men away at war, in Afghanistan, women and children are left to beg. The worst drought for three years in a row has withered wheat crops and ruined pastures. The herdsmen have lost most of their sheep and goats and the irrigation system has been destroyed. There are no jobs, and in some regions, there is no water to drink, much less bathe in. Dams and artificial lakes need to be built, there are no roads, no transportation, no housing. Besides starving women and children, there are only war lords, drug czars and the Taliban."

I was well aware of the plight of the Afghans, a difficult and dangerous situation, a sad and desperate predicament. I would be very happy if the government of Hamid Karzai brought peace and stability to Afghanistan, a nation composed of a patchwork of ethnic groups, Pashtun, Tajiks, Hazaras, Uzbeks and others. The largest groups were Pashtun and Taliban fighters. I could tell by the way he spoke and the fact that he was a soldier that Darya Khan was a Pashtun.

"Last year, after forty years of service, I retired from the army to take care of my wife, Zohara. She had a malignant tumor that spread quickly. She died fast, ten months ago. No parent should lose a child. What ultimately killed my wife was the death of our son. I can't believe that both my son and my wife are gone. It is hard to accept. It does not feel real. Since her death I have had problems falling to sleep at night. Thanks to Allah, now I have this private security job."

Darya Khan did not ask me about my wife. I have not talked about Virginia to anyone. It has been so long ago now. "My first wife, Virginia, died unexpectedly, more than twenty years ago," I tell Darya Khan. "And to think that Virginia is gone is still beyond my belief. Our son, Imran, is in college now. I'm married again and have another son, Raheem, who is in eighth grade." I wanted him to know that life goes on after loved ones die, but I didn't know how to say it.

"I am glad that your sons are well," Darya Khan said sincerely. We sat in silence for a few moments. "Around here," he went on after a small sigh, "there is little central authority to oversee law and order, to bring justice or to mete out punishment for injustice. This is a tribal society in which the commonly recognized law is that of tribal justice or vengeance, depending on which side you belong to: If a member of the Tahari tribe attacked or harmed someone from the Ghorbani tribe, the attack would entitle anyone from the Tahari tribe to retaliate against anyone and everyone from the Ghorbani tribe. It is an unending cycle of bloodshed and violence, a circle far wider than the original crime."

Darya Khan lifted the rifle from his lap and leaned it against his chair. "Last month in a border village, a young man was identified as a United States informer by the villagers and responsible for the deaths of two teenagers and three men in an American raid," he tells me. "His case became a matter of tribal justice: relatives of the dead men made it clear to the informer's relatives that the father either kill his son or the villagers would murder his entire family. So the father of the informer took his son out to their pomegranate field and shot him with an AK-47. No man should have to kill his son, but in this situation the father had no other choice. The worst tyranny in the twenty first century will not come from armies but from their lack, from the lack of capacity and courage to use them wherever they are needed to protect justice, freedom, and truth."

I thought, hadn't President Bush said something like that? It was like saying that if guns were outlawed, only the outlaws would have guns, or is it, guns don't kill people, and then there are people who need people.

Darya Khan continued. "If war is not the answer, then what is? How do we rid ourselves of tyrants or protect ourselves from ideologies or fanatics who attack us with their own principles and weapons?"

I looked out toward the entrance where swarms of mosquitoes were electrocuting themselves against a blue lamp. Private security was big business. It was the other army, the private army. Any job that required carrying firearms was beyond my understanding, experience or ability. During a visit to Colorado Springs last year, I had seen an ad that I thought was strange, bizarre: Dragon Man's Machine Gun Shoot. Anyone twenty-one or older could rent a machine gun plus ammo for ten bucks, and experience the excitement and feel the fire power of shooting M60s, AK47s, HK91s, Uzis and more. There was even a full-size bin Laden mannequin for practice. There was also posted a sign that read, 'Wanted: 85 Iraqi terrorists to hold targets.' And hadn't Mazher just told me that the U.S. government hired forty private gunmen from the American company DynCorp to keep Hamid Karzai alive in Afghanistan? In the Mansehrra district, less then sixty miles north of Islamabad, where foreign journalists were not allowed to travel for the sake of their own safety, there were said to be training camps where American officials along with the Pakistani army were aggressively cracking down on foreign militants, especially the suspected al Qaida, the Taliban.

I was no longer from around there, but I could pretend for another day. One more Saturday night, as the song goes. Darya Khan did not have to tell me too much more. I lived in America, a land of large armies and larger opportunities, and now we had a new enemy that in part we created. A faceless, country-less, shadow-less, ever-present adversary that struck us from the dark, who hated us and our ways, an enemy we called terrorist, a foe that had managed to change the way we lived after September 11, 2001.

It was time, I supposed, to exchange addresses, time to say to Darya Khan, "If you come to Karachi, look me up." But I did not. I didn't live in Karachi and there was no reason to perpetuate more lies. This man had lost his son and his wife. He was lonely, depressed. "I'm sorry to hear of the loss of your son and your wife. Live well, be safe and Godspeed." I extended my hand and he shook it warmly. I knew I would not see him again.

Outside, on the eastern hills and valley, the light was changing. Islamabad, City of Islam, City of Peace was a relatively new city. The site, Potwar Plateau, was chosen in 1959, when Karachi was deemed unsuitable, for reasons of national security, as the capital. Construction started in 1961. A scooter drove by, breaking the quiet. Darya Khan picked up his rifle and walked down the hall to the security office to monitor the cameras. I went to my guestroom to sleep for one more night in the safety of strangers.

305

Printed in the United Kingdom
by Lightning Source UK Ltd.
124456UK00002B/23/A